Also in the Kent Stephenson Thriller Series

Taking on Lucinda

SIMPATICO'S GIFT

A Kent Stephenson Thriller

FRANK MARTORANA

$\mathcal{V}_\nu$

VinChaRo Ventures

Simpatico's Gift
Copyright 2019 by Francis S. Martorana

VinChaRo Ventures
3300 Judd Road
Cazenovia, NY 13035

vincharo.ventures@gmail.com

This book is a work of fiction. Names, characters, places, and incidents either are the products of the author's imagination or are used fictitiously, and any resemblance to actual events or persons, living or dead, is entirely coincidental.

ISBN: 978-0-99893-262-0 (print)
ISBN: 978-0-99893-263-7 (ebook)
Library of Congress Control Number: 2019901389

Cover designed and illustrated by Amanda and
Sebastian Martorana
Sebastianworks.com

Author photo by Rosemary C. Martorana

Printed in the United States of America

In memory of
Richard A. White
Rich loved his family and friends above all.
After that, it's too close to call between
hunting, skiing, and Lynyrd Skynyrd

ACKNOWLEDGMENTS

Over the years that it took to write this series, countless clients, friends, and acquaintances, close and casual, have contributed when, often unbeknownst to them, I picked their brains. I can't possibly name them all without embarrassing errors of omission, so I won't try, but I do thank them all deeply. There are some I just have to give special acknowledgment because they contributed so much and in ways that, if they had not, this book would never have been written, much less published. Thanks to Garda Parker, Rhoda Lerman, and S. V. Martorana, all three world-class authors, for neither laughing nor rolling their eyes when they first read my manuscripts. Thanks to Alicia Bazan-Jemenez, Sylvia Bakker-Moss, Deborah Fallon, Mark Andrews, Felicia Lalomia, Andy Olson, and Jeannine Gallo for assorted advice and technical support. Marlene Westcott, you are truly the Word Wizard. Sebastian and Amanda Martorana, what you do with the covers is amazing. Editors, Celia Johnson and Mona Dunn, I thank you for finding my many errors and doing the polishing. Rosemary Martorana, you get special thanks for always smiling and showing great patience while solving my many logistics issues. Last, but never least, there is my wife, Ann Marie. I don't know how you put up with me through it all, honey, but I'm sure glad you do.

CHAPTER 1

Spring 1986

JUST AFTER DARK, CHALK-EYE TOOK COVER IN the stallion barn at VinChaRo Farm. His clothes were soaked. His shoes sloshed with each step. Water the temperature of snow ran down the back of his neck, pasting his mousy brown hair to his shoulders. Another wet, lonely night. It reminded him of Vietnam — night patrols near Khe Sanh.

He was working his way north toward Ottawa for the summer. He panhandled in Canada during the summer and Florida all winter. Simple. He liked simple. Simple was right for a bum, and Chalkeye knew he was a bum.

He'd used this VinChaRo barn before when he needed a night place. It was safe, and clean, and near a town whose folks didn't roust him. They were pretty generous with handouts, too.

He glanced down the long alleyway. Stalls on both sides. Not a sound. It reminded him of the farm where he grew up in Wisconsin, except way fancier. Just about everything reminded him of something these days. The problem was it all blended into a strange, illogical fog.

He pulled the door shut against the wind and used the orange glow of the security light to find a stack of hay bales in an alcove. He rearranged them to form a cubbyhole where he could hide and sleep.

It reminded him of the forts he and his cousins used to make in the haymow back home. He left just enough of a crack between the bales that he could keep an eye out for a night watchman.

Chalk-eye keeping an eye out — that was a laugh.

Ol' Chalk-eye. He'd gotten that name when he bet his eye patch in a crap game behind the VFW in St. Louis. He lost, as usual. That was twenty-two years ago and he never bothered to wear one since. Nowadays, hell, he didn't even notice when clerks at the hundreds of liquor stores he stumbled into struggled to avoid fixing on his bad eye while he dug into his pockets for change to buy whatever bottle he could afford. He ignored children's stares or parents' terse whispers as they led their kids away. To Chalk-eye's blurred way of thinking, being blemished with what looked like a tiny egg where his left eye should have been wasn't so bad. It was a lot smaller price than a lot of his buddies had paid to get out of Vietnam.

With great reverence, he drew a halfempty bottle of cheap vodka from the pocket of his fatigue jacket, wet his lips while he unscrewed the cap, and took a long pull. Squinting his good eye, he held the bottle toward the light checking how much was left for breakfast. Just enough to ward off the headache he fully expected. He screwed the cap back on. From another pocket he pulled a wad of waxed paper, teased it open and grimaced at the sight of a half-eaten cold-cut sandwich. He lifted a corner of the soggy bread, grunted, then stuffed the whole works back in his coat without taking a bite.

He yawned, bent slowly to his hands and knees, and crawled into his den. The hay smelled sweet. He thought again of his home in Wisconsin and wished he were there. He pulled his collar tight around his neck, tucked it up under his beard, and closed his eyes. The sound of raindrops and the warmth of the booze brought sleep, but not peace. Nightmares of killing fields and hopeless years wandering around America wedged their way between pleasant dreams of the farm and family he still missed after half a lifetime away.

2

Sometime later, much later — he knew because he woke up shivering and he needed to empty his bladder — he heard the muffled rumble of the door at the other end of the barn as it rolled open. He was pretty sure it was really happening because he doubted he would dream the part about having to piss.

Soft, tentative footsteps in the alleyway worked through a blur of sleep and alcohol. He knew the night sounds of a horse barn — straw rustling as thousand-pound bodies rolled to get comfortable, feed tubs rattling when explored by velvet muzzles, occasional fluttering sighs through giant nostrils. These were the nocturnal murmurings he usually heard whispered over the soft purr of the fans. The sound he heard now was not right.

Chalkeye rolled up onto one elbow and aligned his eye for the best view through the crack between the bales.

Movement and inquisitive snorts came from the horses in their stalls. They, too, were aroused by the footsteps, but they didn't seem alarmed.

A shadowy figure, illuminated amber by the security lights, crept to a stall across the alleyway from Chalkeye's den and peered between the bars. The horse within inhaled softly — an identifying whiff — but like the others, seemed calm. Chalkeye heard the latch slide back with a metallic snap and watched the stall door roll open.

He rubbed his spider-veined face, pinched the dryness out of his nose, and tried to focus. No flashlight or key ring jingling, no talking to himself or brash gestures to ward off the loneliness of night duty. This person was not a watchman.

The shadow whispered, "Hey there, Simpatico. How ya doin', big guy?"

With one hand the shadow patted the stallion's muzzle as his other raised a leather halter. Even from his hiding place, Chalkeye thought he caught the scent of its neatsfoot oil.

The stallion sidestepped to the right, and then directed his head into one of the back corners of the stall. His massive haunches that could lay a man out pivoted toward the intruder like cannons on a turret.

A faint whistle of admiration escaped Chalkeye's lips as he watched the shadow ignore the stallion's warning.

"Come on, man. Don't give me a hard time," the shadow cooed. He placed a hand on the stallion's rump, nudged the beast aside, and slid up to the horse's head. "Easy now, it's just a halter. You've worn one a million times. It's just a halter."

The shadow continued his horseman's calming chatter as he slipped the halter over the stallion's muzzle and fitted its leather strap behind his ears. A brass snap clicked, and the stallion was secured.

Chalk-eye watched the intruder teased a plastic bag from a hip pocket and slid it over the stallion's nostrils and mouth. The majestic equine accepted it without resistance.

Deft fingers pulled a drawstring through the halter rings securing the bag over the stallion's face just below his eyes. Then, with one smooth motion, they drew the string snug and tied it. The leadshank was unfastened and the stallion freed.

"Hey, man. This what you get for being the best of the best," the clandestine figure said, and then slipped out of the stall, bolting the door behind.

Chalkeye continued watching, mesmerized, as the stallion held his breath for a long minute. Then, as the air in his lungs was consumed, the horse began to breathe slowly, tentatively. He could exhale without difficulty, but when he inhaled, the bag sucked tight against his nostrils. Gradually, the carbon dioxide began to rise in his blood. The bag kept him from breathing deeper.

"What the hell . . .?" Chalk-eye whispered, but it was lost into the hay.

Another minute passed. The stallion began to tread. He grunted as he strained harder to breathe.

Chalkeye covered his ears, but couldn't make himself stop watching.

The stallion's huge head began to swing from side to side in giant arcs. He dropped his muzzle to his fetlock and pawed at the bag in a vain attempt to remove it. He pitched wildly, reeled, then crashed his muscular shoulder into the hardwood wall with a force that shook the barn. He rebounded onto his hind legs. His poll smashed the ceiling light overhead, sending shards of glass raining down.

The stallion's magnificent brown eyes bulged from their sockets like huge wet marbles and Chalkeye began to cry. Why would anyone hurt such a beautiful animal? He'd seen too much irrational cruelty in his lifetime. The tears descended his cheeks. He hated the shadow-man for what he was doing. He hated himself for doing nothing to stop him.

The stallion careened into the wall one last time, then slid down onto his knees. A shutter waved across his massive body, he stiffened, and melted away from the wall onto his side.

A moment later, the great stallion was dead, and Chalkeye, still frozen with fear, only watched.

The stall door latch snapped again, and the shadow figure crept in. He hesitated a moment over the stallion's lifeless body, then snipped the drawstring, removed the bag and halter, rolled the door shut, and was gone.

Chalkeye knew he couldn't stay. Rain or not, he couldn't sleep in this barn tonight. Not in the presence of death.

He pushed his way out of his haybale lair and, without taking time to brush away the sprigs that clung to his damp clothes, he slipped back out into the night.

As he closed the barn door, he stared out into the rain, pulled the vodka bottle from his jacket and emptied it down his throat. Who could kill such a beautiful horse? *Death follows me*, he thought. He stared at the bottle in his hand. *It's why I need this. Now I can never, never come back to this town.*

He slogged north toward Ottawa.

CHAPTER 2

KENT STEPHENSON DREW IN A DEEP BREATH OF spring air as it blew in through the window of his mobile veterinary unit. He straightened his arms against the steering wheel, and stretched back into the seat. After last night's rain, the weather was perfect — warm and sunny, with the sweet smell of soil and emerging vegetation. Any day was a good day to be a large animal veterinarian, but springtime was special, when the sun was getting higher each day, and the mares were foaling.

"Today is Emily's birthday," he said to Lucinda, the Redbone hound on the seat beside him. "Don't let me forget."

Lucinda pulled her nose back in through the window, gave him her usual expression of infinite loyalty, and wagged her tail.

Emily was Kent's daughter. Cake and ice cream tonight. Fourteen years old! How could that have happened so quickly?

He leaned over and inspected himself in the mirror — not too worn for having a teenage daughter. Thankfully. If anything ever happened to him, Emily might have to go back to her mother. That prospect gave him a chill. He knew it chilled Emily, too. Mary had divorced him and bailed out of their lives years ago. It was the low point of his life — it was what drove him into the darkness — but he had survived. Neither he nor Emily cared to have her mother a part of their lives again.

The half-ring half-buzz of his mobile phone snapped him out of his musing.

"Just finished the swollen fetlock at Fowlers. Heading up to Lark Ridge to check out the sore eye," he said, anticipating his dispatcher's standard first question. Instead, he was surprised to hear Aubrey Fairbank's voice. She was one of only a few clients who had his mobile number — because she was much more than a client. Even so, it was unusual for her to interrupt him while he was working.

A few years back, Aubrey had shown up in Jefferson with a bevy of animal rights activists protesting the use of live animals to test products at the local cosmetic company — which happened to be the town's largest employer. A warm, comfortable feeling wafted over Kent as he recalled how their relationship, a small town vet and a high profile Hollywood actress, had gone from blood enemies to respect and commitment. When the dust settled, Aubrey had parlayed her knowledge of horses, gleaned from her childhood years on an Iowa farm and later turning in the Hollywood horse set, into a position as farm manager at VinChaRo. In no time at all, she, along with her teenage son, Barry, had become a permanent fixture in Jefferson.

He could hear her breathing hard into the phone as if she had been running.

"Kent, we need you over here right now."

"What's going on?"

"Simpatico. We just found him. In his stall. Dead."

"That's not funny."

"I'm not kidding."

"Jesus. What happened?"

"We don't know. He's just lying there. Can you come right now?"

"I'm on my way." And just like that, his comfortable feeling vanished.

Kent slapped the phone onto its dashboard bracket and pulled his truck to the shoulder. He glanced for traffic and was about to pull a U-turn when he had a second thought. He let the truck sit on the side of the road, grabbed the mobile phone again, and punched 'one' into its memory. His housekeeper/stand-in grandmother to Emily answered.

"Margaret. Tell Emily I'll be there in five minutes. I've got a call at VinChaRo. I know she'll want to come along. Pack her a lunch, too, will you? We'll be out for a while."

"Sure," Margaret said. She was accustomed to the urgencies of her boss's dual role as single father and veterinarian, and took such requests in stride. "I'll have her ready, lunch in hand."

Kent reached over and ruffed the hair on Lucinda's back.

"The person who can make my day with the sound of her voice just ruined a perfectly good morning."

Lucinda looked up at him, trying to fathom why she caught agitation in his voice. Any day spent doing horse calls with Kent was a good day as far as she was concerned.

Kent's mobile unit was one of five in the Compassion Veterinary Center's fleet. Each was a sleek, white fiberglass body mounted on a pick-up truck frame and stocked with state-of-the-art veterinary equipment and medicines. He ground his teeth at his helplessness. In spite of all the supplies he had on board, he had nothing that could help Simpatico. He stomped the accelerator and headed to pick up Emily.

Simpatico gone. The thought was like a kick in the gut from a draft horse. Simpatico, The King, the standard bearer of all New York Breds was dead.

"Long live the king," Kent said, under his breath.

Lucinda turned to him and whined softly.

Kent had always felt a sense of pride in being Simpatico's personal veterinarian, but suddenly he felt an irrational anger toward the great horse. "You picked a great day to die," he said. "Happy birthday, Emily."

● ● ●

Kent eyed the familiar sign that read PINE HOLT FARM where his driveway retreated into a grove of white pines. The thought of naming his home had been way over the top to his way of thinking, but in time he had accepted the sign, and maybe even liked it, because it had been Emily's idea.

His ranch-style house was nestled among the trees to disguise its size. There was a clear, green pond surrounded by lawn out back and to one side. Beyond that was a barn, the kind we remember from our childhood stories. A half dozen Polled Herefords loafed near it inside a board fence.

As he pulled to a stop in front of the house, the door opened, and Emily emerged. Glancing down to fix the position of the top step, she started toward her dad, keeping a grip on the railing and placing her foot carefully on each step. Once she had reached the flagstone walk, her pace quickened. Kent leaned on the fender. Lucinda leaned on Kent. Both observed Emily's approach.

She was tall for her age, but the bend in her knees made her appear more average in height. She had big blue eyes, a little nose, freckled across the bridge, and a smile that was warmed by her habit of cocking her head when she flashed it.

Emily had been born with a spinal deformity that bent her lower back and affected the nerves to her legs. Like most girls her age, she was aware of her appearance and tried hard to improve her posture by forcing her shoulders back and swinging her legs straight through as she walked. Despite her efforts, the sharp curve in her lower back forced a bend in her knees. Her walk may have been awkward, but when Kent looked at Emily, all he saw was a wonderfully bright young mind peering alertly out of those brilliant blue eyes. It delighted him to no end that everyone else who knew Emily saw her the same way he did.

How unfair nature could be, Kent thought. Simpatico, a horse — a special one, admittedly, but just a horse really, and having no more sense than one — was the picture of physical perfection. While Emily, the essences of warmth and loving intelligence, was trapped in a crippled body. He pushed the thoughts out of his mind. He learned long ago, that dwelling on such things accomplished nothing.

"Happy birthday, Em,", Kent said. "Fourteen, huh? Almost a grown-up."

"Thanks. I thought you'd forget." She gave him a peck on the cheek, and Lucinda a pat on the head.

"Never. Margaret was supposed to tell you we'd have a birthday cake at dinner tonight."

"She did. I get to open my gifts then."

"If you get any."

"Whatever."

"Big problems at VinChaRo," Kent said, his tone serious. "I figured you'd want to come along."

"Yeah, Mrs. M told me. Thanks, I do," Emily said, picking up on her father's tone. "What happened?"

He opened the passenger door of his mobile unit, and Lucinda, right on cue, hopped over into the back, while Emily pulled herself up and in.

"I'll tell you while we drive. Do you have a lunch?"

She held up a brown bag. Kent took it and waved to his housekeeper who watched from the porch. "Thanks, Margaret."

"See you for supper. You two be careful."

Emily gave Margaret a don't-be-ridiculous scowl.

"Catch you later, Mrs. M."

As they headed down the driveway, she asked, "So, what's happening at VinChaRo, Doc?"

Kent knew Emily was way beyond the sugar-coated version. "They found Simpatico dead in his stall."

Emily turned to her father, a stunned look on her face. "Simpatico is dead? No way!" Her voice trembled.

"Aubrey found him this morning. They want us to see if we can figure out what happened."

"Jesus. What's next?" Emily said.

Kent glanced at Emily, and saw her face blanch. He wondered what connection she was making? Did she sense some evil god was, once again, bearing down on her? The one who had created her infirmity, now had taken Simpatico, too? Kent knew Simpatico was Emily's favorite. And, he knew Emily drew strength from Simpatico's physical perfection.

They had taken her to doctor after doctor when she was young. None could come up with a cause, or treatment plan, for her spine. Surgery, yes, but what type? The doctors did agree on two things, however. One, that any surgery would be extremely risky. Attempting to straighten her back could make it worse, even leave Emily paralyzed. And two, that any attempt at correction should be held off until she finished growing. Kent admired her for the way she had not let her physical challenges define her. Instead, they seemed to fuel her personality, make her plucky, mature beyond her years.

"Honey, I'm sorry. I should have asked. Maybe you don't want to go with me. It's just that..."

"Of course I want to come along," Emily said, drawing herself up. "I've seen dead animals before. It's not that. It's just that it's Simpatico. He is so...special. Thinking of him gone is..." Her voice trailed off. Then she asked, "Now what are we going to do?"

CHAPTER 3

VINCHARO FARM WAS A SHORT RIDE OUTSIDE
of Jefferson, around the west side of Heron Lake. Within minutes,
Kent, Emily, and Lucinda were turning on to its macadam lane. The
entry was a wrought iron gate surrounded by splashes of spring flowers and emerald shrubs. On the gate, a sign with gold lettering read
simply:

VinChaRo Farm
Thoroughbred Horses

Ancient maples formed a canopy over the driveway, and
beyond the trees, on each side, were rolling pastures enclosed by
white board fences. On the left, chestnut and bay brood mares dot-
ted a sea of green. Next to the dark bulk of each mare was a smaller,
leggy replication. To Kent, they were more than beautiful little creatures that he had helped bring into the world, they were living testi-
monials to the New York State Thoroughbred Breeding and Racing
program's success.

The *New York bred program*, as it was usually referred to, was
near and dear to Kent. Back when it was dreamed up by lawmak-
ers as a way to stimulate the state's sagging Thoroughbred industry,
Kent had fought hard for the breeders. He realized that it was vital

to insure that racehorse *breeding*, not just racing, was kept profitable in New York. In the end, his victory guaranteed that a percent of the winner's purse would go to the owner of the winner's dam. That meant serious money for the breeders.

Kent was the longest sitting member of the program's board of governors, and he considered it to be his contribution to his profession and his community. All of New York benefited from the program, and so did the state's veterinarians. Big time.

In less than a decade, the program's infusion of cash had resulted in New York's Thoroughbred breeding industry growing and flourishing beyond all expectations. *New York breds* were winning major stakes races, and farms were selling stock throughout the United States and even in the lucrative Japanese and Middle East markets.

As they drove up the lane, Kent watched the foals nuzzle under their mothers, and then buck and run with their playmates. Life is smoke and mirrors, he thought. Those little creatures don't even know their father, Simpatico, is dead. They don't realize what a blow has been struck against the New York bred program.

On the other side of the driveway, yearlings looked up from their grazing and, anxious for any excuse to run, bolted across the pasture in a tight group, more like a school of fish than a band of horses.

Lucinda fixed her laser stare on the running horses and trembled with excitement. What a blast it would be to chase them.

Emily's stare carried right through them, as if she didn't even notice them. Then, in a soft voice, she said, "Boy, what I wouldn't give to be able to run like that."

They drove past VinChaRo's stone mansion and headed to the barns. There were three in all, each a long rectangular building with outside Dutch doors for the twenty or so stalls it contained. One barn held mares for breeding. One was for foaling. VinChaRo's business office was in the third barn, which was also home to the six mature stallions that stood at the farm. It resembled the other barns, except for a cavernous center pavilion, the breeding shed.

They pulled to a stop in front of a door labeled *office*. "You stay, girl," Kent said to Lucinda, as they got out of the truck.

Horses, especially mares with foals, tended to be wary of strange dogs. Hence, Kent's rule: When he went into a horse barn, Lucinda stayed in the truck. She knew the rule, but just to make sure Kent knew she wasn't happy about it, she let out a half-whine half-grunt sound. Then she turned herself around on the seat, flopped down, and resigned herself to wait.

Aubrey came out to greet them. She was nearly six feet tall, and slender. Her thick, black hair was pulled back into a ponytail that fell down her back. Her skin was smooth and dark, partly from Native American ancestry, and partly from long hours on a horse farm. She radiated a poise and confidence that made it easy to imagine her in her previous life as an actress. But today her eyes pooled with tears as she gave Kent and Emily a sad smile.

"Hi," was all she said.

"Anything new since we talked?" Kent asked.

She wiped her cheek with the back of her hand. "Nothing."

He searched her face for more clues as to how she was handling the catastrophe. All he could read was deep sadness.

"We'll get through this," he said. It sounded awkward and inadequate.

Her lips narrowed and she nodded, eyes cast down. But when she remembered Emily, she forced a brighter smile.

"I know this sounds sort of weird at the moment, Em, but happy birthday."

Instantly tears filled Emily's eyes and spilled over. They hugged, and let the tears fall.

A few years ago when Emily had asked to take riding lessons, the doctors were aghast that her father would even consider such a thing. But Emily had argued fiercely that she could handle it. Aubrey had come to her rescue by agreeing to take time out from her role as farm manager at VinChaRo to be Emily's personal riding instructor. Reluctantly, the doctors agreed, admitting that as long as she was under close supervision, riding probably would do no harm. They reasoned that if straddling a horse caused her too much discomfort, she would decide to quit on her own.

But riding changed Emily's life. She rode every free moment, and there was no discomfort. When she was on a horse she was like everyone else, the same four powerful legs beneath, no awkwardness, no looks from strangers.

Aubrey was a patient but demanding teacher. When Emily's frustration boiled over, Aubrey knew just how, and how hard, to push. "Are you a wannabe or a gonnabe, girl?" she'd say, and Emily would sigh deeply, mumble the teenage equivalent of *you ol' battle-axe* under her breath, and then try again. Kent knew it was a mutual thing — Aubrey drew strength from her young student's fierce determination.

"Elizabeth is waiting for us in the office," Aubrey said. As she led them that way, she said, "Simpatico gone. It's surreal."

"No kidding. I can't believe it. What could have killed him?" Emily said.

Aubrey nodded toward Kent. "We're hoping your dad can tell us that."

● ● ●

Elizabeth St. Pierre's office was a large, comfortable room naturally lit by floor-to-ceiling windows. It was decorated with antique furnishings and a lifetime of horse racing memorabilia. There were matching walnut desks for herself and her son, Charles. A conference table stood to one side and a leather couch was across from it.

15

Elizabeth was standing in front of her desk. The sleeves of her blue cotton blouse were rolled up, and her khakis had a few sprigs of straw clinging at the knees, no doubt from kneeling next to Simpatico. A coil of silver hair on the back of her head was more disheveled than usual, but as always, she wore just enough jewelry to assure any observer that this hardworking woman was also a lady. She looked distraught.

Charles sat behind his desk, surrounded by his shadow, Burton Bush, and several other hirelings. Burton's shepherd dog, Ninja, lay curled at his feet.

In recent years, advancing age and the sheer volume of work had forced Elizabeth to relinquished much of VinChaRo's management responsibilities to Charles, a small man with wavy black hair, combed straight back. His trademark was his open-necked shirt and gold chain around his neck.

"Anybody got any ideas as to what happened to our guy?" Kent said.

Heads shook, glances went to the floor. No one spoke.

Kent could see further questioning was going to get him nowhere. He cleared his throat, "All right then, let's go see what we've got."

As Aubrey led the group into the stallion barn, Kent caught Charles studying the sway of her hips. Instinctively, Kent stepped in front of him, blocking the view.

Burton Bush cursed and swung a foot at Ninja, who had exploited the moment to sneak into the barn. The dog was infinitely loyal to Burton for reasons no one could fathom, except perhaps for their mutual unfriendliness and ill tempers. Ninja retreated back into the office.

"Did he seem sick to anyone?" Kent asked the group.

A general negative murmur.

"Who saw him last?"

"I did," said Osvaldo, VinChaRo's chief hand. His Hispanic voice was surprisingly strong for his slight build. "I did late check last night. He was fine then. They were all fine."

Kent knew VinChaRo's protocol. "That would have been about two o'clock, right, Osvaldo?"

"Yes. Exactly two o'clock."

"Who did the ten o'clock?"

"Me. It was my night," Osvaldo said. "The same person does ten and two checks, and gets to sleep in the next morning." He scanned the group for accusatory glances, but none appeared.

Kent studied the barn as they walked. Immaculate, as always. "Was there any change in Simpatico's routine yesterday?"

"No," Aubrey said, her lips drawn tight in an expression of frustration. "We've all been wracking our brains about that while we were waiting for you. He bred two mares yesterday afternoon, but nothing unusual happened. He handled same as usual. His attitude was good. He ate all his feed last night."

When they reached Simpatico's stall there was a momentary hush as each person braced for the sight to come. Osvaldo rolled back the door, and Kent surveyed the scene. Someone had covered the body with a tarp. It gave the stall an eerie blue hue as it reflected morning sunlight that entered through a window above. Four black hooves and the brush of a black tail protruded from under the tarp.

"Nothing much I can do here," said Charles, queasiness apparent in his voice. He turned and headed back to the office.

Burton rubbed the mayonnaise-colored crescent of skin that showed between his jeans and T-shirt. "Yeah, I'm outta here too."

Several others in the group uttered lame excuses and departed.

Simpatico lay close to the back wall. By the contour of the tarp, Kent could tell the horse was on his left side, and the head was facing away from him. He noticed that the ceiling light was broken and two of the hardwood wall planks had been broken and pushed completely through into the next stall.

"Definitely looks like he was violent. Maybe he colicked. Osvaldo, you didn't hear him rolling or pawing last night?"

"No, sir, Doc. I looked in each stall. Everybody was quiet."

"He got the same thing to eat he always gets, right?"

"Yes," Aubrey said. "We haven't changed a thing in weeks. No new deliveries of grain. Same hay."

"Well, he sure trashed this stall. All the other horses are okay?"

"For the most part. We gave them all a good look over. Hubris was pretty freaked-out, but that's understandable, him being next door. I mean, he did get his stall wall pushed in."

Kent set down his black leather grip and looked over at Emily who stood quietly to one side. She seemed to be holding up under what would have crushed an average kid.

"Emily, in the back of the truck there's a tray with some specimen bottles. Would you get it for me, please? And a pail of water with disinfectant."

Emily nodded and slipped out of the stall.

Kent turned back to the tarp, lifted a corner, and peered beneath. The odor of body fluids and death had already accumulated under it. Simpatico's eyes, always animated in life, full of personality, wonderfully devious, were now devoid of expression. Kent stepped back, leaned against the wall, and waited for his knees to stop quivering.

Elizabeth noticed and stepped to him, threaded her arm through his. "Kent, are you sure you can do this?"

"No. But I'm going to try like hell."

He stepped into a pair of coveralls that he pulled from his grip, rolled the sleeves to above his elbows, and slipped on a pair of rubber gloves. He took the tray and pail from Emily, and set them next to the corpse. "You can stay and watch if you want," he said, as a warning to the few remaining onlookers

"Step in at the office when you're finished, Kent," Elizabeth said, over her shoulder as she turned to leave. Others followed until only Emily and Aubrey remained.

As Kent withdrew a large postmortem knife from his grip and knelt next to Simpatico, his face collapsed into a look of utter sadness. He gently patted the horse's shoulder. "I'm so sorry, buddy," he said. "If there was any possible way I could avoid doing this to you, I would."

CHAPTER 4

THE BARN WAS QUIET EXCEPT FOR THE OCCA-
sional rustle or snort from horses in nearby stalls as Kent knelt next
to Simpatico's body, meticulously dissecting it, and carefully searching for clues to how he died. Within minutes a dark band of sweat
appeared across the back of his coveralls.

Emily rested against the wall at a good angle for observation
— but she looked away. Aubrey donned a pair of gloves. Over time
spent with Kent, she had become an able assistant — Yet another of
her traits he found amazing.

"Remember the day we confirmed Lady in Linen was pregnant
to Ever Up?" Kent said. "Remember what it was like?"

Aubrey angled so Kent could see her face, but Emily could not.

"I think we celebrated with a bottle of chardonnay, and a roll in
the grass," she whispered, letting her eyes dance.

Kent flashed Aubrey a soft scowl, and a nod toward Emily.

She returned him a *like-she-doesn't-know-about-such-
things* look.

He sat back on his heels, letting his gloved hands rest on
Simpatico. His mind drifted to earlier times. Silence hung while
Aubrey let him have his moment.

After a while he resumed his work, and said, "Everyone thought
Elizabeth was crazy to pay so much for Lady in Linen."

"She knew what she was doing," Aubrey said, as held back a fold of skin.

"Over a year of studying pedigrees, talking to agents, going to sales — she knew what she was doing, all right."

"She was creating a dynasty."

"The reign of Simpatico," Emily said.

Kent had almost forgotten she was there, and her voice startled him. "That's right, Em."

Kent puddled through slippery coils of intestine.

Aubrey held out a specimen bottle, and Kent turned to deposit a piece of tissue in it. In the process, his elbow brushed the curve of her breast. She didn't pull away.

In the revolting environment of that moment, the touch strengthened both of them. She was the one person with whom he shared his innermost feelings. Secretly, he wrestled with the wisdom of asking her to commit. He wanted to, for sure, but sometimes he questioned whether she preferred her own space. One thing he did know for sure, Aubrey was a beacon of light for him and Emily.

"Remember how he was?" Aubrey said. "The way those beautiful black legs unfolded when he was born. From the first time he lifted his head out of the straw he was different from the rest. His eyes. It was like he could see right through you."

"Back then he was just Lady in Linen's colt. Didn't even have a name."

"Count on Elizabeth, the master of weird names, to come up with *Simpatico*," Emily said. "I had to look it up."

"It was perfect for him," Aubrey said, as she continued to hold out jar after jar, some empty and some containing formalin, for Kent to drop in sugar-cube size pieces of liver, kidney, muscle, brain, stomach contents, and everything else.

"Winner of eleven major stakes, Horse of the Year twice, and retired healthy with earnings over a million. Good thing he transmitted his genes to his offspring."

"Thank God. Hopefully he packed it all in Hubris."

They had been at it just over an hour and a half when Kent stood, peeled off his gloves, and laid them on the tray stacked with specimens. He wiped the sweat off his brow with his forearm. Then he blew out a sad sigh.

"Done," he said.

He let his eyes drift over Simpatico's remains — one last slow-take of what was once his favorite patient, even more than that — his friend. His eyes burned.

"Goddammit," he said, as he arranged the tarp to hide the body. "This may be the last time I actually see this, but I guarantee, I'll see it in my mind every time I close my eyes for a long time to come."

He heard a soft sniffle and looked over to see Emily, head down, crying, her tears dripping into the straw.

His heart went out to his daughter as he stepped over to her, and he extended his hand to help her stand.

"I know you are scared at the thought of not having Simpatico around anymore," he said, as he wrapped her in a hug. "We all are. He was so important. But we'll get through this. I promise."

He shifted so they were face to face, and wiped a tear from her cheek. "You believe me, right?"

She nodded weakly. Then sniffed again, collecting herself.

To reset her mind, Kent said, "Would you take the instruments out to the truck and rinse them off? Leave the samples. I want to handle them myself." He turned to include Aubrey. "I'm going to get cleaned up. How about I meet you ladies in the office."

When Emily was gone, he said to Aubrey in a soft tone, "Riesling,"

"What?" Aubrey said, caught off guard.

"We had a bottle of Riesling, not Chardonnay, that time we celebrated Lady in Linen's pregnancy."

Aubrey squeezed his arm and smiled. "You know, things like that are the reason I keep you around."

He walked toward the washroom. His legs felt weak, tingly from kneeling too long.

He stood six-feet even and weighed one-eighty, just as he had in college. Even so, these signs of age bothered him. He reminded himself again that he was going to have to get on a regular exercise program. But that would have to wait. In the next few weeks, maybe months, he was going to have his hands full dealing with the many ramifications of New York losing its top Thoroughbred stallion. Worse yet, in the next five minutes, he had to figure a way to tell the folks waiting in VinChaRo's office that he had no idea what killed their horse.

●　●　●

When he entered the office, Elizabeth, Aubrey, and Emily were sitting on the couch. Charles was again behind his desk. Burton Bush leaned into the corner. They all held looks of anticipation, except Burton, who stared blankly down at Ninja. His red hair scattered from his head in all directions. It was the reason why the other farm hands called him "The Burning Bush."

Kent stepped toward a chair three feet in front of Burton. Ninja considered that too close and emitted a soft growl until Burton changed it to a yelp by thumping the dog's ribs with the side of his foot.

"Don't kick the dog," Kent said, and gave Burton a look that registered his anger. "It doesn't help anything."

Kent refocused on the crowd. He raised his hands at his sides, palms up. "I wasn't able to determine what killed him," he said. "I did as complete an autopsy as possible and couldn't find anything." His frustration was palpable.

"What about any injuries?" someone asked.

"He does have a fractured left scapula just above the shoulder and quite a few cuts and bruises around his head. None of that had much swelling or hemorrhage, so I'm thinking they were from him slamming around the stall. They weren't what killed him.

"Can you tell what time it happened?"

"Based on lividity, I'd guess he's been dead for close to eight hours. It's about ten o'clock now, so I'd put the time of death at soon after the two o'clock check."

When no one could come up with any more questions, Kent said, "I'm taking a bunch of blood and tissue samples back to the diagnostic lab. With a little bit of luck, they will be able to tell us something." He paused, tried to think of something else to add but couldn't, so he finished with, "I'm very sorry, Elizabeth."

"Yes. Well, we all are," Elizabeth said. "We'll just have to wait and see." She sounded exhausted.

"I'll put a rush on everything, of course," he said, and then he had another thought. "Did you talk to the insurance company, yet?"

"They'll be sending some papers and I'll need a statement from you. They were very nice about it. They didn't see any reason to prolong things after you made your examination. As far as they are concerned, we can dispose of the body as we see fit." She glanced at her son. "Charles and Burton will bury him on the ridge."

In the beginning days of VinChaRo, Elizabeth and her husband, Ward, had designated a farm cemetery in a grove of sugar maples on the ridge behind the mansion. Each grave was marked with a granite boulder. A brass plate bearing the horse's name, age, racing record, or any other information they felt worthy of mention, was secured to the rock. Kent had always thought it was a wonderful tribute to VinChaRo Thoroughbreds and an honorable final resting spot for them. Still, it was too early for Simpatico.

"I'll get a marker plate made up," Charles said.

Elizabeth nodded in acceptance of the offer. Charles was the middle of Elizabeth and Ward's children. Their first was Vincent, who, after graduating from the Air Force Academy, had perished in a bombing raid over Laos. Their third was Rosemary, who never showed much interest in the farm. She pursued a life as cellist in the New York City Philharmonic. It was from the names of the three children that they had derived the farm name — VinChaRo. Charles was the heir apparent.

Kent pushed himself to his feet. "I'll plan on taking a walk up to the ridge when you've got the plaque mounted. I'd like to see it." He glanced at Emily. "Probably we all would."

After the group broke up, Kent circled back around to fine Aubrey, who had slipped out early. He found her in a quiet section of the barn half-heartedly grooming Hubris.

When she saw him approaching, she set down her brush. "It doesn't seem possible that the absence of one horse could make this huge barn feel so empty."

"Not knowing is a bitch," he said.

"You got that right. I want to be the first to hear anything."

"You will be. I promise."

● ● ●

The second Kent and Emily were back in the truck with doors slammed for their departure, Emily began bombarding her father with questions.

"Doc, what do you really think?"

"You heard everything I said."

"I mean, if you had to guess."

Kent face folded into a baffled look. "I don't know, Em. There're a lot of possibilities."

"Like what?"

"Well, at first I was thinking colic, but I should have seen evidence of that during the autopsy. So, the next thing that comes to mind is some kind of a stroke. Or, horses can have acute heart failure, a lot like a heart attack. That's a possibility. Both are really hard to diagnose during an autopsy. The tissue samples may help us, though."

Lucinda hung her head over into the front seat. Her eyes half closed as Emily stroked her velvety ears.

"It's weird," Emily said. "He hasn't been sick. I mean, at least no one thought he was. You just gave him a check-up before breeding season, and he was fine. Right?"

"Yep. I gave him a complete physical. Granted, that doesn't show everything, but he seemed healthy as a horse."

Emily didn't acknowledge his weak pun, so he went on.

"His blood work was fine, too. The whole idea of doing all that is to try to anticipate problems. Obviously, it doesn't always work."

Kent turned and watched the rural scenery pass by for a long moment. Finally, he said, "I'm still thinking colic is high on the list, even though I didn't find any sign of it. I could have missed it. Colic fits. It's common. It can come on without warning. You've seen enough cases. You know how violent they get when the pain in their belly becomes unbearable. There is no question in my mind that Simpatico was violent. At least at the end."

"Do you really think the diagnostic lab can tell what happened?"

"I'm counting on it. Dr. Holmes is the best of the best. If anybody can figure it out, he can."

● ● ●

After VinChaRo, Kent and Emily visited several farms and examined horses with garden-variety coughs, lameness, and skin problems. They checked a few mares for breeding soundness and made out shipping papers for a colt sold to a racing syndicate in California.

As they climbed back into the truck, Kent checked his watch. "It's noon already. Let's stop in Mattson for lunch. Want to?"

"Good with me," Emily said. "I'm starved."

Mattson was a tiny hamlet, not much more than a four corners where, a century ago, there had been a gristmill. Not much remained. However, it did have one outstanding feature — their favorite place to eat lunch — the Mattson Cemetery.

He guided his truck into the cemetery through a break in the stone fence, and wound his way between ancient trees shading the tombstones. A thick mat of myrtle kept the grass at bay without mowing. The headstones were mostly simple gray rectangles, weathered to illegibility, and tilting in all directions — cozy and secluded, perfect for a picnic.

He pulled to a stop on the circular lane that wound through the headstones, and opened the door to let Lucinda out for a run. Kent and Emily each picked a marker with enough grass around it for a good seat cushion, and just the right tilt to serve as a comfortable backrest, and sat. As they had done many spring days before, they spread the lunches Margaret had prepared for them onto their laps.

For a while they ate in silence, content to watch Lucinda chase a fat gray squirrel away from whatever he was burying under one of the maples.

Finally Emily said, "It's going to hurt the program."

It took Kent a second to refocus on Simpatico.

"Yeah, well, the New York Bred Program is not built on one horse."

She gave Kent her *I'm-not-buying-it* look. "He was our most important stallion."

"The others will have to pick up the slack."

"Which ones?"

Kent crumpled an empty potato chip bag. "Well, off the top of my head, Cedar Cut's got Charter Oak and there's Solar Wind at Keuka View. They're both super stallions."

"What about VinChaRo?"

"Hubris moves to the number one slot now."

"Think he can do it?"

"He's Simpatico's son, he packs Simpatico's genes. He'll do fine."

"His first crop of foals is just getting to the track now. We don't really know."

"Yeah, but those that have raced have won big. It's looking like he's got what it takes to be a great stallion."

Lucinda wandered back and flopped down next to Kent.

"Hubris is the man now."

CHAPTER 5

IT WAS AFTER FIVE O'CLOCK WHEN KENT, EMILY, and Lucinda made it back to the Compassion Veterinary Center, the mega animal hospital that was Kent's pride and joy.

He had broken ground on the CVC a few years back, soon after he and Aubrey met, and she had pulled him out of his dark period. They were in the intensive care unit at the Cornell University vet school at the time, watching Lucinda recover from a gunshot wound, when the idea struck him. Right then and there, he pledged to rebuild his tiny, outdated animal clinic into a state-of-the-art veterinary medical center. Jefferson's cosmetic manufacturer, who was eager to show her gratitude for all he had done to save her business, pledged a pile of money. Aubrey reached back to her former life as an actress and picked the pockets of her wealthy Hollywood friends. And even the animal rights group, Freedom of Animals Movement, which had brought Aubrey to Jefferson in the first place, made a huge donation. The project had consumed Kent, but the outcome was spectacular.

Today his satisfaction was tempered. Today, neither he nor the CVC had been able to help Simpatico.

He scanned the client parking area. It was jammed with cars. "Looks like office hours are in full swing."

The frenetic activity level within confirmed his suspicion. Half a dozen doctors quick stepped in and out of exam rooms. As many technicians shuttled samples to the lab, and reported back with results. Canine toenails clattered on the quarry tile floor as owners were dragged behind huffing, tugging dogs. Cat owners clunked over-size carriers into door jams and cabinets as they worked their way in and out of the reception area.

Just then a pair of gangly teenage boys came down the hall carrying a stretcher with a huge Basset Hound on it. One was Aubrey's son, Barry, and the other was his best friend, Nathan.

"Hi, fellas. What you got there?" Kent asked, as he made room for them to pass.

"HBC," Barry said, not breaking stride. "Just arrived. We're hoping it's a fractured pelvis, not his back."

Kent's cringed. *Hit by cars* were never good, but better a pelvis than a back.

"You guys are getting to be quite the diagnosticians. All your hard work is paying off."

Both boys beamed.

"Maybe," Barry said," but we're going to let the real doctors say for sure."

"Probably smart."

"Very smart," Emily said, teasing the boys.

Barry's eyebrows rose in a look of false indignation. "Hey, Em, we've got this place ticking like a Swiss watch."

Emily's glanced around. "Yep. Run-of-the-mill chaos."

Lucinda pushed her shoulder against Kent's leg to keep from being run over.

"Afternoon, Sally," Kent said to his hospital director, when she caught up to him. "Looks like the ship's on an even keel?"

Sally's short-cropped hair was mussed. Her Irish cheeks glowed. She bent and gave Lucinda a pat on the head. "Busy. Very busy. But I'm not complaining."

"Just the way we like it. Right?"

"Keeps the bills paid." Then the freckles merged across her forehead. "Anyway, what happened at VinChaRo?"

Kent told her how they found Simpatico, about the autopsy and what little they knew at this point. Already it seemed he'd repeated the story a hundred times. And, already he hated the empty words he put together to really say nothing. He ended with a shrug that signaled she would have to wait for the pathology report like everyone else.

"You might as well tell the rest of the staff," he said. "They're going to find out anyway, and maybe we can keep the rumors down." Then he had another thought. "And, we'll probably be getting a lot of phone calls about it, so remind everyone that all requests for information go to you or me."

"I'll tell Kathy. She's handling the phones now." Sally disappeared down the hall.

Kent and Emily weaved their way through the building to the diagnostic lab where they unloaded the specimens to a technician who began inventorying them in. After guarding them all day, Kent was relieved to pass them on.

As Emily handed each item to the tech, she studied their contents. There were pieces of heart, lung, liver, spleen, kidney, intestine, and muscle clinging to the inside of zip-lock bags like thawing dinner. There were samples of blood, stomach contents, urine, and joint fluid in glass vials and tubes.

"It's gross to do this to Simpatico," she said, giving her father a guilty look.

"I agree," Kent said. "But we need to know why he died."

"Who died?" Peter Murphy, the CVC's head equine surgeon, asked as he entered, and pulled himself to a seat on the lab counter.

Peter was right out of James Herriot's *All Creatures Great and Small* — a gangly six-foot-four, an uncooperative head of sandy hair, and lots of tweed. He was raised outside of Birmingham, England, the heart of foxhunt country, and educated at the Royal Veterinary

College. There was no better equine surgeon in the United States, and no one Kent trusted more.

Before Kent could answer, Peter, intrigued by the mound of specimens, picked up one and read it.

"Oh, the VinChaRo thing," he said, "I heard a few murmurings about it earlier today. Sorry."

Peter was the consummate professional. Kent knew Peter would not bother to ask the next obvious, but unanswerable question.

Kent eased back onto the counter across from Peter. "I honestly don't know what happened," he said, without prompting. "I've considered everything from accidental electrocution to poison, to…" He held up his hands in frustration. "To — you name it. About all I can say for sure is that Simpatico was violent at the end. He had a nasty scapular fracture and a bunch of lacerations and contusions on his head. That's it."

Peter toyed with one of the vials for a moment. "Any chance of foul play?"

"I'm not ruling it out. Or anything else for that matter. But nothing really points to it."

"Well if there is anything you need from me, just ask," Peter said, then added, "How is Elizabeth holding up?"

"She's okay. You know how stoic she is. Of course, it's a huge loss. She loved that horse. But the farm will go on." Kent hesitated. "Charles, on the other hand, I'm not sure. He's hard to read. My guess is he feels it more as a personal financial blow than as the loss of a great horse."

"Yeah. I get that. How about Aubrey?"

"She's hurting. She was real close to Simpatico. She's going to be messed up for a while."

"No doubt."

Kent looked around and saw that Emily had finished giving the samples to the tech and wandered off. "I've had enough for today. I'm going to find Emily and get out of here. See you in the morning."

"Good idea," Peter said, pushing himself off the counter. "I have a couple of post-op checks, and I'm right behind you."

Kent found Emily in Sally's office highlighting names on a computer printout.

"Taking my helper?" Sally said, with a faux frown.

"Yep. We have a birthday dinner tonight."

"Oh, that's right. Happy birthday, Em."

"Thanks. I didn't make it all the way down this list."

Sally waved it off. "No problem. You don't sound too excited about your birthday."

Emily didn't respond.

Sally gently clasped Emily's chin, and turned her to look her in the eye. "Hey, young lady, don't get hung up on things out of your control. None of this Simpatico stuff is your fault. Your birthday is your birthday. You celebrate."

Emily smiled weakly. "Thanks, Sally."

● ● ●

Kent and Emily drove home to Pine Holt — to Margaret, the cows, and Emily's pony, Flame.

Margaret had prepared a birthday feast as promised. For her sake, they worked hard to maintain a party mood. Even so, it seemed forced. He hated it when his work interfered with his family, but he knew Simpatico's death was going to be wedging its way into his life for a long while.

CHAPTER 6

THE INTRUDER DUCKED INTO THE BARN through a feed room door at Cedar Cut Farm, flattened his back against the wall, and squinted at the luminous face of his watch. Just after three. Right on schedule.

He slipped a hand into his pocket to be sure the all-important vial was still nestled there. It was. Of course it was. Everything had been planned perfectly.

Easing across the feed room, he paused to peek down the main alleyway. These barns were all alike at night — dark, silent, giant beasts lurking — creepy as hell. Every odd noise made him jump. He was wired. He needed a drink, bad. He wiped his palms on his thighs and told himself to be cool.

For a moment he thought back to Simpatico with a twisted sense of pride. Damn fool had stood right there and let himself be suffocated. He exhaled a soft laugh, and then he swallowed hard as fear crept in again.

This one would not be so easy. This stallion had a nasty rep — real nasty if he wanted to be — downright dangerous.

The intruder moved slowly down the row of stalls. Next to the last one on the right. Hell, a couple of beers at Kolbie's Tavern and the idiot farmhands had told him everything he wanted to know.

A brass nameplate on the stall door read *Charter Oak*.

A loud snort came from inside and the intruder glanced between the bars to size up his victim. Charter Oak flattened his ears against his head, bared his teeth, and came at the bars like a snake.

"Ugly bastard," the intruder whispered.

He dropped to one knee in front of Charter Oak's stall, pulled out a zip lock bag full of horse feed, opened it, and set it on the floor. More carefully, he took the small vial from his pocket, unscrewed its cap, and mixed the amber fluid into the grain.

Maintaining a low voice, he said. "There we are, Your Highness. Your special treat is ready." He held it toward the horse at arm's length and entered the stall.

Charter Oak caught the sweet scent of molasses. His nostrils flared.

"Ha. Even you can be bought. Now you just take it easy while I slip this little snack into your feed tub and I'll be out of here so fast it'll make your head spin."

The intruder kept a sharp eye on the stallion, moved cautiously to a corner of the stall, and deposited the grain mix into the feed tub. Then he stepped back out, eyes still on the horse.

Charter Oak turned to the tub, sniffed inquisitively, and began eating.

A satisfied grin crept across the intruder's face.

He remembered what he had been told. Forty-eight hours and that horse wouldn't be worth shit. *Two down.*

CHAPTER 7

KENT TOOK A LATE AFTERNOON EMERGENCY call for a Quarter horse that had come in from the pasture three-legged lame. They shot a few radiographs with the portable machine and confirmed the coffin bone was fractured. He waited around to help the farrier get a bar shoe on the guy, and then he cast the leg. Before he left, he informed the owner that they would be seeing a lot of each other for a while.

He arrived back at the Compassion Veterinary Center late, as usual. Dampness in the air was accentuated by a gusty wind that blew tiny tornadoes across the empty parking area.

A week had passed since Simpatico's death and, surprisingly, life had gone on pretty much as always. There were still animals to treat and family matters to juggle.

A chill rattled down his spine as he entered the quiet warmth of the building. Hot dinner, hot shower. That's what he needed. A hot woman, that's what he wanted. He wondered what Aubrey was doing at the moment.

The hospital was silent, in its night mode, with just a skeleton crew. He glanced through an observation window into the main equine treatment room, and smiled. He could see a horse standing in the stocks. Next to it Barry was on his knees, helping a young veterinarian dress a wound. As she worked, she was teaching Barry the correct way to bandage a horse's leg.

When he got to his office, he found his desk littered with veterinary journals, bills, invoices, statements in need of review, correspondence requiring his approval and signature, and little yellow stick-up notes. It was pretty much the way he had left it that morning, except for one new addition. Taped to his lamp in the place that had evolved as the spot reserved for items needing immediate attention was a small note:

4:30 p.m.

Ed Holmes is looking for you. Wants to talk about Simpatico. Will be in the dx lab till 5:30.

Sally

Finally, some information about the tissue samples. It seemed as though the lab had taken forever to process them. Kent glanced at his watch.

"Damn," he said, as he picked up the phone. Why hadn't Sally called him on the truck phone? Then he remembered that he'd been in a barn, away from the truck from about 4:00 till closing. She had probably tried.

He dialed the extension for the diagnostic laboratory and got a recording.

He was tempted to try Ed's home number, but then reminded himself how much he disliked such arrogant exhibitions of self-importance when they interrupted him at home. No, he was doomed to wait till tomorrow.

● ● ●

At Pine Holt, Kent fed the cows, then washed up and put on a tattered guayabera Emily had given him a few Christmases ago.

Emily updated him on school and her progress with Flame. She was developing the little pony into quite the dressage horse, and he was learning quickly. School was boring. And today a letter arrived from Maria Castille, an Ecuadorian girl who had become a family friend when she did an internship at the CVC a year ago. In her letter, Maria said she wanted to come back for the summer. Emily had written her back immediately — of course she could, it was a great idea.

Kent smiled and feigned interest at the appropriate times, but he couldn't get into Emily's running conversation.

"I'd like to have Maria around again," he said, without much enthusiasm. "She's a lot of fun, and she was one of our best interns we ever had." He gave Emily a five out of a possible ten stern look. "You probably should have asked me first."

Emily was just starting to catch on to her father's glum mood, and not liking it, when Margaret stuck her head in from the kitchen.

"Evening, Kent. We waited dinner for you. Lasagna. It'll be ready in a few minutes."

"Thanks, Margaret."

"Also, I know you hate phone calls at home, but Dr. Holmes called about 45 minutes ago. It sounded important. He said you'd probably want to call him at his house this evening, and that it was okay. He made me promise to give you the message. Sorry." She reached into the pocket of her apron and took out a grocery receipt.

"Here," she said, handing it to him, "his number is on the back."

Margaret and Emily expected a groan from Kent, and gave each other perplexed looks when he snatched the note and said, "Can you hold dinner ten minutes? Just ten minutes. That's all I ask."

"Sure. No problem," Margaret said. "Wow."

"I'll just make this call and be right back. I mean it." He disappeared into his study, and a moment later had Dr. Holmes on the line.

"Ed, I appreciate your calling me at home. Sorry to bother you at night, but you're right, I am eager to know what you found."

"No problem. Here's what we've got." Holmes's voice dropped into an analytical drone. "All tissues were histologically normal except lung and heart. As you noted, there was petechial hemorrhage on the lung surfaces and some pulmonary emphysema. The lung histo just confirmed it. So that's not too enlightening. But, I did find quite a bit of hemorrhage on the surface of the heart. You probably would have seen it on the gross, except that it was buried in pericardial fat. That was about it." Holmes paused for Kent to take in the information, then he started again. "So, when I have a happy, apparently healthy horse that dies suddenly, and bleeding on the surface of the heart is all I can find, I start thinking, A, toxins, or B, acute anoxia."

Dr. Holmes paused again, no doubt expecting a response from Kent. When none came, he continued in the same objective tone. "The pulmonary emphysema, plus what you told me about the fractures and contusions, would support your suspicion that he died violently, too."

"So you're thinking poison or suffocation?"

"Right."

"I know there was nothing poisonous within a mile of the guy. Whatever. What kind of poison could cause the stuff you found?"

"Plant poisons like bracken fern or sweet-clover would do it. Maybe chemicals like arsenic — unlikely knowing where he was. Maybe endotoxins."

"What about the stomach contents or the blood samples, any poisons there?"

"I was getting to that. I had my techs run tests for everything I could think of. Nothing panned out. But remember, endotoxins would be virtually undetectable, at least with what we can do here."

"But wouldn't endotoxins require an initial infection, or colic, or some sort of nasty sickness to set them off?"

"Usually."

"There wasn't any."

"Right. So, let's say we can rule out endotoxins. That pretty much takes care of possibilities in our first group, poisons. Any chance of anoxia?"

"I checked that horse's airway from nostrils to alveoli. It was clear all the way, no obstruction anywhere."

"And his stall was well ventilated, right?"

"Ed, come on. This was a multi-million dollar horse. He lived in the lap of luxury."

"Just asking. I'm grasping for anything here. Take it easy."

"Sorry. I was hoping for a cause of death that was totally out of our control. You know — some weird act of God, so that we could put this thing to rest."

"You're dreaming."

"Asking quite a lot, isn't it?"

"I'd give it to you if I could. Unfortunately, things hardly ever work out that neatly."

"I know you're doing your best. You *are* the best."

"I'll get you a written report that summarizes everything. Officially, the cause of death is *undetermined*."

Kent blew a humorless laugh through his nose, too soft for Dr. Holmes to hear. Then he said, "Thanks again, Ed, for letting me bother you at home. You keep me posted, and I'll do the same for you."

"You got it. Good talking to you."

When Kent returned to the kitchen, a hot meal and warm company was waiting. He hardly noticed either.

CHAPTER 8

KENT'S LEATHER-HEELED SHOES CLICKED ON the freshly buffed floors of the Syracuse airport terminal. Emily's sneakers squeaked softly as her gait caused her foot to twist with each step. The drone of a maintenance worker's vacuum cleaner harmonized with the hum of a huge ventilation system. Predawn blackness outside made the terminal windows reflect like enormous anthracitic mirrors. The security guard operating a metal detector dozed on a stool beside her machine. She still had an hour till the real hustle and bustle began.

Within minutes Kent and Emily would be reunited with Maria Castille, and that thought raised Kent's spirits. A mix of impatience and warmth roiled in his chest like a parent waiting for a long-absent child. He looked over at Emily. She hadn't stopped talking about Maria since the letter arrived a week ago. Now she was beside herself.

"Why do you figure Maria left her job in Kentucky?" Emily asked, as she dropped into a chair near the gate. "She didn't say why in her letter."

Kent shrugged. "She'll tell us when she gets here."

He was wondering the same thing. After graduation from Clinton College, Maria had taken the perfect job at Hector Figurante's Farm, Criadero Del Jugador. It was one of Kentucky's premier

Thoroughbred horse farms. An occasional letter from her had indicated all was going well. Why would she give that up?

Maria was the eldest daughter of one of Ecuador's wealthiest men. Her father sent her to Clinton College, in Jefferson, because, even though it was a small school, it offered strong programs in both equine studies and business, which fit perfectly into Señor Castille's plan to have Maria manage the family's horse farm outside of Quito when she returned to Ecuador.

During the spring semester of their senior year, all equine studies students at Clinton were required to work in a horse-related field. Maria pulled down a much-sought-after internship at the CVC. Since spring was the foaling season and generated so much night emergency work, Kent had arranged for her to stay at Pine Holt. That way she could accompany him on night calls, where the real action was. Maria and Emily had become instant pals.

"There she is, Doc," Emily said, pointing through the glass. "That's Maria." She broke for the arrival gate, and yelled for him to hurry up.

He waved for her to go ahead. He loved seeing Emily so happy and was content to watch the girls reunite from a distance.

The double glass doors swung open and a herd of passengers pushed through splitting left and right to hugs of loved ones, car rental desks, and the bag claim area. Two heavyset businessmen peeled off, and there was Maria. Her normally springy stride was encumbered by the weight of two oversize carry-ons. The hem of her light wool coat nearly dragged on the floor with each step. Kent chuckled at the sight of her struggling. When Maria saw Emily, her face broke into a radiant smile. He had forgotten how captivating that smile could be.

He saw instantly that Maria had matured in the year she was away. She had grown slightly taller into delicately framed womanhood. The erratic body movements of youth were now replaced by fluid grace. The foal had become a beautiful filly.

Maria wrapped Emily in a swaying, sighing, from-the-bottom-of-the-heart embrace. Then, for a long moment they held each other at arms length, smiling and laughing, oblivious to other passengers skirting around them.

Maria was endowed with utterly smooth black hair. Her mahogany eyes were embellished with long lashes and the Kentucky spring had changed her olive skin to a silky bronze.

"Can I help you with your bags, Miss?" Kent said, and his greeting startled both girls.

"Doc," Maria said, forcing herself to show restraint. "It's good to see you." She extended her hand, politely.

"Don't give me that formal stuff," Kent said, as he pushed her hand aside and lifted her in a bear hug. "If you're going to be a member of our family, you'd better start acting like one."

Emily applauded. "Yeah. That's what I'm talking about."

Maria returned the hug eagerly. "I'm so glad to be back with you guys."

Her carry-on bags were jammed drum-tight. Her hanging bag resembled a half inflated life raft.

"I see you carried everything on the plane," Kent said. "No need to stop at the baggage claim, right? You really didn't have to pack your saddle, Maria. We have extras, you know."

"This is just my makeup. I hope you brought a van."

Emily stuck her tongue out at her father.

"Oh, so that's how it's going to be this summer. Two against one."

At the baggage claim, Kent began to wish he had brought a van as he hauled several more laden bags off the rotating platform. Emily heaved each onto the courtesy cart, laughing at her father's dismay.

● ● ●

The three of them chattered and reminisced for the forty-five minute drive from Syracuse to Pine Holt. Margaret fixed brunch and joined them for more stories, updates, and planning for the summer, as they devoured omelets and fresh melon. The only somber moment was when they told Maria about Simpatico.

The second the last fork was laid to rest on its plate, Emily stood up and began clearing the table.

"What's the big hurry?" Kent asked, surprised by his daughter's sudden eagerness to do cleanup.

"I want to take Maria out to see the horses."

Kent winked at Margaret. "You ladies go ahead. I can help here."

He waited till the girls were gone, then asked his housekeeper, "What do you think?"

"About what?"

"About Maria staying here for the summer?"

"I love it! She's a wonderful girl, and welcome anytime, as far as I'm concerned."

"It'll be fun having her around again."

Margaret stopped organizing dishes. "Young girls should have someone to giggle with and tell secrets to. You know, Kent, Emily is growing up fast. She needs a girlfriend she can talk to. Someone to go shopping with, teach her about makeup — and boys."

Kent's face crumpled into a mock look of total lost. "I thought you covered the girlie stuff."

Margaret's eyes rolled. "You don't get it. I help with the motherly advice."

"Whew. I was worried there for a second."

"What I'm talking about is different."

"A big sister?"

"Right. Maria is perfect."

"She's a good role model," Kent said, as he carted an armful of dishes into the kitchen and returned with a soapy sponge. "Why do you think Maria came back to Jefferson? Doesn't it seem odd that she'd come back for the summer after accepting one of the best jobs offered to anyone in her graduating class?"

"Probably because she doesn't have to work at all," Margaret said. "She's a rich, gorgeous young woman. She can do whatever she wants, whenever she wants."

Kent wiped off the table. "Uh-huh."

Then Margaret added, "She said her father expects her to run the family horse farm in Ecuador. She probably wants to bounce around a little before she goes back home."

"Makes sense. Anyway, like you say, having her around will be good for Emily. Me too, for that matter. She's always a willing hand on farm calls." He shook some soap into the chambers on the door panel and closed the dishwasher. "Done. You need me anymore?"

"I'm fine. You go see what the girls are up to."

● ● ●

Kent caught up with Maria and Emily as they crossed the lawn headed toward the barn. He noticed that both had changed into riding clothes.

"Flame and I have taken up dressage," Emily said to Maria. "He's an amazing pony. I mean he's always been cool about doing whatever I asked, but he's getting old now and I thought he might not like the discipline. Turns out, he loves it." Pride shown in her eyes. "I taught him to do pretty good half passes, and sort of a piaffe."

"That's great, Em," Maria said. "I want you to show me." She scanned the birds by the pond and the cattle loafing near the fence. "This is a wonderfully safe place," she said, with a peculiar sadness in her voice.

45

Kent was about to question the remark when Emily said, "There's my boy!"

Flame's chestnut face appeared over his Dutch door in response to the approaching voices.

"As handsome as ever," Maria said.

Then she was startled by a second head, darker, with a splash of white on the forehead that emerged out of the adjacent door. "Who's that?"

"Oh, man," Emily said. "That's Neapolitan. He was supposed to be a surprise. Remember him from over at Mrs. Hanover's? She and her husband decided to move to Florida, so we bought him — for you. So that you would have something to ride this summer."

Maria stepped to Neapolitan. She stroked his muzzle as he nuzzled her, registering her scent. Then she touched her cheek to his. "Thank you, guys. He's fantastic!"

Kent said, "He moves well. And he's well-schooled. He'll be a good ride for you this summer. I'll vouch for his soundness, too. But he's no plug. You pay attention to what you're doing when you're up on him."

Emily looked over from her place at Flame's head. "I'll watch out for her, Doc."

"How's ol' Flame this morning?" Doc stroked the Welch pony's neck at arm's length as his trained eye gave him the quick once-over.

Emily eased Flame out to the cross ties. "He's ready to go."

Kent stood back as the girls tacked their horses and led them outside. Maria swung herself up onto Neapolitan with one smooth motion. Emily guided Flame to a mounting block that he had built for her, then by folding herself across the saddle and pivoting on her stomach, she forced her arms and shoulders forward, and her legs down into the stirrups. It was a Herculean effort. Kent noticed Maria watching too, and her expression told him that she was experiencing the same angst that he felt. He quickly forced it out of his head.

Once she was up, Emily gathered the reins with surprising dexterity, and then glanced back at Maria. Satisfied that her companion was ready, she tapped her heels against Flame's flanks and headed him away, unaware that she had aroused even the least emotional response in her observers.

"We'll be back in a couple hours," she said, over her shoulder.

"Okay. Remember, Neapolitan isn't familiar with the trails yet."

"Yep. We've got it covered."

Kent watched the tandem sashay of the horses' rumps as the girls guided them across a field and into the woods.

Why had Maria come back to Jefferson? She could go anywhere in the world. Even from a distance her loveliness shone. She was as suited to lounge on the French Riviera in a string bikini as ride horses in upstate New York.

● ● ●

Neapolitan proved to be a perfect trail horse. He proceeded unfazed past the myriad of obstacles and distractions found in the woods. Before long, the horses were at the periphery of the girls' consciousness as they lapsed into a mix of silly chatter and meaningful conversation.

"You seem stronger now," Maria said.

Emily struck her thigh with a firm fist. "I've been working on these legs of mine."

"You're riding with more confidence, too."

"You think so? Aubrey says I'm a natural. She says I have the hands of an Olympic rider."

"Aubrey is a good teacher. If she says it, you can believe it."

"If the stupid doctors would let me get an operation now, instead of after I quit growing, I think I'd have a chance of getting really good." Emily's voice took on a dreamy tone. "Can you imagine

— me at the Olympics?" She glanced at Maria, searching for signs of doubt.

"Easily," Maria said. "But, you've got to listen to the doctors. If they say it's too risky to operate now, then it's too risky."

"But when I'm eighteen it will be too late." After a pause, Emily said, "Let's talk about something that's not such a bummer. Tell me what it was like in Kentucky."

"Hot this time of year. Really hot."

"I don't mean the weather. I mean the horses, the people, the farms, you know, the cool stuff."

Maria was quiet for a moment. "Well, you wouldn't believe the farms. They're all spectacular — awesome barns, huge pastures, and lots of white fence. Everywhere you look there are amazing horses."

"The horse capital of the world. Right?"

"Yep. You know all those really famous Thoroughbreds that won the Kentucky Derby and stuff? There're a lot of them around."

"What about the farm where you worked? Criadero Del Jugador? Is that how you say it?"

Maria chuckled at her friend's Spanish. "Yes. Criadero Del Jugador. It means High Roller Farm."

"Like a gambler?"

"Exactly. It's awesome, too. Big, but more modern than most of the others. It's only been in business for maybe ten years, compared to some of the old farms down there that have been around since horses had four toes on each foot. Even so, Criadero Del Jugador has managed to get some top horses. They bought a lot of them, but they've bred a lot of them, too."

Emily squirmed in the saddle at the very thought of working with such amazing horses.

"Did you learn a lot?"

"Definitely. It's hard not to when you're there. I learned more about breeding, training, and racing Thoroughbreds last year than I did my whole time at college."

They rode in silence for a while. Finally, Maria said, "I learned a lot about people, too."

"You mean horse people?"

"People in general."

Emily twisted to face her friend. "Sounds like there's a story you're not telling me."

Maria didn't answer for several strides of the horses. When she did, there was a forced levity in her voiced.

"Never mind. It's too nice a day to ruin with bad thoughts."

CHAPTER 9

LOUISE STANFORD SAID HER STALLION LOOKED bad when she called, but now, studying the dismal beast, Kent knew that was an understatement. Charter Oak was extremely sick — possibly dying.

Kent did not even try to approach the horse. Instead he set his grip down in the alleyway, propped himself against the stall bars, and signaled Emily and Maria to keep a safe distance.

"He was this bad when you found him?" Kent asked, trying to conceal his astonishment at the severity of the horse's illness.

Louise's usually confident voice trembled. "Yes. I called you the second I saw him."

"How was he yesterday?"

"Like I said on the phone, he didn't clean up all of his grain last night. He ate maybe half his normal ration. So I took his temperature. It was up a little — a hundred two and a half — but he wasn't colicky or anything, so I figured, since you were already scheduled for today to palpate some mares, I'd just have you check him out when you got here."

"Did you take his temperature this morning?"

"It's a hundred six."

Kent hoped Louise didn't see him wince.

"What about his legs? Did you notice any swelling in his legs last night?"

"No, Doc, I didn't. We groomed him early afternoon, as usual, and he seemed fine. And, like I said, he was a little off feed last night, but I didn't notice any swelling."

"They look like stovepipes now. That's an unbelievable amount of edema to occur overnight. See that swelling under his belly? That's edema, too. Same with his eyes lids and lips."

Of all Kent's equine patients, Charter Oak was the one he least liked to deal with. The stallion was extremely wary, and when provoked or overly restrained, he became defensive. With no warning he'd been known to transform into twelve hundred pounds of kicking, striking fury. But now he was totally subdued, slumped in the corner, hip resting against the wall, swollen face hanging to within inches of the straw. As they watched, a string of saliva drizzled from his lower lip.

Kent toyed with the stethoscope that hung around his neck. This was no ordinary sickness. Kent had been Cedar Cut's veterinarian since the farm started, and he knew their way of doing things. He knew they considered each horse to be family, and cared for each like a child. Nothing came to mind that would explain the horrible symptoms he was looking at. But, he did know one thing — if he didn't do something, and do it fast, the Stanfords were going to lose their prize stallion.

"What's happened different in his life within the last few days?"

"Absolutely nothing."

"Any exposure to toxins? Fly spray? Dewormers? Coat conditioners? Anything?"

Louise shook her head, "No medicines. Same old grooming stuff. Nothing new."

Kent rattled through his usual list of questions. He asked the same question in different ways, hoping to jog Louise's memory, probing for any information that could shed light on the nature of

Charter Oak's ailment. When he was convinced that he knew all that Louise could tell him, which wasn't much, he stepped cautiously across the straw and took Charter Oak's halter. He got no resistance, which worried Kent even more. When Kent coaxed him, it was all the stallion could do to step away from the wall so that Kent could examine him.

Louise watched quietly as Kent poked and prodded, shined his penlight, and listened with his stethoscope. He swabbed over Charter Oak's jugular vein with a cotton ball soaked in alcohol, inserted a needle, and collected several vials of blood which he passed through the stall bars to the Emily and Maria. The whole time, Charter Oak stood motionless, seemingly unaware of any of it, except to lift his head slightly when the alcohol fumes aroused him from his stupor.

When he finished, Kent released the halter and resumed his position against the wall. Silent, biting his upper lip, he stared at the pitiful horse. This one could go either way.

Finally, Louise broke the silence. "What's happening to him, Doc?" Her voice begged for an answer.

Kent continued to watch Charter Oak without a word.

Tears filled Louise's eyes. Embarrassed at her own lack of self-control, she wiped them away with the back of her hand. The matriarch of Cedar Cut Farm straightened herself, sighed, and resolved not to interrupt the doctor's train of thought again.

She and her husband, Walt, had dealt with countless setbacks in their fifteen years with Thoroughbreds. As charter members of the New York State Thoroughbred Breeding and Racing Program, the Stanfords had been among the trailblazers.

In the beginning, the whole venture had been a risk — even more so than now. Adversity was expected and accepted, met head on with the vitality engendered by the challenge. Horses had been Walt's escape from the stress of his automobile business. For thirtytwo years he had built an empire of car dealerships until he finally decided he needed a change. He convinced Louise that they should put up a couple of barns and plunge into the world of Thoroughbreds. She had never regretted their decision. Charter Oak had been their ultimate gambit. Walt and Louise had taken a whole winter to convince themselves that they could afford such a stallion.

Louise looked at the suffering animal.

"It's hard to believe he holds a record at San Anita. He so sick."

"Louise, I'll tell you outright, I don't know what's happened to him." Kent stepped over and put his arm around her shoulder. "Yet," he added, with more confidence than he felt.

"How do we find out?"

Kent waved a hand toward the girls.

"Hopefully, those blood samples will tell us. In the meantime, I think you better have Kevin bring a trailer around. Charter Oak is going to need to be at the CVC."

"Right."

Kevin, Cedar Cut's foreman, Kent, and the girls pulled, pushed, and cajoled until they had Charter Oak loaded — one slow step at a time. When he was secure, Kent gave Kevin a final warning about driving slowly, and then headed for his mobile unit. As they climbed in, the girls opened fire.

"Holy schmoly, Doc. He looks like he could kick off at any second!" Emily said.

"Yep. That's why we're bringing him to the CVC."

"Don't you have any idea what's wrong?"

"You heard what I told Mrs. Stanford."

Maria pushed Lucinda's muzzle away from her ear. "First Simpatico, now Charter Oak."

"Yeah. Not good."

"If we lose the good stallions, we don't get the bookings for the best mares, then we don't get a super foal crop, and then the program goes down the tube."

Kent's voice took on an edge. "We haven't lost Charter Oak, and we'll do our damnedest to see that we don't. We're not going to let anything happen to the New York Bred Program either. That's a promise."

CHAPTER 10

KENT ROTATED SLOWLY BACK AND FORTH IN HIS desk chair at the CVC, telephone to his ear. Throughout their entire phone conversation, Dr. Holmes had sounded totally confident. It twisted Kent's intestine into a curling mass of snakes. How could Ed be that sure, making such an outrageous diagnosis? Equine Viral Arteritis! You gotta be kidding.

"But now you want to *double check*?" Kent said.

"It's pretty bizarre."

"You can say that again."

"We need to get this right."

"You've had two days."

Dr. Holmes's voice took on an edge. "A couple more won't hurt. It's my reputation, too. You know what I'm saying? It's too weird, and has too many repercussions, to say we're dealing with EVA based on one set of tests."

Kent could see he wasn't going to win this battle.

Dr. Holmes veered the subject. "How is Charter Oak doing now, anyway?"

"He's no great ball of fire, but compared to the way he looked two days ago, I'd say he's doing great. I'll tell you one thing for sure. In light of what you've just told me, I'm glad we put him in isolation."

"So am I. You may have prevented an epidemic of EVA. Actually, that could turn out to be the most important thing you did with this mess."

The praise helped.

"I'd like to stop over and check him out myself," Holmes said. "Maybe this afternoon. Actually, I'd like to bring a few of my residents to see him, too. Is that all right?"

"Of course. Let me know when. I'll try to be there."

"In the meantime, Kent, could you have somebody dig out copies of Charter Oak's EVA screening tests? Just to be sure they are all negative. We'll need the dates, too."

"They'll be ready when you get there."

"One other thing." Dr. Holmes's voice dropped to an ominous tone. "We need to get out in front of this. I think you should quarantine the farm. It's never a very pleasant task, but in this case I think it's warranted, at least temporarily. If this all pans out, the state guys will insist on it anyway, and they'll be glad we got out ahead of it."

Holmes's words came through the phone like a black fume.

"That'll be a first for me."

Quarantine. The word had shocking implications. It invoked visions of typhus and plague. It conjured images of a panicked populous, mass exodus, communal cremation fires billowing smoke into the night air. If news of it ever broke on the horse breeding grapevine, and it surely would in spite of the diagnostic lab's policy of confidentiality, Cedar Cut Farm would be an absolute pariah. Regardless of the outcome.

"Are you still there?" Dr. Holmes's voice pulled Kent back from his nightmare.

"Yes. I'm with you. Okay, I can quarantine the farm." Kent was trying to remember if he even had the necessary forms. He was pretty sure they were tucked away somewhere in the cabinet where he kept bureaucratic documents.

"Thanks. One last thing. Keep your eyes open for other horses showing symptoms. With EVA, if there's one, there's probably going to be more."

"Will do."

"Then I'll see you this afternoon." The line went dead.

Kent felt sick. "Where in the hell could Charter Oak have picked up EVA?" he said to his empty office.

"Who are you talking to?" Peter Murphy asked, his surgery-capped head leaning through Kent's door.

"Peter, come in, you're not going to believe this. Ed Holmes says Charter Oak has a sky high titer for EVA!"

"EVA? You're kidding. Where the hell would he get EVA?"

"That's what I want to know."

Peter slumped into a chair. "Is Ed sure?"

Kent looked side-long at Peter. "We're talking Ed Holmes here."

"He's sure."

"But he wants to repeat the serology."

Peter sank into a chair across from Kent, and pulled his surgery cap into his lap as if to free his mind.

"All stallions get tested each spring, right? That's a regulation set by the Breeding Program."

"Yep. Charter Oak has tested negative every time."

"Has he been off the farm for any reason in the last few months?"

"No."

"So no exposure, that way. And all the mares that were bred to him showed negative for EVA, right?"

"Yep."

"Do you suppose there could have been a false negative on one of the mares? Charter Oak does draw a lot of out-of-state mares. There is an occasional pocket of EVA some place or another in the United States."

"It's a possibility, I guess. The test isn't perfect. That's one of the things Holmes is considering." Kent leaned back in his desk chair, intertwined his fingers behind his head, and looked at the ceiling. "You know something else that's strange? Charter Oak's showing such severe symptoms of EVA. Way worse than usual."

"I'm not sure I follow you."

"Usually the horses are a little sick. Kinda flu-like."

"Yeah, okay."

"There is an occasional abortion. But a lot of horses that blood test positive show no signs at all." Kent spoke slowly, pulling musty facts from the corners of his mind. "Back in the fifties there was a really nasty outbreak. In Ohio, I think. A lot of horses got as sick as Charter Oak is, and there were abortion storms. That outbreak convinced the Feds and breeders just how devastating EVA could be, and got them moving on a testing program."

"Yes, but didn't that super-strain disappear over the years?"

Kent made a cynical laughing sound. "Everyone thought so."

Peter mulled that over a few seconds. "What happens now?"

"Ed wants me to quarantine the farm."

Peter moaned and rubbed his eyes with the heels of his hands. "Wait till that gets out. We're going to see some serious backpedaling on the part of the owners who have mares booked to Charter Oak."

"They'll have to pull out. They have no choice."

"No bigtime mares means no New York Breds."

"Uh-huh. I've been thoroughly reminded of that already."

Both doctors sat in silence for nearly a minute, until Kent broke their trance by standing up abruptly.

"If you need me, I'll be at Cedar Cut," he said. "Executing a quarantine order." He headed for the door.

"Oh, man. There's a task I never want to perform."

CHAPTER 11

KENT CAUGHT LOUISE LEADING A PAIR OF SLEEK Thoroughbreds from the paddock to Cedar Cut's main barn. Her face showed pleasant surprise when she recognized his truck.

"I thought I'd stop by and give you an update on Charter Oak," Kent said, as he got out.

"Thanks for the personalized service," Louise said, and turned the horses over to one of the stablemen. "How's my boy?"

"Better. His temperature held at just a whisker above normal overnight and he's eating and drinking again. His legs are still swollen, but a lot less. He's even getting grouchy. For him, I'd say that's a good sign."

Louise chuckled. "Sorry. I apologize for my boy's bad manners, but I'm glad to hear they are returning."

"Don't worry. When he gets too ornery to treat, I'm sending him packing right back home to you."

"The sooner the better."

Kent paused for a moment then continued, choosing his words carefully.

"Ed Holmes, from the diagnostic lab thinks the blood tests are suggestive of EVA." Actually, the samples had shown an astronomical antibody level. "But, before he draws any conclusions, he's going to look the guy over for himself. Probably he'll repeat the tests."

Louise's face ashened before Kent's eyes. Her knees quivered and he braced to catch her. She stepped back to a stone border around a perennial garden and sat. Louise knew the ramifications of EVA.

"When?" she asked.

"When what?"

"When is he going to check Charter Oak out?"

"He's shooting for this afternoon."

"Do I need to be there?"

"No, but you can if you'd like. I'm sure he's going to want to come out here and see the farm, too. I told him I didn't think you'd mind."

"No, of course not."

Kent drew a trifolded form from his pocket.

"You know how important it is that we get to the bottom of this, for Charter Oak, and you, and all the New York Breds, right?" He unfolded the sheet slowly, deliberately. "And if there is any EVA around, we need to nip it before it spreads. I know you understand that. So," the words tightened in his throat, "I'm asking you to sign this order to quarantine the farm until we're sure everything is okay."

Louise dropped her face into her hands and began to cry.

Kent touched a hand to her shoulder. He could feel her quake with each sob. He was forced into the role of being a bully and he hated it. By Dr. Holmes's own admission, the evidence was not conclusive.

"Louise, this may turn out to be a big false alarm, it's just . . ."

"I understand." She waved off his apology, and pulled a tissue from the pocket of her jeans. "It's just so frustrating and humiliating. I feel so helpless. And Walt. Walt is going to be crushed."

"You and Walt can't blame yourselves. I know you are meticulous about the care and protection of your horses. I also know you've followed every health regulation and recommendation to the letter. No one could do more than you have. Listen, if you think it will help, I'll be glad to talk to Walt. That way we won't risk any misunderstandings from third party communications. In fact, he's welcome to stop by the CVC when Dr. Holmes checks Charter Oak, too."

Louise searched her tattered tissue for a dry corner. "That may make it easier. Maybe he can get over there." The possibility seemed to mollify her for the moment. She looked at Kent with an embarrassed, red-eyed smile. "Sorry."

Kent shrugged. "Hey. I feel like doing the same thing."

She drew in and released a deep breath. "I guess I'm going to have to give the syndicate members a call. I don't look forward to that. They've been on the edge of their seats since I first told them Charter Oak was sick."

"He's their horse, too," Kent said. "They have a right to know, but it won't be any fun telling them."

"Yeah. It's just that most of the five of them are purely investors. Sure, they'd say they like horses if you asked, but mainly, Charter Oak is an investment, made with the sole intent of turning a profit." She sniffed deeply, and wiped her nose one last time. "I guess I shouldn't be so self-righteous. They really are nice people. They just aren't handson, get-sweaty-and-dirty, horse people. You know what I mean?"

"I see the type every day."

"The only one of the bunch who has any horse background at all is Charles St. Pierre, and he's not exactly your classic horseman."

The mention of Charles St. Pierre in connection with Charter Oak sent a prickle racing up Kent's back. He didn't know why, or what significance it had, he just felt that jittery feeling that an unsettling thought causes.

"I didn't know Charles owned part of Charter Oak," he said.

"Actually, Walt and I own fifty-one percent, then Charles comes in with the second biggest share. The other three members only own about fifteen percent all together. So, how much does that make for Charles?"

Kent had the calculation before she finished the question. "Thirty-four percent. Thirtyfour percent," he repeated slowly.

"Seems like Charles is having a tough year. First Simpatico, now Charter Oak."

"Aren't we all?" Louise said.

CHAPTER 12

AS USUAL, THEY WERE RUNNING LATE WHEN
Kent wheeled the mobile unit into his spot at the CVC. In the space
next to his was a midnight blue Lincoln with dealer plates. On the far
edge of the lot was a white Cadillac Seville.

Blue — Walt Stanford. White — Charles St. Pierre.

"Damn," Kent said. "They beat us."

"You go ahead," Maria said. "Emily and I can restock the truck."

Kent flashed both girls an appreciative smile. "Thanks.
Sometimes I think having you two around is worth all the grief you
cause me."

"Yeah, right," they said, together. Then Emily added, "Like
we're the ones who cause the grief."

Kent made a quick detour into the hospital's isolation unit.
One last check on Charter Oak. He didn't want any surprises when
he brought his guests back to see the stallion.

He watched the horse through an observation window for a
moment — thin and rough, asleep on his feet. A few sprigs of hay
dangled from his still swollen lips. A crystalline intravenous line
spiraled from his neck upward to a mammoth jug suspended from
the ceiling.

Kent's heart sagged at the weight of what he saw.

"You know what, buddy?" Kent whispered, his face close to the glass, "Normally, you are one of my major pain in the ass patients. But right now, I feel for you. If I could do anything more to help you out, I would."

He grabbed Charter Oak's file and headed to the reception area. As he pushed through the door, he slowed, inhaled a deep breath and released it, easing himself into his professional demeanor. He brought up the best smile he could muster, and silently reminded himself of his longstanding motto — *Never let them see you sweat.* In Catholic congregation fashion, all in the waiting room rose as he entered.

"Hi, Ed," Kent said, extending his hand to the nearest person. Dr. Holmes was a blocky man with a head so bald Kent could make out reflections of the globed ceiling lights. He had eyes that caught and held a person's attention, and a smile that put them at ease.

"Afternoon, Kent," Dr. Holmes said. Then he introduced the three young lab assistants he had with him.

Kent lifted a hand onto the shoulder of the distinguished gray-haired man who had taken a position next to him. "Ed Holmes, I'd like you to meet . . ."

"Walt Stanford," Holmes said. "We've met." He gestured toward Charles, adorned in an expensive sharkskin suit, open at the neck. "I've also met Charles. I heard Sally call them by name when they came in, so I took the liberty of introducing myself."

"Good, that makes things easy," Kent said. "So I suppose you'd all like to see our star patient."

Kent leaned hard against the push rail of a heavy door, and led Charles and Walt, the two men who had the most at stake, down a corridor to the equine unit. Dr. Holmes followed with his helpers. The confluence of eagerness to see the patient, and fear of what they would see, was palpable among the group.

Outside the isolation area they donned coveralls and disposable overshoes.

"He might not look that hot right now," Kent warned. "But he's one hell of a lot more alive than he was a couple of days ago."

As quietly as he could, Kent rolled open the stall door.

Slowly Charter Oak raised his head and edged back deeper into the stall. Eyes that had been glazed since his arrival, flickered a warning as the big horse braced to defend himself. The snort he let out was weak, but it made his point.

Kent stopped the procession with an out-stretched arm. Charles took a step back.

"Walt, he knows you best. How about you hold him while Ed gets a few samples? Go in slow, okay? Looks like he's a little nervous about the crowd. Which, to tell the truth, I'm happy to see."

Walt stepped in cooing silly words from deep in his throat, the way horsemen do. "Hey there Mr. M, you've got ol' Doc scared to come in here." The others glanced at Kent and chuckled. "But we are all glad to see you're getting your old piss and vinegar back. We are all real worried about you."

The familiar voice relaxed Charter Oak.

A few minutes later Dr. Holmes and his assistants had completed their examination and collected blood.

"Christ, Ed, you could have left some in the horse," Charles said, as they all stared at a pile of blood tubes that could fill a wheelbarrow.

"Actually, he looks better than I expected," Dr. Holmes said, stepping out of the stall and sliding the door. "But as you and I discussed before, Kent, he's way sicker than I'd figure for a typical case of EVA."

"Any explanation?"

"Not really. Could be just an individual variation. It happens. His resistance may have been down for some reason so that the virus really got a foothold. Odds are that's what happened. Or, it could be a different strain of EVA. We'll repeat the serology to confirm EVA, then, if it is, we will do some other tests to try to identify the strain."

Walter kept studying Charter Oak through the stall bars. "Where would a new strain come from?"

"Probably a mutation — random variation."

"Mother Nature at work."

"Right. She's always a step or two ahead of us. Always trying to find ways for her creatures to cope."

"It seems to me that becoming more harmful to the host might not be a better way for a virus to cope," Walt said. "But let's not worry about that now. What's our next step?"

As they all pulled off their foot gear and washed, Dr. Holmes said, "First, if it's okay with you, Walter, I'd like to stop over to Cedar Cut and have a look around. Check out the other horses. Sometimes it helps us to get the whole picture. Better yet, maybe you could give us a tour."

"Absolutely," Walter said. "Whenever you say."

"Now would be perfect, if it fits your schedule."

"I'll make it fit."

Charles turned to Dr. Holmes, his face clouded with concern. "I've got a question before you fellows leave. Tell me about *shedders*. They always talk about *shedders* with EVA. What are they?"

"Right, Charles. Good question." Dr. Holmes said. "You've been doing your homework. Actually, shedding is the big problem with EVA. Once a horse becomes infected, one of three things can happen." He ticked off the possibilities on his fingers. "One, he gets sick and dies, which is rarely the case nowadays. Thankfully. Two, the horse's immune system totally eliminates the virus. He may have been sick, or he may not have shown any signs of illness at all. That's what happens in most cases and, of course, is the best outcome. Or three, the horse's immune system is able to keep the virus under control enough that the horse doesn't get sick, but it's not able to totally eliminate the virus. That's a shedder. They show no signs of the disease, but they can pass the virus to other horses."

Charles nodded understanding, then had another thought. "Can you tell a shedder by looking at him?"

"No. Only by blood testing."

Kent said, "That's why New York requires EVA screening for all breeding mares and stallions."

"Exactly, to identify the shedders before they can spread the virus."

"How long do they shed it?" Charles asked.

"We don't know for sure. Some for a few months. Some apparently for years."

Walter frowned. "Isn't there any medicine we can give him to kill the virus?"

"Unfortunately, no. Viruses are not killed by antibiotics or any other medicine. Anything strong enough to kill the virus will also kill the host."

"So you're saying we just have to wait for his system to fight it off? That is, if it will. Otherwise our boy becomes a shedder."

"That's about it."

Maria and Emily had finished restocking the truck and rejoined the group.

"I thought there was a vaccine," Maria said, and immediately covered her mouth with her hand. "Sorry." Her eyes showed surprise and embarrassment. She knew better than to break Kent's cardinal rule that the girls remain silent when he was talking to clients.

Emily gave her friend the side-eye. "Nice work, Maria."

Kent turned to Maria and said, "I'd like you all to meet Maria Castille. She is spending the summer with us. You may remember her as the Clinton College Equine Studies intern who rode on farm calls with me a year or so ago." He gave her his best stern look. "Sometimes her curiosity gets the best of her. It bubbles out like a burp."

Even looking sheepish, Maria's smile disarmed the crowd.

"A vaccine?" Dr. Holmes said. "Yes, there is an EVA vaccine. But it has problems. In fact, any veterinarian who wants to use it has to get a special permit. That's because there is some evidence that the vaccine can actually *cause* the disease. Also, remember that in Charter Oak's case a vaccine would do no good because vaccines only block the *invasion* of a disease organism. Once the bug is in, it's too late."

"Could we use the vaccine on the other horses at our farm?" Walter asked. "Which is worse, the disease or the vaccine?"

"We could. We might. But usually we try to control the outbreak without it. We'll be able to give you more info on that after we check out the other horses and get these tests back."

"What happens to Charter Oak now as far as breeding is concerned?"

An uncomfortable look crossed Dr. Holmes's face. "We'll have to assume he's a shedder until proven otherwise."

"What does that mean?"

"First, he'll remain in quarantine. We'll inform the office of the New York Breeders Program that his negative status has been revoked. Then, in a month or so, if and when he appears to be healthy, we'll begin provocative testing."

"Which is what?"

"We get a group of inexpensive mares, test them for EVA to be sure they are negative, then we breed them to Charter Oak. After that, once a month, each mare gets tested for EVA. If any of them seroconverts, that is becomes positive, Charter Oak is a shedder. If not, he's okay and gets released."

"I suppose the owner supplies the test mares." Walter said.

Dr. Holmes's lips pressed into a thin line. "I'm afraid so."

Walter turned and put his hand on Charles' shoulder. "Charlie, for the first time since we got Charter Oak, I'm glad he's syndicated."

Charles smiled, but without much amusement. "Uh-huh."

"I'm also glad you talked me into all that insurance," Walter added, with obvious relief in his voice.

"You had to be *talked into* insuring a horse of this caliber?" Ed Holmes asked, disbelief in his voice.

"Not exactly. The syndicate did intend to insure him, but for mortality and medical like most other horses. I must admit I was the chief advocate of that strategy. I figured we would save a bundle in premiums." Walter gave Charles another thankful look. "Charles insisted that the risk was too great and argued, successfully, thank God, that we should insure him for loss of use. The premiums are more than three times as high, but now, it turns out, absolutely worth it."

For a split second admiration flashed into Kent's mind. This was further evidence of Charles's business acumen and knowledge of the horse world. Then that uncomfortable feeling returned to his stomach.

CHAPTER 13

KENT GAVE THE OLD QUARTER HORSE ONE LAST reassuring pat on the neck.

"Domino, ol'man, you're going to be fine," he told the horse, loud enough that the anxious middle-aged couple dressed in carriage driving attire and standing a few steps away could hear. "But in the future, you may have to back off this marathon thing. You ain't as young as you think you are."

"Thanks, Doc. We get your point," the man said. "I guess we figured Domino would go on forever. He loves marathons. He's been coming here to the Ledyard Competition for the last fifteen years."

"It happens to the best of us," Kent said, trying to keep it light. The owners felt bad enough already. They didn't need to be scolded. "He just overdid it. He doesn't want to admit his age. Sometimes I have the same problem. Better have him stick to the ring events from here on out."

"We can deal with that," the woman said. "We'll help him make the adjustment into old age." She elbowed her husband. "Like you say, Doc, 'It happens to the best of us.' We just want him to be all right."

"Walk him until he cools down. The shot I gave him will keep him from stiffening up. Make sure he gets lots of water and electrolytes."

They thanked him again, and led Domino away.

Kent was confident the old horse would be fine. It was the kind of outcome he liked — happy horse, happy owners. Humming *Stars and Stripes Forever*, he marched back toward the show's veterinarian station.

A few weeks had passed since the Charter Oak crisis, and, while he still anguished over Simpatico's death, the day-to-day routine of his life had pretty much returned to normal. Today was a perfect early summer day, and he was volunteering his services at the driving competition. Emily and Maria were wandering around somewhere, and Aubrey had said she and Barry were planning to attend. He'd find them. What could be better?

The Ledyard Carriage Driving Competition was Kent's favorite equine event of the year. It was held each summer on the rolling lawns of the historic Ledyard estate overlooking Huron Lake. It drew the best driving horses and the most elegant horse-drawn vehicles in the eastern United States to Jefferson for three days of show-ring classes, obstacle courses, and a marathon. For Kent, being the veterinarian-on-duty was more play than work since the ailments tended to be minor and there were long lapses for him to visit with friends he saw only once or twice a year.

He heard the screams before he actually saw the runaway. Instantly, the peaceful murmurings of the horseshow turned into pandemonium. Spectators dove for cover like the crowded street scene of a cheap sci-fi movie.

The runaway was a young Hackney gelding. Gray. Sleek with Sho-Sheen, running full-on, and wild-eyed with adrenelin. He was between the shafts of a beautifully restored cariole that bounced and pitched behind him. Its rattling frame and flailing reins egged him even faster. Kent could see that the seat of the delicate two-wheel carriage was empty.

The pony charged through the exhibitors' area, miraculously avoiding rows of horse vans, trailers, and buggies. Nearby exhibitors held tight to their own horses, speaking calming words, and struggling to control them as they reared and snorted in response to the excitement. One of the cariole's wheels slammed into a metal watering trough, sending out a low ring like a Chinese gong. The Hackney sped up.

Kent rose on his toes for a better look. The pony's head was as naked as a mustang — he'd slipped his headstall. Kent watched the cariole go up on one wheel as the pony made a galloping turn out of the exhibitors' area and onto a long macadam driveway that led from the mansion's portico to the highway. If the pony made it to the busy road, there would be a disaster for sure.

Kent spun to his left, and at a dead run he cut between two horse trailers, vaulted a split-rail fence, and pawed his way through a swath of pines that separated the lawns from the driveway. If he could get to the driveway in time, he might be able to intercept the pony.

He was in full stride when he broke out of the trees, jumped the ditch and landed on the drive a heartbeat in front of the pony that was coming at him like an F-16 fighter jet on a runway. He raised both arms and yelled, "*whoa!*" But it was too late. The pony was too close and moving too fast. Kent sidestepped an instant before he would have been trampled, grabbed the left shaft as it brushed by, and held on.

He might as well have grabbed an F-16. He was yanked off his feet and dragged along the macadam, inches away from hammering hoofs and churning wheels.

He shouted, *whoa!* half a dozen more times, but it was useless.

If he could use his body weight to turn the panicked pony, he might be able to prevent the horse-automobile crash that no doubt would occur if they reached the highway.

He leaned out, letting his legs scrape along the ground to increase drag. It started to work. The pony veered to the left a few degrees, and may even have slowed.

If they had just had a few more feet — but they didn't.

Steel clad hooves skated onto the macadam surface. Cars parked on the shoulder blocked their way a few yards ahead. Kent held a split-second longer, then released, rolled to avoid the cariole's wheels, and came up in the ditch just in time to witness the spectacular crash.

The pony jumped in a valiant attempt to clear a parked Lexus. He went up, in Grand National form, and had enough height that he probably would have made it over the hood, had it not been for the carriage he had in tow. It caught on the car's front quarter panel. The pony stopped dead in mid-flight, then crashed down and through the windshield.

Kent groaned and looked away, then back.

The pony's struggling made it worse. Horse blood, auto glass, and cariole splinters flew in all directions.

Kent ignored his skinned palms and the aches that were exploding all over his body. If he didn't get the thrashing pony's legs out of that windshield, the little horse would shred himself beyond hope.

He charged forward, fishing for the Barlow knife in his pocket, as he ran. By the time he reached the carriage, his blade was ready. He scaled the Lexus's demolished hood dodging hooves and slashing harness like a bushwhacker.

Get control of the head, he reminded himself. *That's the only way to control a crazed horse.*

When he was close enough, he lunged, grabbing the pony's flailing head in a bear hug. He pulled it to his chest, and then let his full weight press it to the hood. The pony grunted loudly but relaxed, seemingly glad to be in Kent's arms.

Out of the corner of his eye Kent caught sight of a dozen other horsemen rushing to help.

"Get the carriage out of the way," he shouted, and held on.

When he heard someone yell, *all clear*, he began giving instructions in a calmer voice.

"Okay. He's too heavy to lift. We'll have to roll him to get his legs free, then we can lower him to the ground. Grab a hold wherever you can, but don't get kicked. The poor guy is terrified. He can put you in the hospital or worse. Ready? On three. One, Two, Three."

Within minutes, they had the pony off the windshield and on the grass. To everyone's astonishment, he was able to stand on his own. Barely.

Several onlookers slapped Kent on the back, others yelled congratulations, but Kent ignored them. A halter appeared out of the crowd and he helped a woman strap it on the pony.

He took a few steps back and assessed the trembling, blood-soaked little horse. "He's going into shock."

"I never saw one torn up so bad," the woman with the halter said.

Kent manipulated one of several flaps of skin draping from lacerations on the pony's legs.

"He's a mess, all right."

Maria and Emily arrived and handed him his grip.

"Sorry, Doc. We'd have been here to help sooner, but we were on the far side of the ring watching the show," Maria said.

"That's not your fault. I'm glad you thought to bring my grip."

He pulled a vial and a syringe from his grip. "This will help the shock," he said, as he injected. "Anybody know who the owner is?"

A thirty-ish man pushed through the crowd. He had perfectly moussed, razor-cut hair, and was wearing a crisp Oxford shirt with expensive khakis.

Kent instantly dubbed him Slick.

"We are. I mean, she is. Patina Dewey," Slick said, and he motioned toward a woman behind him. She was a mix of designer clothes, expensive jewelry, and plainness.

"Florentino," Patina said, moaning his name. She kissed the pony's muzzle. With her cheek pressed against the pony's face, she said to Kent, "I took his headstall off while he was still hitched."

"What an idiotic thing to do," Slick said, and rolled his eyes.

"He's always so good," she said back to him.

"You broke a basic rule of horsemanship!"

"How was I supposed to know that someone would let a bunch of dogs run loose?"

Kent didn't speak, Slick was saying it all, and being plenty hurtful about it. But for a second Kent's thoughts shifted to Lucinda, and how she had protested being left at home that morning as he prepared for a day at the show. He had literally had to tug her, whining and giving him every pitiful expression she could muster, from her usual perch on the seat of the truck. He had almost given in, now he was glad he hadn't.

"That's why it's a rule — because you never know what's going to happen," Slick said. "What a mess. What do you think, Doc, put him down?"

"No!" Patina wailed.

Kent bent, hands on knees. He studied the tattered legs a moment more. Finally he straightened and said, "I think we can put him back together."

Slick grimaced. "That will cost a fortune."

"We've got to try," Patina said.

Slick shrugged.

They led Florentino carefully to an area of relative seclusion between two horse trailers. Emily held the pony, Maria assisted, and within minutes Kent began the arduous process of cleaning, debriding, and suturing the wounds.

"Where's your home?" he asked Patina, as he sewed.

"Ohio."

"Must be your first time at the Ledyard Competition. I think I would remember you."

"It is. We thought we'd kill two birds with one stone," she said, her voice still coated with guilt.

"How's that?"

She squatted for a closer look, but grimaced each time Kent drew Florentino's skin together. "We dabble in driving horses as a hobby. Mostly Hackneys. Florentino is the best."

Kent put in a few more stitches. "So what's the two birds with one stone?"

"The Hackneys are for fun, and they add some color on our farm, but our real business is Thoroughbreds. Racing."

"Oh."

"Actually, it's my father's farm. I run it. John, he's our trainer. He helps me." She looked around, then nodded toward Slick who was on the periphery of the crowd that had gathered to watch Kent work.

He noticed John chatting with Aubrey. Too close. All smiley. Too much eye contact. Aubrey feigned interest.

An hour-and-a-half after he started, Kent smoothed the last piece of tape over the last bandage. As he stretched the kink out of his back, he said, "There you go, Ms. Dewey. He's back together and ready to do it again."

"God. I hope not."

Kent patted Florentino's neck. "Take him home. Have your vet check him in a day or so. I'll send you with some antibiotics and pain meds, and some notes on what I did."

"I can't thank you enough, Doctor Stephenson. For the last year or so, John and I have been reading such good things about the New York sires that we decided to see for ourselves. So we entered the driving competition as an excuse to come east and look at stallions for our mares." Her expression darkened. "That was before our first choice died."

"Simpatico, you mean."

"Yes, terrible news. Then we heard about Charter Oak." She shook her head and clucked her tongue. "I guess as long as we're here we'll look around, but I'm afraid it's back to Kentucky. Again. Too bad, I'm getting tired of their bloodlines and their hubris."

Kent's eyes narrowed. "I'm going to give you a little free advice — don't be too quick to give up on New York horses. Yeah, we lost Simpatico and Charter Oak may be out, but the New York breeding program wasn't built around two horses. We can still go head-to-head with Kentucky or any other state."

Patina's eyebrows lifted. "You sound confident."

"I am. And with good reason. Funny you used the word hubris. While you're here, I'd suggest you check out Simpatico's son, Hubris. He's at VinChaRo Farm. As a matter of fact, Aubrey Fairbanks, the farm manager, is the one John is talking to."

Patina glanced toward her trainer and Aubrey. "Hmm. Maybe he really *is* conducting business. I'll go see." She rose on her tiptoes and gave Kent a peck on the cheek. "Thank you again for saving my Florentino. You're the best."

"That's what I'm here for."

"Well, I'm glad you are. And thanks for the Hubris tip, too."

"Good luck with that."

Kent's conversation with Patina Dewey swirled in his head as he scrubbed himself in the restroom behind the show office. He threw on the spare shirt and pants he kept in the mobile unit — wrinkled, but clean. Emily bandaged his palms and the show secretary came up with some aspirin. Was the New York program that decimated? Could the loss of two stallions have such impact? Would Hubris be able to pick up the slack? "Let it go, Kent," he said under his breath. He knew better than to try to second-guess the horse breeding game.

CHAPTER 14

BY THE TIME KENT GOT CLEANED UP AND BACK out to the driving competition festivities after the runaway pony fiasco, it was pretty much like nothing had ever happened. Carriages circled the ring in front of the judges while spectators, sitting in lawn chairs, watched and applauded for their favorites. He was making his way back to the veterinarian station and waiting for the last of the adrenalin to wash out of his system, when he came upon a group of locals. They were leaning on the rail, watching the show, and making small talk.

Fred Jenkins, Jefferson's mayor, saw Kent first. "Hey, Doc. Finished sewing?"

Kent gave him a thumbs-up. "Little rascal looks like new, if I do say so myself."

"That-a-boy. What did you do for the Lexus?"

"Euthanized it."

"Would never happen to a beat-up old Ford, would it."

"Ain't that the truth?"

"You could have gotten killed."

Kent held out his bandaged hands and smiled. "I'm glad you didn't tell me that beforehand."

"No. I mean it," Fred said. "Great job, Kent. Really."

"Thanks. So what's up with you guys?"

"Just shooting the breeze. Charlie St. Pierre is the current juicy topic." Fred nodded toward the heavyset, rosy-cheeked woman next to him. "Beth was just telling us he's broke."

Kent gave her a questioning look. "Being Town Clerk, you ought to know. He file any papers with you?"

"No. Nothing that bad." She, in turn, nodded toward the Ichabod Crane look-alike next to her. "Lester, here, was the one that told me."

Lester McCarthy was one of Jefferson's current lawyers. For over twenty years he was Jefferson's only lawyer.

"We invited Charlie to talk to our investment club," Lester said. "The more he talked, the more apparent it became that he lost his shirt last year."

Kent shrugged. "So is Charlie in financial trouble or did he just lose a pile of money?"

Lester sipped on a straw stuck down in a tall drink with lots of ice. "He said he lost a lot, for sure, but I guess he stopped short of saying he was in trouble."

Kent detected a note of malicious satisfaction. "It better not be true. VinChaRo goes under, we're all up shit creek."

"A big farm like that does pump a lot of money into the town," Beth said. "Equipment, supplies, employment, services."

"To say nothing of taxes," Fred added in agreement.

"I was thinking more about the prestige," Kent said.

Beth's face fell into a look of accord. "There's a lot of history there, no doubt."

"Damned right, there is!" Kent said. "VinChaRo has one hell of a reputation. How many times have you been traveling and you told someone that you were from Jefferson, New York — What did they say? 'Jefferson. Isn't that where that big horse farm is?'"

Several heads nodded.

Kent waved a hand toward the activity around them. "And having VinChaRo in our backyard certainly hasn't hurt the driving competition. If you remember, it was the year that Charlie chaired this thing that the governor saw fit to make an appearance."

"It was an election year."

"You know what I'm saying."

"Yeah, yeah, Kent, we get your point. None of us want to see anything bad happen to VinChaRo."

"Good." Kent felt his belly growl. "I'm going to find Emily and get something to eat."

Beth nodded toward the mansion, "I saw her over by the mansion house a while ago. Wow, is she ever growing up, Kent."

"Tell me about it."

He strolled past an arrangement of perfectly white patio tables, each shaded by a yellow umbrella and surrounded by four or five people who had returned from the buffet line. There was boisterous chatter and lots of laughter. Kent was just starting to feel more lonely than hungry when he was saved.

"Kent. Kent, over here."

He turned to see Aubrey coming toward him, her muscled vibrancy unconcealed by her flowing skirt and patterned vest. She beamed. "I was looking for you. What do you say we get something to eat?"

"My plan exactly. I was going to find the girls and hit the buffet line."

"They are way ahead of you, Dad." Aubrey pointed to a table along the hedge where Maria, Emily, Barry Fairbanks, and several others in that age bracket were half eating and half clowning around.

"I guess they can do without me for a while."

"Nothing personal, but I'd say they'd *rather* do without you for a while." Aubrey took his elbow. "Elizabeth is holding a table. She wants us to join her."

He followed her gaze and saw Elizabeth watching them, Charles next to her concentrating on his food. He waved *hello* across the crowd, and said, "Sounds good to me."

At the buffet tent a queue of plate holders treaded impatiently and craned for a view of the line ahead. At the other end, a trickle of people exited with laden plates.

"Kent?" Aubrey held him back with a gentle tug of his arm. "Let's wait a few minutes. The line is too long."

"Good idea."

"Want to walk the woods path? We can ... " her voice dropped to a tongue-in-cheek whisper. "We can check out the flowers."

Together, they descended into the coolness and shade of the woods. To his delight, the mansion's groomed forest path was deserted.

"I've been thinking," Aubrey said. "Maybe it's time for you and me to step up the pace a little. You know what I mean?"

Kent's brow furrowed. "No. Not really."

"Come on, Lover-boy. Help me out here. I'm not all that good at throwing myself at a man. What I'm saying is, I think it's time we make it official we're a couple. Fish or cut bait as they say. Both of us are way past our divorces. And I'd say we've got a pretty good feel for each other. Pardon the pun. Right?" She leaned forward to study Kent's face as they walked.

In that moment, Kent no longer felt his scrapes and aches. A warm glow filled his chest. It grew and spread through his body. He smiled inwardly, but kept his eyes forward, his stride steady, and his expression neutral.

When Aubrey felt she had given him adequate time to respond, and he had not, she pulled him to a stop, stepped in front, and locked eyes with him. "Don't make this one of my all-time biggest embarrassments, Kent," she said, with an edge on her voice. "Are you with me here?"

"I don't know, Aubrey. It's a busy time for both of us. Foaling season and all that."

Aubrey threw her head back and groaned loudly. "Kent, no!"

He let a silent pause hang as long as he dared. Then, slowly, he twisted his face into the mother of all dumb looks.

"On the other hand, you are the most wonderful woman I have ever known."

It took her a moment to catch on. When she did, her eyes glistened with a mix of relief and anger. "You're an asshole."

"Absolutely."

"I should wring your neck!"

"Absolutely."

He took her in his arms, held her tight, and gave her a long, slow kiss. She leaned into him.

"You were great out there today," she whispered between kisses.

He pulled back just far enough to give her a questioning look. "What?"

"With the pony crash, I mean."

"Oh, that. No big deal."

"Heroism turns me on."

"Like I was saying, I could have been killed. Extremely daring on my part."

They kissed again.

Finally, Kent said, "Leave it to you to say what I've been thinking for a long time. I love you, Aubrey. It's time for you to know that. For everyone to know that."

They kissed one last time then headed back to the buffet line.

● ● ●

Kent and Aubrey took seats next to Elizabeth as they greeted Charles and the couple sitting across from them.

"Elaine and Arthur," Kent said. "Nice to see a Keuka View contingent." He held up his bandaged hands. "I'd shake, but I'm currently under repair."

"It's a pleasure to see you both, too," Arthur said, rising slightly from his chair. "Yeah. It was amazing the way you handled that pony. Everyone's calling you a hero."

Kent felt Aubrey's foot tap his shin, even while she maintained polite eye contact with Arthur.

Arthur Kelsey was the gray-haired, third generation owner of Keuka View winery-turned-horse-farm. His eyes were warm and playful and, after a half-century of chewing on his pipe, his smile displayed a mouthful of teeth, worn and yellowed like corn kernels.

"It wasn't that big a deal," Kent said. He flicked a glance to Aubrey, and then said to the Kelseys, "I trust you are having a prosperous year."

The silence that followed was palpable.

"What?" he said, finally.

"Well, as I was mentioning to the others here at the table, we've had a terrible thing happen at the farm," Arthur said, and he was no longer smiling. "Solar Wind is missing, to put it briefly."

Kent instantly lost interest in his food. In pin-drop silence, the others let Kent and Aubrey absorb the news.

Solar Wind was Keuka View's top stallion and the one who had transformed the tiny winery into a full-fledged Thoroughbred farm. Solar Wind boasted a stellar racing record. His lifetime earnings were off the charts. But most important, he had that ever-so-rare genetic ability to transmit his talent to his progeny. He, like Simpatico, was an elite member of New York's breeding program.

A shudder worked its way up Kent's back. "What do you mean *missing*?"

"He disappeared almost two weeks ago, during the night, pure and simple." Arthur said, as if he were announcing the loss of his best friend.

"How could that have happened? How come we haven't heard about it?"

"The working theory is that he was stolen. The police have asked us to keep it quiet, for now."

"Stolen!"

"At least the police are looking at it that way. Actually, theft, call it horsenapping, is probably the best of the possibilities. At least he could still be alive." Arthur pulled his pipe from his coat pocket and stared into its black bowl. "There are still a lot of unanswered questions. I'm keeping an open mind. Why would anyone steal him? The only plausible reason would be for ransom. Yet, we've received no ransom demand. Every day we expect one, but nothing happens. There's no other reason for someone to take him. Without his papers and a sale registered with the Jockey Club, he's worth no more than a backyard plug, dog food price, six hundred dollars." The thought caused Arthur's voice to crack.

"That's true," Aubrey said, thinking aloud. "Without a ransom note, the kidnapping — horsenapping — theory doesn't make much sense. Unless, maybe they chickened out."

"That's what the police suspect. I guess there's no way to disprove that."

Arthur performed the ritual of tapping, packing, and lighting his pipe. "The other frustrating thing is the insurance investigation. A dead end there, too."

"Same as the police?"

"Right. I'm sure they consider Elaine and me suspects."

Aubrey rocked back in her chair. "What? Idiots!"

"Whatever. They won't settle the claim."

"*Corpus delicti*," Kent said.

"You got it."

"How long can they hold out?" Elizabeth asked.

"According to our lawyers, there are legal limitations. At least, technically. But by tangling the thing up in court, they could hold out for years."

Kent remembered how Elizabeth's insurance company's handling of her Simpatico claim had been hassle-free. "That's ridiculous."

"Obviously, the best solution is to find Solar Wind."

Elaine leaned over and nudged her husband gently. More to change the subject than as a point of information, she said in her soft voice, "Dear, now may be a good time to ask Kent if he can come over to Keuka View to ultrasound those mares."

Arthur took the hint. "Yes, right. Kent, would you be willing to do the same thing you did last year — Come over for a long weekend, spend a half-day scanning mares, then spend the rest of the time goofing off? Maybe we could discuss Solar Wind more then."

"Emily told me she'd love to come see us again," Elaine said. "I ran into her in the food line. Maria, too. But Barry said he'd pass." She flashed Aubrey a quizzical look. "Said he had to work."

Aubrey scrunched her face. "Don't blame me." She jerked a thumb at Kent. "It's all his fault. He's got my son all caught up in the CVC. Barry absolutely loves the place. Spends every minute there. Hardly takes time out to eat, which is really something for Barry. I had to twist his arm to get him to help out at the around here today."

"What about you, Aubrey?" Elaine said. "We're hoping you can come, too."

Kent brightened at the possibility, but his hopes evaporated when he saw Aubrey's expression.

"No. There's too much going on at VinChaRo right now. Wrong time of year for me. I'm going to have to pass. Thanks."

"Like mother, like son," Kent said.

She nudged his leg with her toe.

Kent sighed. "Well, I'm in. It was a great little getaway last year."

"Except for a few hours of hard work," Arthur reminded him.

"Maybe you could call Sally at the office next week and line up a time. I'll let her know we talked."

"Excellent. Elaine and I look forward to it."

"I know Emily will be delighted to see Keuka View again and it will be a real treat for Maria." He also knew Keuka View's lavish accommodations would only heighten the loneliness he'd feel without Aubrey there to enjoy it with him.

He took a mouthful of Jell-O salad and let its summery flavor melt over his tongue. Solar Wind made three. *Our top three stallions out of commission.* He swallowed, then tossed his fork onto his plate. *Come on, man. Get your head out of the sand.*

"Yeah, Arthur. A visit to Keuka View sounds like a real good idea."

CHAPTER 15

THE SUN WAS JUST RISING IN THE EAST AS KENT'S
mobile unit rumbled west on Route 20. He had scheduled himself
out of the CVC for Friday. Three days of R & R. He'd get Arthur's
mares ultrasounded first thing, then enjoy a Finger Lakes mini-va-
cation. Arthur and Elaine had a huge home and they were gracious
hosts. It would be great. One of these times he'd have to find a way
for Aubrey to join them.

Kent sat behind the wheel and the girls shared the passenger
seat. Lucinda hung her head over from the back seat as they chatted
about the rural New York scenery that flashed by.

Going through Cardiff, Emily told Maria the story of the Cardiff
Giant hoax, and how, in the 1800s, a clever farmer and his sculptor
brother-in-law egged the faces of the world's greatest archaeologists
by convincing them that they had found a petrified giant man.

They rounded the north end of Skaneateles Lake and wound
through Auburn. They crossed through the Montezuma Wildlife
Refuge which brought on a philosophical discussion of whether or
not the animals that lived there were truly wild.

Route 20 paralleled the Erie Canal, and as they drove through
Seneca Falls, their conversation turned to whether a boat could get
from Seneca Lake to the Atlantic Ocean. Kent cataloged that trip
into his long list of things to do with Emily.

They turned south onto Route 14A toward Penn Yan and the conversation waned for half an hour. Emily was first to see Keuka View's sign looming ahead.

"There's the farm," she said.

Kent turned into the driveway and eased to a stop adjacent to a watchman's cubicle.

"Pretty tough to sneak in here," Maria said.

Kent suspected she was thinking about their Thoroughbred stallion problems as much as he was.

An elaborate iron gate spanned the driveway. It was anchored at each side into the thickest, thorniest hedge of multiflora rose Kent had ever seen, an impenetrable wall of vegetation running in both directions and surrounding the farm.

A white-haired attendant in a pressed gray shirt stepped from the booth. He leaned toward the window and did a slow take of the mobile unit. A faint smile cracked his otherwise straight face when his eyes hit Lucinda who was staring back with equal intensity. "Welcome folks. Mr. and Mrs. Kelsey are expecting you," he said. As he pushed a button and the gate rolled open, Kent saw him speak into an inconspicuous intercom.

"I was about ready to show him my visa," Maria said.

"Don't take it the wrong way," Kent said. "The people at Keuka View are all very friendly. You'll see. It's like a summer resort."

Maria pointed to a gigantic wooden barrel. "What's that?"

The barrel stood as a centerpiece in the lawn, varnished brown, displayed in a bed of flowers. It had the volume of a good-size hot tub.

"That's a hogshead."

"A what?"

"An old fashion wine barrel. That stone building behind it is the original Keuka View winery. Arthur's grandfather started it over a hundred years ago."

"Do they still make wine?"

"A little. For their own use, mostly. In the mid-seventies, the wine industry got hit by several corporate take-overs. They were big on quantity and didn't give a damn about quality. At least that's what Arthur thought, so he opted not to go with the flow. That's when the Kelseys got serious about the Thoroughbred business."

The driveway curled to where they could make out the red bricks of the main house's federal-style architecture. Elaine waved from the porch as they pulled up to one of several stone hitching posts that designated each parking place. Seconds later, Arthur's wine-red Mercedes slid in next to them.

"Richard buzzed me, too," Arthur said to his wife, and then to his guests he said, "It's wonderful to have you here. How was your trip? Come in and have a drink and something to eat."

The next hour was spent visiting and getting settled into rooms. The adults had regrouped in Elaine's wide-open country kitchen when the girls bounced in.

"I am going to show Maria the lake," Emily said. When Kent gave her a scowl, she turned to Elaine. "That is, if it's okay with you, Mrs. Kelsey."

Elaine nodded a smile to Em and a wink to her father.

● ● ●

Arthur seemed to be in no hurry to ultrasound his mares. Kent let him set the pace as they ambled toward the barns. Lucinda ranged ahead, happily exploring every bush and culvert along the way.

"Aside from Solar Wind, things must be going pretty well at Keuka View," Kent said. "I mean, really, I see a new pool even with your lakefront *and* a new wing on the barn? Such opulence."

Arthur gave a short sad laugh. "They were going well until, as you say, Solar Wind disappeared."

"Right. I hear you."

"We need more barn space for mares coming in to breed. The pool is for Elaine."

Kent eyed the barn as it came into view around the bend. Two long buildings ran parallel, joined in the middle by a breeding shed and office. Neatly groomed lawn and shrubbery appointed it. Except for the area excavated around the new addition, the entire estate was groomed perfectly.

The sonograms proceeded uneventfully as the hired men lead up mare after impressive mare to be examined. Kent extended his gloved arm — ultrasound probe in hand — into each one's rectum, viewed the uterus on a monitor for a few moments, and confirmed the presence of a healthy fetus.

At noon, Emily and Maria appeared with lunch. It was in a wicker basket the size of a laundry basket.

"Mrs. Kelsey knew you guys wouldn't stop for lunch, so she sent us down with some sandwiches and a jug of lemonade," Emily said.

"I married well," Arthur said, and took the basket from her. He pointed down the alleyway. "Let's eat in the office. It's air-conditioned."

As the four of them walked through the quiet barn, their voices echoed as if they were in a cave.

Arthur said, "I was looking for an excuse to take a break. I can't work like your dad anymore. You ladies see the sights?"

"Yes, we did," Maria said. "Your farm is fantastic."

"Oh, yeah? What makes you say that?" Arthur drew out the compliments.

"For one thing, the shoreline is like something in a magazine. I love that seawall! Why did you put in a pool? The dock is perfect for swimming."

"Elaine wanted it. She's got some problems in the joints. Swimming seems to help. The lake is okay for playing, but not so good for serious swimming. Plus, since the pool will be heated, it'll extend the season a lot."

They took seats around a heavy oak table in Arthur's office. Lucinda retreated to a corner with a bone the size of a man's wrist that Elaine had included in the basket.

Kent's eyes were drawn to an oil painting of a horse. It hung on the wall just above their heads. He'd never paid much attention to it before, but now the brilliant eyes of the dark stallion grabbed him and held. The horse stood like a lord studying his subjects — neck crested, chest out. It was Solar Wind. Kent felt his heart sink as he admired the painting. *Such a loss.*

Arthur followed Kent's gaze, and momentarily stopped passing out sandwiches. "He's something special, isn't he?"

"Yes, he is."

"He sired a lot of nice foals, too."

"He's a pillar of the New York Bred Program. We owe him a lot."

"Thanks for saying so. I'm very proud of that fact. For Elaine and me, it's like we've lost a child."

"The hedge goes all the way around the farm, doesn't it?" Kent said.

Arthur put a potato chip in his mouth, and took his time chewing and swallowing it, weighing the abrupt change of subject. He answered cautiously, knowing Kent's mind had returned to Solar Wind's disappearance.

"Yes. Except along the beach."

"It goes around the whole compound?"

"Uh-huh. All of the land we use for the horses is within the hedge. About fifteen acres. All of our buildings, too. We have a few hay fields and the vineyard outside of it."

"You lease most of your vineyard to one of the big growers, right?"

"Right. But they stay outside the perimeter. That hedge is, for all intents and purposes, an impenetrable barricade. My father wanted all his possessions under one roof, so to speak. I added the gateman when we got into Thoroughbreds. Someone is on duty twenty-four hours a day. I thought we were well ahead of the security curve, and it was working great — until it wasn't."

Kent glanced out a window, studied a section of the hedge. This time of year it looked like a billowing cloud of pink blossoms, but the eight-foot high, four-foot thick entanglement of thorns and ropey stems was a formidable barrier to anything larger than a stray cat.

Arthur rambled in the dazed way of one baffled by defeat, all the time his eyes on the painting of Solar Wind. "The hedge forms three sides of a rectangle, and the lakefront is the fourth. The main gate, of course, is up on the highway, and there is a smaller gate on each of the other two short sides. They're chained and locked at night and only the gateman, Richard, and I have keys."

"Do you have any kind of an alarm system?"

"Fire alarms? Everywhere. For intruders? There's an alarm system in the house and office, and motion detectors along the shoreline. But nothing in the barns. We do night watch instead."

"Really?" Emily said, curiosity obvious on her face. "I didn't see any security stuff on the beach."

"It's pretty well hidden, I don't like looking at it. But if you look closely, you'll see the sensors in the shrubbery. We installed it several years ago when we had problems with patio furniture and some other stuff disappearing from the beach. The police figured it was probably kids coming in on boats at night."

Kent took one of Elaine's homemade chocolate chip cookies.

"So if anyone crossed onto your property from the lake it would trigger the alarm?"

"Right."

"Who would be alerted?"

"Richard and I have monitors in our houses, and there is one in the gate house."

"Is it a reliable system? I mean, pretty hard to breech?"

Arthur shrugged. "If you talk to the sales reps it is. It was supposedly the best on the market. Who knows? I think any of them can be disarmed. As far as the police could tell, there is no evidence that it was tampered with."

"You'd know if Solar Wind had been walked through it, right?"

"Absolutely. But the police considered it a possibility anyway. They thought maybe he got loose from his stall, jumped into the water, and drowned. Absurd, if you know horses, but they combed the shore for hoof prints. None. The insurance company even hired a boat with underwater cameras to search the area. Nothing."

"What about closed circuit televisions?"

"Only in the foaling stalls to monitor the mares. Not for security. A watchman makes rounds every two hours."

"Do you trust the gateman? What's his name?"

"Richard Parker. Been here since he was a boy. His dad worked in the winery for my dad. He was a few years behind me in school. Rich is as honest as the day is long."

"He works the night shift?"

"Midnight to eight. He was about to go off when you arrived this morning."

Kent washed down his lunch with a long drink of lemonade. "How the heck could anyone get a horse out of here?"

A small silence ensued. No one answered.

Finally, Kent tossed his napkin into the trash, basketball style. "What do you think? Should we get back to work?"

"I guess so," Arthur groaned, and stood stiffly. "Another hour or so and we'll have it licked."

"Maybe less if we can get some work out of these girls," Kent said.

Emily gave him an exaggerated frown.

Maria nudged her with an elbow. "We'll help."

CHAPTER 16

"QUIT YOUR GROUSING," ARTHUR SAID TO KENT, as the group strolled back toward the car. "They beat you fair and square."

It had been Arthur's suggestion that they catch the afternoon horse races at Lake Country Raceway, and, of course, everyone had agreed enthusiastically. Kent and Emily had not yet been to the races this season, and it would be a first for Maria.

"I can't believe it," Kent said, then made a grunting noise loud enough that they could all hear him. "I studied the program before each race. I was analytical, objective, calculating. Maria and Emily picked their horses because they liked their name, or color, or — whatever, for Pete's sake — and they did better than I did. They won more than I did. I ask you, is that fair?"

"There is no justice in horseracing," Arthur said. "Do an extra dog spay when you get home. You'll make it up."

"Thanks for your sympathy. My price for ultrasounds is going up next week."

Emily, Maria, and Elaine joined in the tease until they reached the car. Then Kent swung the subject to evade the bombardment.

"Seriously. You know what impressed me the most today? There are a lot of Kentucky bred horses coming up here to run, and the New York breds are doing great against them. That's pretty good evidence that the New York Program is going strong."

"Absolutely," Arthur said.

Kent felt a sense of pride. The industrial North, long ravaged by the lure of the sunbelt, was rising again, to use the southerners' phrase.

They drove through the gate at Keuka View as a furious sunset silhouetted the west hill vineyards and sent lines of orange glistening across the water.

"I could use a swim before dinner," Kent said. "It's either that or a nap."

Elaine glanced at her watch. "Okay, but we're due at the Keuka Mist pier at eight o'clock. That gives us just over an hour. Better make it quick."

"Sounds good to me, too," Emily said.

"I'm in," Maria said.

A limb-flailing charge off the pier, a few strokes out, and a dive to wash away the racetrack dust. The cold, clear lake water erased any need for a nap. Kent and the girls passed the shampoo around and sent soft white suds drifting along the surface when they submerged to rinse. They called and coaxed Lucinda, until finally, even she plunged in.

Kent perched himself on the pier, with his feet still dangling in the water. He stroked Lucinda's dripping coat and watched the girls swim. Maria burst to the surface through the foam, shaking back her black hair, and sending crystalline droplets into the water around her. She swam to the pier, and with a powerful scissors kick, she heaved herself up. The effort delineated her youthful muscles beneath cinnamon skin. She folded herself over the edge, inadvertently displaying smooth buttocks and thighs. Kent tore his glance away. He stood quickly, and whipped his damp towel across his shoulder with a force that bordered on self-flagellation.

"I'll meet you up top," he shouted over his shoulder as he turned to go. "Come on, Lucinda, let's get out of here." He trudged up the hill, longing for Aubrey.

● ● ●

At eight on the dot they parked at the Hammondsport pier. Docked alongside, and bathed in floodlights, floated the Keuka Mist. She was snow-white with two open decks appointed in brass and teak. A huge black stack belched smoke and an orange paddle wheel fifteen feet in diameter idled at her stern. She was a perfect replica of the steamer that traversed Keuka Lake between Hammondsport and Penn Yan in the late 1800s. Walking up her gangway was like crossing back in time.

Throughout the evening, Kent, the two girls, and the Kelseys dined on the top deck, and enjoyed a nautical tour of the vineyards, the bluff, and the elegant homes along Keuka Lake's shoreline. When they sailed passed Keuka View, guests at nearby tables *oohed* and *aahed*. Emily and Maria directed teasing giggles at Elaine and Arthur when they overheard one woman spreading a rumor that Billy Joel recently bought the farm.

But then, gazing at his estate, Author washed away the humor. "Strange how peaceful it looks from here. Who could have imagined?"

All five of them stared at the farm across the water. Each harbored their own thoughts.

"New York's top three stallions out of commission. One of them from right there," he said.

Kent took a sip of wine. "Sounds like you're connecting the three."

Arthur shrugged. "What do you think? Do you suppose they could be related?"

"How?" Elaine asked. "Why?"

"Who would benefit?" Arthur asked. "Nobody that I can think of. That's the problem."

Kent slowly rotated his glass and watched the light play through the wine. "Well, we'd better figure it out pretty soon. We've got a lot at stake."

● ● ●

The clock down the hall struck three. Kent hadn't slept a wink. He reached down and stroked Lucinda who was dead to the world beside the bed. None of his usual techniques for lulling himself into drowsiness worked. The best he could do was get to that uncomfortable plane of consciousness where worry dominates. He tossed. His skin tingled. He climbed out of bed and crept along the hall to the bathroom, hoping that stretching his legs and emptying his bladder would re-set his mind. He took a sip of water and a few Tums, even though he figured his agitation was way beyond indigestion from the rich food they'd eaten on the Keuka Mist. On the way back to his room, he peeked in on Maria and Emily. He couldn't see them through the darkness, but heard their slumberous duet.

Back in his room he stared out at the lake for a few minutes, then climbed back into bed. Immediately, the fretfulness demons renewed their attack. He groaned, fluffed up the pillows, and folded his arms behind his head.

"All right, you want to think? Then think," he whispered, and gave his mind a free rein. Instantly it fixed on Arthur Kelsey's missing horse.

He rehashed the facts surrounding Solar Wind's disappearance — excellent security, no ransom note, no known enemies. Was the horse alive or dead? How did they get him out of the compound? Kent rolled each piece of the case over and over in his mind without finding a way to fit them together.

"There has to be more," he mumbled, then rolled onto his side, sighed heavily, and closed his eyes.

Suddenly, his eyes snapped open. He sat up, fully awake. They, whoever *they* were, did not breach the security system at all. No way could someone get a horse out of there without detection. They must have kept Solar Wind *inside* the compound! How could anyone do that? Where could they hide a horse?

Maybe they'd stashed him in some secret temporary stall in one of the accessory buildings for a few days, then smuggled him out later. No, there were no such out buildings in the compound. None remote enough that anyone could rely on it for a hiding place. Besides, stallions made a lot of noise. He could be tranquilized. But you'd still have the problem of where to hide him. A retired and forgotten horse van? Maybe, but pretty risky. No, it would be just about impossible to hide a live horse in a fifteen-acre compound when a dozen or more people were searching for him.

Kent considered the other heinous option. What if they killed Solar Wind? How could anyone kill such an animal? For what reason? That's not the point. What if they *did* kill him for whatever reason? How? It was not easy to kill a horse quickly and quietly. Even then, there would be blood or evidence of a struggle. Suddenly, the awful day flashed into his mind when he folded back the tarp and was faced with the revolting image of Simpatico's cold staring eyes.

The vision startled him. "Jesus," he said, then forced the thought from his mind. Say they did kill Solar Wind somehow. Then what? Where would they dispose of a twelve hundred pound body? Winch him onto a truck? Hide him under a tarp or plywood or something like that? Maybe they could sneak him through the front gate. Maybe even under a load of sand or dirt. There must have been trucks entering and leaving on a regular basis as part of the construction project for the pool and barn addition. What about burying the body? Couldn't do that with a hand shovel. It takes a *big* hole to bury a horse. The new construction again. Under the pool or the barn addition? Could they do that? Could someone bury a horse by hand in just a few minutes? They could if the hole was already dug. And, if nobody was going to be the least bit suspicious of disturbed earth. Hell, there would have been mud and ruts and freshly dug soil all over the place. What if they walked Solar Wind next to the foundation hole, killed him, and rolled him in. In next to no time they could throw and landslide a foot or two of dirt over the body and no one would be the wiser. What stage was the construction work at when Solar Wind disappeared?

He had a lot of questions for Arthur in the morning. The *killed and buried* theory was plausible. How could he prove or disprove it?

He finally drifted off to sleep with his arm dangling down to Lucinda.

CHAPTER 17

KENT WAS OUT OF BED THE SECOND HE HEARD Elaine rustling around in the kitchen. He reminded himself to exercise self-control, that Solar Wind's burial in the compound was a long shot, and, from the Kelsey's standpoint, it would be a dreadful solution to the mystery. Show some sensitivity. Nevertheless, his stomach fluttered with anticipation.

Elaine greeted him as he entered the kitchen. "My, you're up and about early. I thought you'd sleep in."

He lied. "You know how it is. Your biorhythms say 'time to get up' no matter what."

"I know. Except it's more my arthritis than my biorhythms." She handed him a cup of coffee, and said as a suggestion, "Nice morning for a walk along the lake."

"You're right about that, but I want to talk to Arthur first thing," he said.

His tone caused Elaine to turn from the stove and look directly at him. There was concern on her face. "Problems?"

"Hunches."

"About what?"

Kent glanced down the hall. "Arthur awake yet?"

"Yes. He'll be down in a minute."

"I'd rather talk to you both together."

"Okay." Elaine went back to her skillet of bacon. A long moment later, Arthur walked in still buttoning his cardigan. "Morning, Kent. Sleep well?"

"Not really."

"Too much good food last night?"

"Too much coffee and spices for sure, but that's not all. Actually, I was mulling over Solar Wind's disappearance and I came up with some ideas I'd like to talk to you about."

Arthur sighed wearily. "Let me get a cup of coffee first."

Kent didn't wait. "Did you — or somebody — search the *whole* farm when you noticed Solar Wind missing?"

"Yes, of course. We had everyone on the place drop what they were doing and start looking."

"Are there any outbuildings that you don't use, or even an old horse van where he could have been hidden?"

Arthur took a seat at the table, pulled out his pipe, and began filling it, all the time shaking his head *no, no, no.* "Kent, believe me, we searched everywhere. I mean *everywhere* — from pump house, to boat house, to hay mow. There was no horse, or any hoof prints, in any of them."

"You walked the perimeter, right?"

"Personally? Twice. Richard at least twice, the police once, the insurance investigators a couple of times. All gates were as they should be. No indication that anybody or anything had entered through the hedge."

"Okay. Was there any lapse in security at the front gate with all the confusion?"

"No," Arthur said, with enough force that Elaine turned from the stove. "On the contrary, when the shit hit the fan, security was tightened. Nothing came or went through that gate without a thorough inspection."

"Then there is no reasonable possibility that Solar Wind, or his body, could have been transported out?"

"Not once we knew he was missing. And probably not at any time before."

For a long minute Kent stared out through the kitchen window at the lake, still misty from the night air. "How about a struggle. Any signs in his stall? Damage?"

"None. Not a goddamn thing out of place. Solar Wind's bedding wasn't even mussed. No blood or hair either. "

"How about his stall door?"

Arthur finished lighting his pipe, and tossed his spent match into a large ashtray on a side table. "It was open when we found it. With the latch unbolted, which you know can only be done from the outside."

"Right."

"What are you getting at, Kent?"

"I'm not sure. But I spent a lot of last night trying to come up with a logical scenario for what happened."

Elaine refilled their coffee cups. "And?"

"Now that you've answered my questions, I have a theory. I know it's a long shot, but it's a theory, and I can't come up with anything better."

Arthur pulled the pipe from his mouth. "Let's hear it."

"In a nutshell, I'm thinking Solar Wind is still *in* the compound." He waited for their reaction and got blank faces. "Somebody killed him. I'm sorry to destroy your hopes of getting him back alive, but I honestly believe that. Then they buried him within a few minutes of his death. They probably walked him to the site, then killed him."

"What site?" Elaine and Arthur blurted at the same time.

"Either the pool or the barn addition."

Arthur looked up at his wife, then back at Kent.

Elaine placed a hand on Arthur's shoulder, steadying herself. "You're saying that someone sneaked into the barn, took Solar Wind out of his stall, walked him to the pool or the barn, killed him somehow, and buried him?"

"That's right. Could it have happened that way?"

Arthur and Elaine stared at each other for a long moment.

Finally, Arthur said, "I suppose so."

Elaine slumped into a chair. "It did drizzle a little rain that night. Not enough to obscure tracks on dirt or turf, but enough to wash them off the macadam driveway."

"It would explain the open stall door, and the fact that the perimeter was undisturbed," Arthur said. "But the pool is too close to the house. It would have to be the barn." He drew on his pipe a time or two, thinking. "How long would it take to do all that, Kent? Could they get it done between watchman rounds?"

"Well." Kent sipped his coffee. "Say the bastard sneaks through one of the side gates on foot. That could be done, right?"

"Yes. A man couldn't get through the hedge, but I suppose someone could squeeze between the rails of the gates."

"Okay," Kent continued. "So then I figure it's five minutes tops to the stallion barn. He puts a halter on Solar Wind and they're out of there in three to five minutes more. Five more down to the barn construction, then ten seconds to kill him with a silencer-equipped gun or three minutes with an injection of euthanasia solution intravenously. Then the hard part; rolling him into the grave and burying him. One man could do it, but it'd be tough. Maybe they walked him into the hole then killed him. I'm not sure. One man with a shovel, working from above in soft dirt, could cover a horse's body lying flat, at least enough to hide it, in, I'm guessing here, twenty minutes, if he's got his adrenalin pumping."

"Dammit to hell," Arthur said. "That theory makes me sick to my stomach."

"How long is that?" Kent asked Elaine, who had been keeping tally on a note pad.

"About thirty-five to forty minutes," she said. The pencil fell from her hand. "It could be done between watches."

Arthur jerked his pipe from between his clenched teeth. "It is possible, but is it likely enough to justify tearing up a newly completed half-million dollar barn addition to find out?"

"I thought about that, too. You may not have to do anything that drastic." Kent was starting to feel a little more confident in his theory. "You probably have something around that has Solar Wind's scent on it. A blanket maybe, or his brushes? Something like that?"

"We have everything," Arthur said. "His stall and his grooming gear are exactly the way they were the day he disappeared."

"Good. We can start after breakfast."

Neither Arthur nor Elaine dared ask what it was they would start.

Elaine walked back to her stove. A few minutes later she served up the kind of country breakfast farmers eat before a big day in the fields. No one tasted a thing.

● ● ●

It was halfway to noon by the time Kent and Arthur arrived at the barn to test Kent's theory. By then, the girls had made their first appearance for the day, had breakfast, and joined them. Elaine had decided she would rather wait to hear the results afterward.

When Arthur opened the tack room door, its odor wafted out. It was a good smell — a wonderful mix of old cedar, oiled leather, and mentholated liniments. Arthur pointed to the closest of a dozen blankets hanging on large wooden dowels cantilevered off the wall. They were all alike — wine red with gold trim. The one Arthur pointed to was monogrammed *SW* in ornate letters.

"There's his blanket. That's probably your best bet. In that chest underneath are his grooming supplies. Take your pick."

Kent stared at the blanket from a few steps away. It felt wrong to disturb anything.

104

"Go ahead," Arthur urged. "Whatever you need."

Kent lifted the blanket from its rack and unfolded it reverently. He brought the coarse material to his nose and inhaled softly, then turned it to examine its underside. "This ought to work," he said.

He held it so Arthur could see a filmy mat of horse hair caught in the felt fibers of the blanket. "Lucinda should be able to get Solar Wind's scent from this."

Arthur's brow creased. "Lucinda?"

"Yep. She's got a great nose."

Lucinda, alerted by the sound of her name, smiled up from her position against Kent's knee.

Arthur gave her a dubious look, then said, "Well, if there's a body buried around here, it can't be too deep."

"My thought exactly," Kent said, giving his dog an admiring look. "Redbone Hounds have amazing noses, and Lucinda's nose is amazing even for a Redbone. Her real thing is coon hunting. I've seen her in action many times. But I'm sure she can find Solar Wind, if he's there."

He knelt down in front of Lucinda, draping the horse blanket across his knee. He let the big hound rest her muzzle directly on the haired surface. She sniffed deeply several times.

"Where is he?" Kent goaded her. "Find Solar Wind! Go on. Go find the horse!" He took a couple of false steps toward the door and stopped abruptly to let Lucinda rush past him. She disappeared out into the main barn.

"Now we'll see if I know what I'm talking about," Kent said.

The four of them took off after the excited hound.

Kent scanned the long alleyway through the barn. Lucinda wasn't in sight. They headed for the daylight streaming in a large door at one end. Still, she was not visible.

A strange mix of optimism and fear crept over Kent as he followed Lucinda. He could tell by the trudge of the old man's stride and the crease in his brow that Arthur had the same feeling.

As they approached the corner of the barn, they heard Lucinda's high-pitched yelp.

"I think she's at the construction site," Arthur said.

"Sounds like it."

By the time they rounded the corner, Lucinda had excavated a feed tub-size hole along the footing of the new barn.

For a long moment, the group stood silently watching her dig furiously, using here front feet to throwing wads of earth between her hind legs.

Arthur sighed, long and dejected. "I know a guy with a backhoe. I'll give him a call." He headed for the house without another word.

Kent called Lucinda away from her hole. He squatted so that he was nose to nose with her. Ruffling up her ears, he said, "Good dog, Lucy! You are my awesome girl. What would we do without you?"

She received her commendation with sparkling eyes and lolling tongue. Then, still vibrating with excitement, she settled to her haunches against Kent's leg.

● ● ●

In less than an hour Arthur's neighbor arrived in a tired-looking red dump truck with a yellow lowboy trailer and backhoe in tow. Arthur flagged him down in front of the addition, and a few minutes later digging commenced.

Elaine, who could no longer stand the suspense, had joined Emily and Maria as they treaded nervously at an observation point nearby.

The man operated the bucket as if it were his hand. With the deftness of an archaeologist brushing away earth from an ancient artifact, he guided the four-inch silver teeth to expose one thin layer of dirt at a time, always watching Arthur and Kent's signals out of the corner of his eye.

The women craned their necks to see into the hole, trepidation on every face. The bucket descended deeper and deeper with each pass. Finally, after many slow minutes, it rattled through a pocket of rubble, vibrated the ground, and dislodged a section of earth from the side of the cavity. Simultaneously, all five observers reeled back as nauseous vapors of decomposing flesh mixed with pungent earth and summer mugginess rose up, rendering a stench that coated their throats and teared their eyes.

Maria gagged hard, hands on knees, then stood and wobbled away to better air. Emily turned instinctively to Elaine and hid her face against the old woman's chest. Both wept. Arthur removed his pipe, pulled a red bandanna from his pocket, and covered his nose and mouth. He was determined to see the revolting scene played out to its end. Kent, more accustomed to the repugnance of death and fortified by the success of discovery, continued to direct the digger.

A few more passes of the bucket and a steel-clad hoof, black with decay, draped limply into the hole. The hideous sight was sufficient evidence for Arthur. He turned, coiled Emily and Elaine in his arms, and led them away.

Kent steeled himself against the overwhelming sadness that enveloped him, and worked with the excavator for another hour. Finally, they delivered Solar Wind's body from the grave and transported it to a secluded location in a machinery building. Kent rolled back the horse's spongy upper lip and made the mandatory tattoo identification. He prepared himself for another exhausting post-mortem exam, then glanced at the horse's blank eyes and sighed deeply. Instead he opted to just confirm what he was sure he would find, a bullet hole in Solar Wind's forehead. Afterwards, he covered the regal beast with a canvas to await Arthur's instructions for proper burial.

● ● ●

Kent found Arthur on the veranda. He could see the old man was in shock, swaying back and forth in a rattan rocker. Kent's footsteps on the porch roused him from his trance. Without looking Kent's way or speaking, Arthur gestured toward a bottle of scotch on the table next to him.

Kent poured himself two fingers and took the next rocker over.

After a long silent, his eyes still fixed on the waters of Keuka Lake, Arthur said, "Shot, wasn't he."

"Between the eyes."

Both men studied the vista for a long time, sipping and thinking.

Finally, Kent said, "How did you know?"

"Because you've been right all along."

Kent poured them each another.

"Arthur, we're going to get the bastard who shot your horse. That I promise."

With his eyes still fixed on the lake, Arthur tossed back the scotch, then let out a low, sad noise that strengthened Kent's resolve.

CHAPTER 18

KENT LET HIS EYES DRIFT AROUND MATTSON Cemetery. "Come on, guys," he said to Emily and Maria. "You're going to have to give me something new." He crumpled an empty potato chip bag and flipped it at the gravestone across from where he sat. "It's been a week and you keep saying the same old thing."

Emily stood and brushed dry leaves off her bottom. "I'm telling you, it makes sense, even if you won't admit it."

"You haven't convinced me."

"No kidding?"

"I keep an open mind. All we know for sure is that foul play was involved in the death of Solar Wind. We have no evidence that Simpatico's death or Charter Oak's illness was anything but natural. Besides, what motive would Charles have?"

"Money!" the girls said in unison.

"Are you talking about what the townies said at the driving competition, about Charles' investment losses? Pure hearsay, totally unsubstantiated. Half those people are so jealous of the St. Pierres, they'd spread any rumor they could get ahold of."

During the silence that followed, Kent watched a fat gray squirrel chase away a blue jay that had raided one of its winter caches. Then he said, "And even if he did kill Simpatico for the insurance money, like you say, how would he cause Charter Oak to get EVA? And why would he kill Solar Wind? He has no interest in Solar Wind."

"We're working on that," Emily said, not wanting to admit she had no idea.

"Maybe he wants to knock out competition from other top ranked stallions," Maria said.

"Right *after* he kills his own number one stallion? Not likely. And you're still left with the problem of how he *wished* Charter Oak to get EVA."

The girls fumed, aware they'd need more facts before they could sell Kent their Charles St. Pierre-did-it-for-the-money theory.

"Listen," Kent said more sympathetically. "The Solar Wind thing has got you going. Okay, me too. After all, we know for sure that somebody *did* kill him. I saw the hole in his head myself, and I've seen enough gunshot wounds to know that's what it was before I removed the slug. We'll see if the police ballistics guys can tell us anything about the gun it came from. Then we'll see where that leads us, but in the meantime, don't let your imagination run away with you. We have no proof that any of the cases are linked."

Kent grabbed the gravestone that was his backrest, pulled himself to his feet, and instructed the girls. "Keep an open mind. Stay objective. That's the way you untangle something like this."

"It was Charles," Emily said.

Kent turned to Lucinda, and shrugged, his palms up. "They're hopeless," he said.

● ● ●

When Kent, Emily, and Maria arrived back at the CVC, the girls went about restocking the truck while Kent headed to his office to see what chaos the day had wrought. Among the clutter on his desk there were several notes with names and numbers to call for one reason or another, but it was the one from Ed Holmes that caught his eye.

He strummed his fingers impatiently as the phone rang in his ear. Finally, Dr. Holmes's voice came on the other end. "Ed, Kent here. Sorry I missed you when you called."

"No big deal, I figured you'd want to know what we came up with on the Stanford horse."

"Absolutely."

"This is going to sound really strange."

"Why am I not surprised?"

"Yeah, no kidding. So we repeated all the tests. I would stake my worthless reputation on this."

"On what?"

"First, we did the serology and, not surprisingly, we got the same results as from your initial samples positive for EVA. A definite positive."

"Right."

"So then I asked the lab to isolate the virus."

"Any luck?"

"As a matter of fact, yes."

"Were they able to identify the serotype?"

"Yes, that's the strange part. It turns out it's the VanMark strain of EVA virus."

A moment of silence passed between them. Kent listened, expecting Holmes to continue. He did not. So Kent nudged him.

"Is that particularly significant?"

"Absolutely. The VanMark strain is not a *field* strain. It's a *research* strain, cultured and maintained at a few research facilities and veterinary vaccine companies throughout the world. I had a couple of my interns check it out. The VanMark strain has never been reported in a natural outbreak of Equine Viral Arteritis."

"Then where did it come from in the first place?"

"Actually, it's a mutant strain that was discovered accidentally back in the 1950s by one Doctor Bernard VanMark, a guy who was researching EVA. The important thing that he noted was that it stimulated better immunity in test horses than the natural strains."

"In other words, it made a good vaccine."

"Exactly. And that was back when there was a real push to develop an EVA vaccine. As it turns out, there were other problems with it." Dr. Holmes's voice dropped to a hollow tone, "Not the least of which was that it caused severe symptoms of EVA in some horses that were vaccinated with it."

Kent's lips shifted into a thin smile of satisfaction as another piece of the puzzle fell into place. "That would explain why Charter Oak got so sick."

Dr. Holmes did not veer. "So, it really never went anywhere. But, to this day, the VanMark strain is maintained at places that study EVA or make vaccines because it's the model for EVA virus immune stimulation against which all others are compared."

Kent thought for a minute, assimilating the new information. "The obvious question is: How did it get into Charter Oak?"

"Yep. That's the big one," Holmes said. "Has he been off the farm at all?"

"Not in a long time. Not since he raced. And he's been tested negative for EVA several times since then. Where could he have gone that he could have picked it up?"

"Kentucky is the only state in the U.S. where there is any VanMark, as far as we could find out."

"Charter Oak hasn't been to Kentucky in years." After a thoughtful pause, Kent said, "You were going to test the other horses at Cedar Cut Farm. Did any others test positive?"

"We tested every horse on the place. All negative."

"So, it wasn't brought in by one of those horses."

"Right. But there were mares that came in for breeding and left before Charter Oak got sick. We haven't retested them yet, so we can't rule them out."

Kent doodled *"EVA"* on his desk blotter. "They all came in with a clean test. It should have shown up then."

"How many outside horses came in and left this spring? Give me an estimate."

"Probably twenty-five. Give or take. It's not a big farm."

"Can you get me a list of their names and where they came from? I'll have my interns track them down."

"For sure. I'd really appreciate it, and so would the Stanfords. I don't know where else it could have come from. I'll have Louise Stanford call you with the list tomorrow. I know she'll be glad to do it."

"Good. Tell her I'll be waiting for her call."

After Kent hung up, he sat for a long time mulling over what Dr. Holmes had told him. How could Charter Oak have picked up such an unusual strain of EVA? He held out next to no hope that Holmes would find it came in through one of those early mares. If it was exclusively a research strain, not found in nature, someone would have had to get it from a research lab, then get it to Charter Oak. That would require planning — premeditation — on someone's part. If that were true, harm to a second of the three horses was intentional and malicious.

"Oh, man," he mumbled to his empty office, "I can hear the 'We told you so' from Em and Maria already."

The worse part about it was, they were starting to sound less crazy.

● ● ●

On the drive from the CVC to Pine Holt, Kent told Emily and Maria what Dr. Holmes had said. As anticipated, the attack on Charles St. Pierre began again with renewed vigor — and carried on right through dinner.

"Outside mares, no way!" Emily said, then filled her mouth with a bite of Margaret's pot roast. She waved her fork in the air to hold the floor while she chewed and swallowed. Then she said, "Now we know that somebody gave Charter Oak EVA. And I'll bet anything that Dr. Holmes's test on those outside mares will back me up. They'll all be negative." She gave Kent a sharp look. "Maria and I have said all along, somebody killed our horses. And I'm telling you, it was Charles St. Pierre."

"You don't know all those mares will be negative."

"I know it."

"Uh-huh. You might lack facts, but you don't lack confidence. I'll give you that."

Emily toned things down with a cagey smile. "You watch and see."

"That's what we are going do," Kent said. "But, for the sake of argument, say the blood tests on the outside horses do come back clean. Given that fact, how would that make a case against Charles?"

"Because he needs the money. We went through this before."

"Except there's no money for him in Solar Wind's death, and even if there was, it's not a strong enough motive for him to do something so drastic. I've known Charles for a lot of years. Granted, he has the personality of a fence post, but I would have gotten some sort of a read if he were trying to pull something like that. He'd have left signs. Maybe slyly ask me about how to kill a horse like, 'Hey, Doc, I read in the paper about these guys who tried to kill a horse by feeding him stuff that would make him colic. Is that possible?' That kind of thing. Besides, did he have the opportunity? Think about that. Sure, he could have gotten to Simpatico at the home farm, but can you imagine Charlie, the pseudo-horseman, slinking into half-loco Charter Oak's stall at Cedar Cut and giving a horse like that a shot of some weird virus? Charter Oak would knock him into next week. No, I've got a hunch something else is going on."

"Oh. So now *you've* got a hunch," Maria said.

Kent gave her a silly grin. "Poor choice of words."

"He could hire somebody," Emily said.

"Maybe, but I doubt it. For one thing, you're talking coconspirator. You and I both know that in the horse world once two people talk, it's no longer a secret. Someone always finds out. Not the cops maybe, but the grapevine picks it up. Somebody would have gotten wind of it by now. Secondly, it's harder to hire someone to do in a horse than to do in a person. Most assassins don't understand horses, and can't muster up that feeling of superiority they need because they are intimidated by a horse's size and strength. Basically, most thugs are afraid of horses. Plus, the whole farm environment is foreign to them. Your average hit man wouldn't know where to start."

Dinner went on in silence for a time. Then Emily brightened. "How about Burton Bush? He's such a loser, always hanging around Charlie and acting all bad."

Kent shrugged. "Burton does know how to work around horses."

"And he's mean enough," Maria said.

It was common knowledge that before VinChaRo, The Burning Bush had drifted from farm to farm, track to track, working for whoever would hire him, and never for very long. His foul mouth, vicious temper, and heavy drinking had usually gotten him, and Ninja, booted in short order. In fact, those traits had landed him in jail more than once.

"He works for Mr. St. Pierre," Emily said.

"It would be incredible," Kent said. "I'll tell you what. Just so we can say we left no stone unturned, I'll snoop around and see if Charles has been putting out feelers for a criminal type. My guess is he'd probably try at the tracks first. I know vets at several. They may be able to keep an ear open for me."

Maria and Emily celebrated their victory with more pot roast.

"Well, Maria, it took us pretty much all night," Emily said, with a sidelong glance at her father, "but now we're getting somewhere."

CHAPTER 19

"MORNING, HUBRIS," AUBREY SAID, AS SHE rolled open the stall door of VinChaRo's new top stallion. "Sorry to disturb you, but there's a young lady in the shed who's eager to meet you." Hubris swung his head around like a great boom. Aubrey swore she saw him smile.

Before her eyes, he went from half asleep to treading with excitement. She had to dance to avoid getting her toes stepped on as she haltered him. He rattled out several loud snorts.

"Take it easy," she said. "I'm going as fast as I can."

It amazed Aubrey how astute these beasts really were. How many times a day was Hubris's stall door opened? Many. And he was always the perfect gentleman. Yet somehow, he could sense when he was headed to the breeding shed — and he turned into a high school boy hoping to get lucky.

The other stallions, who also knew where Hubris was headed, snorted a mix of jealousy and encouragement to him as Aubrey led him down the alleyway. In response he pranced even higher.

Aubrey gave a sharp tug on the lead shank, just enough to get his attention. "Hubris, you keep your wits about you."

Hubris ignored her. He strained forward, shoving Aubrey with his shoulder. Aubrey stopped dead in her tracks, stomped her foot dramatically on the walkway, and wheeled to face him as he skidded to a halt within inches of her. Feigning anger, she snapped the lead shank a little harder this time.

"That's enough!" she bluffed loudly. "Once more and I'm taking you back to your stall." But he was not going back, and he knew it. Her scolding was simply her cue for the big horse to settle down, the daily banter between horse and handler. As they proceeded into the shed, he exercised more self-control.

Inside the breeding shed, Charles St. Pierre moved toward the dark bay mare that Burton Bush held in the middle of the cavernous room. Charles cautiously lifted her upper lip, studied her tattoo, making the mandatory *one last check*. He compared it to the identification on his clipboard.

"Okay. We're good," he said. "Burton, you can put the twitch on."

"I know when to put the damn twitch on," The Burning Bush said. "You don't have to tell me every time."

He took a handful of the mare's silken muzzle and secured it in a loop of rope at one end of a four-foot wooden handle. The mare, familiar with the procedure, showed no reaction until Burton made one final, unnecessarily severe turn that clinched her nose painfully tight. The mare pulled her head back and squinted cross-eyed at the twitch on her nose.

"You best be holding real still or I'll sic Ninja on you," Burton said to the mare, both fists locked on the twitch.

"That dog better not be in here." Aubrey said. "And ease up on the twitch. That mare's behaving just fine."

"Relax. I'm just shittin' her. Ninja ain't anywhere around. And damn right, she's behaving fine. I've got her real good."

"Let up on the twitch, I said, Burton. I mean it."

Burton sighed and begrudgingly let the twitch slacken on the mare's nose. "It's your fault if Hubris gets kicked."

"You let me worry about that." Aubrey knew it was essential to protect the stallions. A stallion's career could be ended in a fraction of a second by a kick from an unruly mare. They couldn't chance it.

But the twitch was supposed to distract the mare, not bring her to her knees. Aubrey managed to ignore Burton's sloppiness and constant run of off-color remarks, but she wasn't about to let him hurt the horses. And that was that.

Hubris screamed loudly to the mare. Every person in the room grimaced.

"Jesus. Shut that guy up," Burton said, as if anyone could.

The equine mating ritual began. The mare turned her rump toward Hubris, raised her tail, squatted slightly, then squirted several pulses of urine.

Hubris followed his cue. He began a rhythm of deep grunts. He pranced in place, neck arched, foamy white saliva bubbling around his lips. Five yards behind the mare, he stopped, raised his muzzle toward the rafters, and rolled back his upper lip, registering the scent from the mare. Aubrey bent, glanced between his hind legs, and confirmed he was ready.

"Okay," she said, and waved in one of the grooms who approached with a stainless steel pail sloshing soapy water. He gave Hubris's underside a quick washing.

"Ready," he said as he ducked to safety.

"Here we come," Aubrey warned Burton.

"In more ways than one," Burton said.

"Turn her head this way a little, Burton. Let her see him step up, so she won't be startled."

"Yes, Madam."

Aubrey eased Hubris toward the mare ever so slowly.

Hubris huffed loudly and surged against Aubrey's firm restraint as he edged toward the focus of his universe. When he was a step or two away from the mare's left hip, Aubrey eased her hand off his shoulder and slackened the lead. He rose into a flailing twelve-foot biped and stepped to the mare. They were done in less than a minute, during which time participants and observers all fell silent.

Afterwards Hubris stood quietly, tranquility returning. Aubrey patted him on the neck.

Burton unwound the twitch from the mare's muzzle. "How'd that feel, Girlie?"

Aubrey gave him a fierce look, but didn't take the bait.

"Okay, that was a good cover," Charles said. "Last one for this morning. Burton, after you take that mare back, get a couple guys and go set up those new troughs. In paddocks one and five, where we talked about?"

"Yeah, I remember. You showed me six times."

"Good. Then get at it."

Burton shuffled away, mare in hand, grumbling as he went.

When Aubrey was sure Hubris was safe and comfortable in his stall, she returned to the shed. Charles was there alone, studying his clipboard.

"Good job done this morning," he commented when he saw her approach. He tapped his clipboard. "Hopefully, we can cross off five more mares."

"Yeah, we cooked right along today. It looks like Hubris is going to handle the number one spot for us." Then she brushed aside the chitchat. "Charles, something really weird happened last night and I think you should know about it."

They crossed the breeding shed toward the office.

"What's that?" Charles said, still studying his clipboard as they walked.

"Osvaldo came up to my place. He hung around for a few minutes making small talk, but I could see he was trying to get up the nerve to tell me something. He was really antsy, and you know Osvaldo — Mr. Mellow. When he finally spit it out, I didn't know what to say, so I'm telling you about it. You know, passing the buck."

Charles looked at her, paying attention now. "So what's his problem?"

"He said Burton and some of the other guys were drinking in his apartment."

"Nothing unusual about that."

"They were playing cards, but they kept getting drunker until it degenerated into a bull session, I guess. Anyway, they got to bragging, and trying to outdo each other. A lot of that 'Oh, yeah, well I blah, blah, blah' crap, you know?"

Charles entered the office ahead of Aubrey. "Yeah, so?"

She was relieved to find it unoccupied. "Burton started blabbing that he killed Simpatico. That's what."

Charles spun around so quickly, Aubrey nearly ran into him. His face twisted. He stared at her with eyes that could not hide his anger.

"*And* he was making a lot of derogatory remarks about you, and Elizabeth, and the farm," she added, but it sounded so like a tattletale child that she immediately wished she had not.

Charles blew out a deep breath, getting control. "Could have been the booze talking."

"It made an impression on Osvaldo."

"So at least he thinks there is something to it."

"Oh, yeah, I could tell Osvaldo believes it, all right. And, any way you cut it, it's way too serious a thing for us to assume it's nothing."

Charles toyed with a gold chain at his throat. "What do you think? Should we call him on it?"

"I spent a good part of last night tossing that question around."

"And?"

She tried to sound confident. "Yeah, I think we should."

Charles gave her a long, thoughtful stare. Finally, he said, "Just ask him outright if he killed Simpatico?"

Aubrey shrugged. "He's your man. I was thinking you could contrive some plan to get him aside, maybe have him go over to the Lake House with you to fix something. It doesn't matter what. Then tell him one-on-one you heard the rumor. You don't really believe it, but being his friend and all, you figured you owed it to him to let him know. Then we'll see what sifts out."

Charles gave Aubrey a doubtful look. "It's hard to believe he's going to come right out and admit it."

"If you can come up with something better, I'm open."

"Not a lot of options."

Aubrey nodded slowly.

CHAPTER 20

THE LAKE HOUSE, LIKE VINCHARO, WAS ON Huron Lake, just a couple of miles closer to town. It had been in the St. Pierre family as long as the farm, but nowadays, since Charles and his sister had little interest in the place, it sat pretty much unused. However, like all St. Pierre property, it was maintained immaculately, at an expense Charles considered exorbitant for the amount of use it got. Several times he had approached Elizabeth about selling it. Each time she refused.

"You never know," she'd say. "Someday I might have grandchildren, then I can put the place to good use. Once it's gone, we'll never get it back."

So, year after year, Charles dumped a small fortune into maintaining the hundred-year-old building and grounds.

He stood along the lakeshore looking back toward the house. Its peacefulness and permanence always made him uncomfortable, but it was worse today. He hadn't slept since he and Aubrey had contrived their plan to question Burton Bush, and he knew nothing was going to put him at ease except being done with it.

He called to Burton, who was unloading tools from a shed while Ninja circled at his feet. Together they walked out onto the narrow wooden pier. Charles pointed out several rotten planks green and slippery with mossy decay. Burton slogged along at his side.

"I hired on to work with horses, not to be some dumb-ass maintenance man."

"I pay you to work. This is what needs to be done," Charles said.

They made it to the end and stood looking out across the lake for so long that Burton began to sense that something was up. He treaded nervously. Charles felt his hired man's suspicion and figured the longer he stalled, the worse it would get. Finally, he blurted the whole story just as he had heard it from Aubrey, except he skipped the names of the individuals involved.

"Which one of those bastards told you that?" Burton said, in a whiny voice. "I'll beat the shit out of him. I didn't kill your goddamn horse, Charles. You believe that bullshit? Come on."

Charles studied his lackey through squinted eyes. "Not necessarily, but the person who brought this to my attention is not a liar."

"Oh, but I am?" Burton's face folded into a tearful expression. "Why am I always the one who gets accused of everything? No one ever takes my side."

Charles shrugged. "Let's hear your side."

"Bullshit! I had no fucking thing to do with any dead horse!"

"Take it easy. If you didn't kill Simpatico, you and I are all good. But I'm telling you, we will catch whoever did it. And, so help me, I'll see them fry."

Burton's eyes widened. He jerked visibly, as if jolted by electricity. His mouth transformed from a pout to a sneer. He moved in, his face inches from Charles's. "Fry? Fucking fry? You son-of-a-bitch! You don't know the meaning of the word."

Charles stepped back.

Burton fed on his employer's fear and let out a nasty little laugh. "All right, you rich fucking asshole, you wanna know how I killed your goddamn horse? I put a bag over his ugly face and watched him suffocate. Slowly. It took a hell of a lot longer than I figured, but I kinda' enjoyed watching him go down." He smiled a hideous smile. "And I'll tell you why I — "

Burton was cut off in mid-sentence by the impact of Charles's fist on his jaw. There was rage on his boss's face. He saw Charles coming at him, hands groping for his throat. Burton ducked, twisting under the smaller man, and allowing momentum to carry Charles past him. Charles braced a foot to recover. A loud cracking sound startled both men as a disintegrating deck plank gave way under Charles's weight. He tried for firmer footing on the algae-laden surface of the old pier, but his feet slid as Burton lunged at him. The pier rocked and, for a moment, it seemed the whole thing would collapse into the water. Charles landed flat and hard on the boards as Burton's colossal weight came down hard on top of him.

Burton felt Charles shudder. It was more like a short convulsion. He scrambled off and crouched a few feet away, braced and ready for Charles to renew the attack. Charles didn't move. Burton stared through terrified eyes. *He's dead, he's not moving.* The ex-con had dealt with death before. Death meant police, courts, and prison. He'd been there and wanted no part of it.

For almost a minute, Burton sat petrified, not knowing what to do, watching. Then he noticed just the faintest movement of Charles's chest — barely visible. Yes, it was there again. Charles was breathing. Relief waved over Burton. "I got to get an ambulance," he mumbled in Ninja's direction, then took off toward the house at a run.

As he stepped from the pier onto the lawn, Burton's pace slowed. He continued for a few more strides, then stopped, hands on hips, his back to the pier.

"That asshole just accused me of murdering his horse," he said to Ninja. "And I just confessed. I told him the whole goddamn story."

He turned and looked out at the pier. Charles had not moved. Burton scanned the shore. No observers. No nearby boats either. He hesitated for one more second, then turned and headed back out over the water. He squatted next to his unconscious employer, made some inaudible curse, and with one heave, rolled Charles's flaccid frame into the water. It floated there, face down, rocking gently on the ripples. The sole witness to the entire gruesome event was Ninja, who seemed totally at ease with it.

Burton watched for a moment, making sure that the water did not stimulate Charles to consciousness. He was no longer running on adrenalin as he moved in the icy, calculating mode of one who had successfully committed murder. He flashed a satisfied smile toward Ninja.

Calmly, Burton left the pier, walked to the shed, retrieved a hedge trimmer, and proceeded to the front lawn. He played out an orange snake of electric cord to the yew near the road and, reveling in his own cleverness, began trimming with enough bravura to ensure that occupants of several passing cars would notice him at work.

Eventually, he eased around the bushes, out of sight from the road, found a suitable maple branch and wedged it firmly between the steel teeth of the trimmer. He pressed the trigger and the little electric motor responded with a brief surge as it strained against the stick, then it settled into a monotonous electrical drone. Burton sat on the ground holding the trigger and waited. Within minutes the acrid smell of an over-heated electric motor wafted up to his nose, then he saw smoke. The drone changed to a whine for a few seconds, and then quiet. Burton picked up the burned-out hedge trimmer, flipped the wood from its blade, and set it in view of the road.

He walked nonchalantly back to the house. It was 11:35 a.m. when Jefferson ambulance dispatchers took the call: Drowning at the St. Pierre's Lake House.

CHAPTER 21

KENT KNELT IN THE FRESH STRAW IN ONE OF
VinChaRo's maternity stalls. His eyes rested on the two-week-old
foal lying in front of him as it gulped air through purplish lips. It
grunted with each painful breath. Kent knew the filly was dying and
he knew he was utterly helpless — to relieve the foal's agony, or to
ease Aubrey's sadness because of it.

"She's lost a lot of ground since yesterday," Kent said.

Aubrey wiped a tear off her cheek. "Uh-huh," she said, her
throat too tight for anything more.

They used a bale of straw to prop the filly upright, hoping that
changing her position would shift the fluid in her lungs and allow
her to breathe easier. All she did was stretch her neck out and rest her
chin in the straw. There was no improvement in her breathing. The
filly's anxious mother nickered nervously to her baby. Osvaldo held
her in the corner and soothed her in Spanish.

This was the part of the veterinarian's job that Kent hated. It
was always the same — he'd give the owner his opinion, and nine-
ty-nine times out of a hundred they would take his recommendation. He'd never been able to rationalize it — *all he was doing was
making a suggestion, it was the owner who made the ultimate decision*
— when virtually all of them went the way he advised them. No, he
was the professional, it was his decision. It was in the best interest of

the patient, he truly believed that, or he would never recommend it, but it was devastating for the owners — and much tougher on the veterinarian than most clients imagined.

He spoke slowly, allowing Aubrey to come to terms. "One day the foal looks better, the next day she is bad again. That's typical of foal pneumonia. And it's what makes it difficult to know when to quit. You've been through it before."

Aubrey knelt next to the frail creature, stroked her chestnut shoulder, and teased a piece of straw from the IV line coiling from her neck. "I know," she said, crying and talking at the same time. "But she was trying so hard. I mean until now, I kept thinking she could fight her way through this."

"I'm sure an abscess in her lung has ruptured into her blood stream. It showered particles of infection throughout her body. That's why she has gotten so much worse overnight."

"She looks so pitiful."

"Yes, she does. And it's not fair to leave her this way. I'm willing to control an animal's suffering for a while, if it looks like there is light at the end of the tunnel, and there has been until now. But if there isn't, then it's our responsibility to see that the suffering ends."

Aubrey stroked the foal and did not reply.

Kent handed her his handkerchief. "You've worked with this filly day and night for how long now? We can honestly say you did all you could do."

"But it didn't work."

"No, it didn't work."

"How much longer would she live like she is? I mean if we kept her on IVs and antibiotics?"

"I don't know. A day or two at the most. She can't breathe. She's drowning in her own body fluids."

"What if we give her more oxygen?" Aubrey's tone was desperate.

Kent bent down next to her, touched her chin, gently turned her to face him, and looked straight into her eyes. "We might prolong things a few hours, but we won't change the outcome."

As Aubrey searched his face for an explanation of why this had happened. He hated himself for not having one. She buried her head against his chest and cried, her body quaking with deep sobs. He wrapped his arms around her and hugged until she was quiet. Then he gently kissed the crown of her head.

Eventually, slowly, Aubrey turned back to the waning foal and petted her again. "Sorry, baby. I love you." She nodded the consent that her heart would not allow her to verbalize, and she stepped out of the stall, leaving Kent and Osvaldo to perform the act of mercy.

Kent stepped across the stall to his grip and extracted a vial of euthanasia solution, the infamous *blue juice*. Its cyanic iridescence was the result of the manufacturer's intentional addition of a fluorescent blue dye. The color was unique and unmistakably different from any other medicine, making it impossible for a clinician to grab the lethal liquid by mistake.

He inverted the bottle over a syringe and glanced once more at the frail creature. Estimating its body weight, Kent drew up the required dose, set the vial back in his case, stepped back to the foal.

"We won't let you suffer any more, little lady," he said, as he delivered the solution into the IV line.

The mare sent a mournful whinny echoing through the barn.

Even before Kent retracted the needle, the foal's rattily breathing stopped and her tortured body slacked into peacefulness.

He closed his grip methodically and turned to Osvaldo. "The sooner we get the body out of here the better for the mare."

Osvaldo nodded. "Right now, jefe."

Kent was glad Maria and Emily had chosen to go trail riding today.

He found Aubrey propped against the wall in dark shadows at the far end of VinChaRo's long barn. She was staring blankly out into the sunlight.

Kent leaned next to her.

"How many times have we been through this?" she asked.

He drew a deep breath and released it slowly. "Over the years? I don't really know. Lots."

"You'd think we'd get hardened to it, wouldn't you?"

"No, Aubrey. We can't ever get comfortable losing any of our horses, whether it's a new foal, or Simpatico, or any other one. They are what we work for. They are a part of us."

As she looked up at him she smiled through red eyes.

He pulled her close, and felt the softness of her hair against his throat as she nestled against him.

"Thank you," she said.

As they were walking back through the darkened alleyway, they noticed a silhouette against the sunlight at the far end. Both of them knew instantly it was Elizabeth coming toward them. She was running. When she was closer, they recognized panic on her face.

"I've been looking all over for you two. I just got a call from the police. There has been a terrible accident at the Lake House. They said Charles drowned!"

"Drowned?" Aubrey covered her mouth with her hand. "Oh, my God. Are you sure?"

"I'm on my way there this minute," Elizabeth said.

Aubrey could see her trembling. How horrible it must be to lose a son.

"My car is out front. Kent and I will take you," Aubrey more ordered than offered.

● ● ●

The Lake House driveway was plugged with emergency vehicles parked haphazardly, roof lights still blinking ominously, two-way radios barking disjointed bits of dispatcher lingo to no one in particular. They parked on the road and walked in. At the pier an ambulance was already backed into position, rear doors swung wide open. The shoreline was swarming with police, EMT's, and other first responders.

Off to one side, away from the confusion, Kent noticed a local cop sitting next to a pair of State Troopers interviewing Burton Bush at a patio table. The local cop was his brother, Merrill. He was quiet. The Staties were doing all the talking. Kent took Aubrey by the elbow and directed her toward the interview as Elizabeth raced toward the ambulance.

When they were within earshot, Kent heard Burton giving his version of the incident. His demeanor — pure shock and grief. One Trooper asked the questions. The other recorded notes on a pad.

"So, I was out front trimming the hedge like Mr. St. Pierre told me. Then, the trimmer started quitting on me. So I . . ."

"What do you mean quit on you?" the Trooper asked.

"Well, it kinda lost power," Burton whined. "It wouldn't cut. And it started to hum funny and smell hot."

"Uh-huh."

"So I figured I'd find Mr. St. Pierre and see what he wanted me to do about it. You know, go get it fixed, find something else to do, like that. The rest is like I told you already." His voice dripped helplessness. "I went around back and found him. Then I called for an ambulance."

"How'd you know where to find him?"

"I guess I didn't really, at first. He just said he was going to be working on the lakeside yard. When I couldn't find him, I remembered he said something about checking out what it was going to take to get the pier fixed up. So I looked around and — there he was — floating." He gave a theatrical shuddered.

"Did you hear anything unusual?"

"No."

"Did you hear him shout for help?"

"No."

"Was he moving?"

"Just floating."

"Face down."

"Right."

"Then you pulled him up on shore."

"Yep."

"Did you attempt to revive him?"

Burton stared down between his knees. "No," he choked out, "I could tell he was dead."

"How?"

Burton looked directly at the cop, his face twisted, recalling the horrible memory. "His eyes. They had that look. I knew he was dead."

He reached into the breast pocket of his tee-shirt, pulled out a crumpled pack of cigarettes, then slowly tapped one out and lit it. He drew deeply, leaning back with eyes closed. When he reopened them, he jerked suddenly, this time for real, startled to see Aubrey and Kent staring at him. His face flushed. Anger shot from his eyes before he could force himself back into character.

Kent could almost see the hairs on the back of Aubrey's neck stir.

"You called from the house phone?" the officer continued.

"Yes."

"Where is it? Where in the house?"

Burton gestured toward the house. "Just inside the glass doors. On a table to the left."

"Why were you and Mr. St. Pierre out here anyway?"

"He asked me to come down with him to do some work around here, like the lawns and pier and stuff. He's the boss, so I came along."

"Was there anyone else?"

"No. Just us."

The interrogation lapsed into a chronicling of details.

Kent nudged Aubrey away to find Elizabeth. They got to the pier and muscled through the onlookers just in time to see the medical examiner complete the grisly task of confirming Charles's death. The examiner nodded to the ambulance crew who zipped the body bag closed, lifted it into the back, and slammed the doors.

Elizabeth turned to Aubrey. "I can't believe this is happening. How can this be?"

Aubrey steadied her with an arm around her waist. "We don't know yet. Let me take you home, Elizabeth. There's nothing more to do here."

Elizabeth followed submissively.

CHAPTER 22

BETWEEN THE FOAL'S EUTHANASIA AND
Charles's drowning, Kent and Aubrey both were in dire need of con-
solation. They decided to meet at her place after work, since Barry
had informed his mother that he had volunteered to monitor a particularly critical patient for Peter Murphy on the night shift at the
CVC, and therefore would not be home till morning.

They made drinks, then made love — several rounds of each.

Kent managed to unwind to that perfect level of post-co-
ital contentment that men live for, but Aubrey remained ill at ease.
Several times she propped herself up, summoned her courage, and
started to tell Kent how she and Charles had planned for him to meet
Burton at the Lake House. But, each time she held back. It sounded
so utterly stupid. Why had they thought there was even a ghost of
chance it could work?

Kent sensed her angst, and would have called her on it, had he
not wanted to hold the moment. Instead, he caressed her, and coaxed
her to relax. After a while, Kent dropped off into a death-like sleep,
Aubrey tossed and turned the night away.

The next morning, as they were sitting in a booth at the Village
Diner, Kent refueled like a farm hand with bacon, eggs, and home

fries while Aubrey took an occasional bite of waffle, but mostly stared into her coffee. She had been so quiet since the night before that Kent was beginning to worry he had done something wrong.

He was studying her, and deciding whether he should say something, when suddenly she sat up straight, took a deep breath, and stared at him hard. For a moment, she did not move, thinking, her face fixed in internal conflict.

Finally, she rocked her head out of the booth, looked to see that no one else was within earshot, and then leaned across toward Kent, elbows on the table.

"I have to tell you something. I should have told you last night. But I couldn't make myself do it. I feel so guilty."

Kent set down his coffee and gave her his full attention. "Okay."

"I know it wasn't an accident, Charles that is. I don't care what Burton says, I know!"

"Wait. You *know* Charles's death was not an accident."

"Yes."

"How?"

"Because Charles and I had a plan. The very fact that he and Burton were there at the Lake House was a setup."

Kent shifted in his seat. "You better tell me the whole story."

Aubrey told him about how Osvaldo had come to her with Burton's admission and her plan to have Charles confront Burton at the Lake House. She admitted she and Charles expected a denial on his part, but not anything like what had happened.

Kent wasn't sure if it was anger or frustration that was causing his blood pressure to rise as he listened. Here it was, happening again: The very impulsiveness that he loved about this woman had backed her into a corner.

"What the hell were you two thinking?"

"I don't know! We wanted to force Burton to make a move, I guess. It seemed like a good plan at the time."

"Jesus. I wish you had asked me. I would have given you a hundred reasons why it was *not* a good plan."

Aubrey stared down into her coffee, studying her own miserable reflection.

Kent stained for a non-judgmental tone. "The question is what are we going to do now?" He tapped the morning paper that lay folded on the table. "Officially, the police have ruled Charles's death an accident, and why not? I believed that myself until this minute. All the evidence would support it, just the way Burton said it happened. The coroner verified that Charles did actually drown. And last night right at the scene, one of the EMT's said there were cuts on Charlie's legs and the back of his head that had small fragments of decking embedded in them. That's consistent with the premise that Charles stepped through the pier, fell and hit his head then rolled into the water. There was the burned-out hedge trimmer and the depositions from the two motorists who saw Burton working in the front yard."

"Did you talk to your brother about it?"

Kent toyed with a salt shaker. "Yeah, I talked to Merrill. He said the State Troopers are handling things. He's only a village cop, so it's out of his jurisdiction. He still knows what's going on, though."

"We need an eyewitness," Aubrey said.

Kent huffed a short laugh. "Fat chance of that. Merrill told me they will be contacting everybody who owns property or a boat on the lake. We'll see. According to him, the Staties figure it was an accident and aren't going to waste much time on it."

The waitress refilled their cups and they sipped coffee in silence.

Finally, Kent said, "*Why* would Burton kill Simpatico? That's the question. Let's think about that, and then work backwards. If he did it for vengeance against the St. Pierres because he hated them and the job and all that, he wouldn't have stuck around. He'd have left town right after he killed Simpatico. You know what I mean?"

"Maybe he stayed to avoid suspicion."

Kent shrugged. "Okay, maybe. But the most likely possibility in my book would be good ole fashioned money. What if someone else wanted Simpatico dead, but didn't want to risk it themselves or didn't know how, so they hired The Burning Bush."

Kent felt that increasingly familiar roll of his stomach. The conspiracy theory again. He could hear Maria and Emily now — *Charles and Burton, we told you so.* But the longer he thought about it, the more it made sense, until it became the obvious scenario.

"The girls were right," he said.

"What?"

"Emily and Maria were right."

"About what?"

"Charles is behind it. He killed the horses. Or at least hired Burton to do it for him. Emily and Maria have been suspicious of Charles right along. They've argued from the beginning that Charles would be the person to benefit most by the death of Simpatico, Charter Oak being out of commission, and Solar Wind dead."

Aubrey gave him an arched look. "Really. How come I never heard any of this?"

"I don't know. You work all the time, I guess. But think about it, Aubrey. It's common knowledge that Charles took a real financial beating last year. He needed money. One of the most common motives for murder, horses or humans, is to recover insurance money. Right? VinChaRo Farm, and therefore Charles, would get the money from Simpatico's death. And Charles was a major shareholder in the Stanford's Charter Oak syndicate. Did you know that?"

Aubrey nodded. "Yes, I guess I heard that one time or another. But, to tell the truth, I'd forgotten."

"Maria and Emily were the first to figure it out. They've been trying to convince me."

"You should have said something to me."

"I know, but I didn't believe it myself until now. What you just told me locks in Emily and Maria's theory." Kent leaned toward her. "Charles stood to collect a lot of money since Charter Oak was insured for loss of use. And the kicker is, I heard this directly from him and Walt Stanford, Charles personally convinced the other syndicate members to get the loss of use coverage." Kent shook his head, angry at his own slowness to accept the obvious. "I'd bet anything that Charles is responsible for Charter Oak getting that weird kind of EVA. I'm not sure just how, but somehow."

"Okay. So why would he kill Solar Wind?"

"That's where things get hazy. I'm not sure yet, but Emily and Maria believe he did it to eliminate competition from other stallions."

"Right after he killed his own best stud?"

"That's exactly what I said to them. Maybe he wanted to have his cake and eat it too. He could have killed Simpatico for the insurance, and then wipe out the competition, banking that Hubris would fill the void. Charles is — was — smart enough to figure that out, and you and I both know Hubris is the best stallion standing on New York soil."

Kent set his crumpled napkin on the table and signaled for the check.

"We know for sure that Solar Wind was killed by someone," he said. "And, if we believe Osvaldo's story, we know that Simpatico was killed by Burton. That just doesn't happen very often in the horse world — the malicious killing of two horses. The fact that they both occurred in the same basic time period and geographic area is way too much of a coincidence. They've got to be connected."

They held that thought while the waitress handed Kent the check, gathered a handful of dishes, and left.

Then Aubrey said, "We all know Burton is — was — Charles's boy. Jesus, it's going to take me a while to get used to the idea of Charles being dead. But I mean, it would make sense that Charles would have Burton do his dirty work."

"True. And think about it. Charles agreed to meet with Burton alone as part of your scheme to trap Burton, the whole time knowing full well how and why Simpatico died. Really he's planning to say nothing at all, or maybe warn Burton to keep his mouth shut when he gets drunk. Then something goes wrong — maybe Burton thinks that Charles is going to turn on him, or maybe Burton tries to black-mail Charles. Who knows? Anyway, they fight, out on the pier. Burton kills Charles, maybe on purpose, maybe not, then stages the accident."

Aubrey let her eyes drift around the diner. "It fits. How can we prove it?"

Kent was quiet long enough that Aubrey knew something was going through his mind. She was just about to prod him when he said, "Maybe we don't want to prove it."

"What?" Aubrey said, loudly enough that other customers looked her way.

"Take it easy. I think we owe it to Elizabeth to talk to her first, tell her what we suspect, and let her decide if she wants us to pur-sue it. After all, it wouldn't surprise me if she is more interested in preserving Charles's reputation than solving the mystery. From the money standpoint, she's already received the insurance money, so the financial loss is minimal. Figuring this thing out only stands to blacken Charles's reputation, and it definitely isn't going to bring Charles or Simpatico back."

"God. When you think about it, that's probably what I'd do. But the thought of that weasel Burton getting away with it makes me sick."

Kent placed the saltshaker on the check with some cash, and then stood to leave. "Me, too."

CHAPTER 23

THE FIRST THING KENT NOTICED WHEN
Elizabeth greeted them at the VinChaRo mansion house was the
steamy redness around her eyes. Her usual energy had vanished,
replaced by a spiritless slouch.

Aubrey ran her finger along the scrolled arm of a French
Provincial chair in Elizabeth's sitting room, searching for topics to
fuel the stalled conversation. Kent sat in a rocker that was so delicate
he didn't dare rock, and did the same. Elizabeth phased in and out,
and seemed to be only half-listening. She contributed nothing.

During one of the long intervals of silence, Aubrey caught
Kent's eye. Her expression asked: *Should we tell her now? Do you
think she can handle it?*

He shrugged.

They made small talk for a while longer, drained the last of
their tea from tiny cups, and were about to give up when a wave of
conviction swept over Kent.

"Elizabeth," he said in a soft but direct tone, " the main reason Aubrey and I came over this evening was to talk to you about
some new information concerning Charles's death. Do you feel up to
talking about that now?"

It actually surprised Kent when she said, "I think so. Go ahead."

He started with Osvaldo's revelation, about how Burton drunkenly admitted to killing Simpatico. Then Kent told her of the plot to trap Burton at the Lake House. He went into the possible tie-in of Charter Oak and Solar Wind, and concluded with a carefully worded version of their hypothesis that Charles and Burton may have conspired to commit the crimes.

"We think that there's a possibility that Charles wanted the insurance money from the horses and he recruited Burton to help him. Then something between them soured, so Burton killed Charles and staged the accident. If this is true, we can't let Burton get away with it."

As they sat in uneasy silence, Kent studied Elizabeth's face. She showed no indication of even having heard his words. Her eyes remained fixed on the fireplace's empty blackness and brass. Uncomfortable silence dragged on into minutes. Just as Kent was concluding that Elizabeth wanted them to leave, she looked up at him, her expression had turned from blank to laser focused. "Would the two of you accompany me to my study? I would like to show you something."

Her words would have brought them relief, had it not been for the seething tone with which they were delivered.

She led them into an adjacent study, then closed an enormous pair of cherry sliding doors behind them. Like a scene from an old movie, Elizabeth stepped to a nineteenth century oil painting of a soldier, no doubt an ancestor, reached up, took hold of a lower corner and swung it aside on concealed hinges. It hid a safe the size of an oven. She twisted its combination lock.

Kent leaned toward Aubrey and whispered, "I didn't think anybody really had that kind of safe."

Aubrey whispered back, "As many times as I've been in this study, I never once had any inkling there was a safe behind that picture."

Elizabeth pulled out a tattered canvas document pouch, a three inch deep oak tray, and a small metal file box. She turned and placed them on a nearby desk. She made no comment about secrecy or privileged information or the importance of discretion. Instead, she simply loosened the string securing the pouch and spilled its contents on the desk. There were several bundles of official look-ing documents, many with vignette margins and gilded seals, all on quality paper.

"Here are some stock certificates for you to look over," she said. "I'm sorry I don't have the really good ones here. They are held at several different banks — one of which the St. Pierre family owns, I might add. Did you know we own a bank?" she asked, but did not wait for a reply. "There are some good stocks in here though," she stirred the pile with her hand. "A few million dollars worth. Pretty good investments to off-set those losses Charles experienced recently that you two are so worried about."

She inverted the wooden tray and a stack of legal documents slid into disarray.

"These are assorted real estate deeds and titles. You are wel-come to look through them if you wish. Again, these are not the best we own, just the best in the house. Estimated value? Oh, I don't even know. The value of real estate in Manhattan changes so fast I can't keep up."

Without waiting for Kent or Aubrey's reaction, she lifted the file box. "I never really understood why Ward insisted on keeping this much cash around since he rarely used it. It must have been some sort of an ego thing. Anyway, the tradition lived on with Charles. A little risky if you ask me." She dumped out a mound of bundled one hundred dollar bills, each wrapped in a proper bank band.

Kent squirmed. There was more cash on that desk than he had ever seen in one place — by far.

"There's a lot of money here," she understated. "I'm showing it to you to make a point."

She reached down to a low file drawer in the desk, pulled it open with much effort, and retrieved still more ammunition.

"Here is our last year's tax return." She talked as she read down through the form, searching for figures to support her now obvious position. "You made one correct supposition. We lost a lot of money in a couple of bad deals last year. Yes, here it is." She folded back several pages to expose Schedule D: Capital Gains and Losses. She held it under the desk light for Kent to see, her finger pointing to line 2c.

He squinted, reading it aloud, "Stocks, bonds, and other securities — minus $1,991,217." He swallowed hard. "Wow."

Elizabeth shrugged. "Sounds like a lot doesn't it? Well, everything is relative." She flipped back to page one and, this time, directed Aubrey's attention to the bottom line.

"Holy shit," Aubrey whispered, as she read Elizabeth's *Adjusted Gross Income.*

A smile crossed Elizabeth's face. "Not a bad recovery after losing almost two million." She reached back into the desk and took out what she knew would be the coup de grace. "This is Charles's most recent financial statement. We can skip past the minutia and look right . . . right here." She pointed to a figure in the lower right hand column. "Net Worth." She moved the document near the desk light and gestured for Kent and Aubrey to come closer.

A cynical gleam flashed in Elizabeth's eyes as she watched them recoil from the astronomical figure. Then she stood silently, letting the full impact whirl in their heads.

When she was satisfied that her buffeting had disarmed those who dared defile the St. Pierre family honor, she said, "It causes me great pain to know that you two, of all people, would come here and malign my son with these accusations based on local gossip and an unfounded conspiracy hypothesis. My whole life, and Ward's also, has been directed toward living a lifestyle that fostered a strong, loving relationship with the community in which we lived. We have strived, at a high cost I might add, to avoid entering into any dealings that could create local animosity or compromise our reputation. By coming here tonight you have made it clear that all of our efforts were for naught." Her stare held boundless disappointment.

"Elizabeth, we would never do that," Aubrey said.

"It appears you have."

"We just don't want Burton to get away with murder."

Elizabeth held up her hand. "I am too upset to discuss this anymore tonight. I suggest we meet at the farm office tomorrow morning, the three of us. We can continue our discussion then." She gestured toward the door. "Now, I would appreciate it if you showed yourselves out."

"Ten o'clock?" Kent offered.

"That would be fine."

Aubrey and Kent retreated from the mansion, feeling like they had been run over by a bus.

When they were back in their car, Kent smiled derisively and said, "I guess the St. Pierre's are worth a lot of money."

Aubrey laced her fingers behind her head, arched her neck back, and groaned, "Thank you, Mr. Perceptive."

CHAPTER 24

KENT TELEPHONED THE CVC EARLY THE NEXT morning. Sally gave him a list of farm calls, and he started out directly from Pine Holt, intentionally avoiding his office with its inevitable delays. He wanted to make sure he would be on time for their meeting with Elizabeth.

He stepped into the VinChaRo Farm office at exactly 10:00. Aubrey and Elizabeth were sitting at the conference table. One look told him neither of them had slept a wink. That put them all on equal ground.

He tested the water. "Good morning."

"Good morning," Elizabeth said, absolutely neutral.

Aubrey gave him an uncomfortable smile, and said nothing.

He poured himself a cup of coffee, even though he did not get his usual invite from Elizabeth to do so, and took a chair next to Aubrey.

When one of the barn workers stuck his head in the door, apologizing profusely for interrupting, and saying that he had a quick question for Elizabeth that could not wait, Kent seized the moment.

"How are you doing?" he whispered to Aubrey.

"Not bad for having someone verbally kick the shit out of me last night."

"Yeah. Same here."

Elizabeth cleared her throat as she turned her attention back to them. She spoke slowly and deliberately as if she were reading a carefully drafted letter. "I cannot accept your contention that Charles was a participant in any plan to kill Simpatico or any other horse. However, inasmuch as I would be remiss to ignore the information you brought to me regarding Burton Bush's possible involvement, I would very much like to determine if there was a conspiracy to harm our horses and, if so, identify and bring to justice the perpetrators. I feel completely confident that any investigation will totally absolve Charles of wrong doing."

Kent hid his sigh of relief. At least they had developed a good enough case that Elizabeth was willing to accept it as a possibility. Even if she didn't consider Charles the mastermind. Time would tell.

Elizabeth continued. "After our discussion last night, the two of you, no doubt, understand how strongly I feel about protecting the St. Pierre name. Since I am aware that your theory would inevitably become part of the public domain and that Jefferson's propensity for rumors would build it into a scandal of proportions guaranteed to persist for generations, I am compelled to see this matter resolved beyond any speculation."

"Thank you," Kent said, although he was not sure what for. "That's why we brought the whole thing to you in the first place, so you could make the decision as to whether or not we pursue it."

"Then my decision is to pursue it to the end." Elizabeth took a deep breath, and as she exhaled, her formality vanished. "Look., this kind of thing is way too much for an old lady like me, and I have no intention of taking it to the police for the reason I just explained. That is my one condition; there are to be no police until we know everything. Even then, only after clearing it with me. That includes your brother. Are you agreeable to that?"

Kent and Aubrey nodded in unison.

"Good." Elizabeth glanced back and forth at her two friends. "I'm turning it over to you. It is totally in your hands. I'll help any way I can, financially or otherwise if you ask, but you are in charge. Again, I say; no police until I say so."

She reached across the table and took both their hands. Her tired eyes brimmed with tears as she spoke. "I'll be honest with you — and blunt. I'm still pissed as hell at both of you. But at least now that I have recovered from the initial shock, I realize your intentions are good. And frankly, I think you are the only ones who can do this."

● ● ●

Through the rest of the morning, Kent couldn't get Charles's role in the horses' demise off his mind. He was used to dealing with problems, and it was a rare one that could distract him to the point that he was unable to give his full attention to his patients, and that made it worse. By midday he decided that he needed to do something about it. He called Aubrey and suggested she and Barry join them for dinner at Pine Holt. They would brainstorm until they had a plan, a good plan this time. No half-ass scheme like the Lake House mess. It was obvious that Aubrey couldn't get the matter off her mind either. She accepted without hesitation.

● ● ●

Dinner at Pine Holt that night was another of Margaret's comfort food masterpieces — eggplant parmesan, which suited Aubrey just fine, and a pile of meatballs for the carnivores.

"Brisk" would not adequately describe the conversation as they argued about who, how, and why — then, what they should do next.

"Elizabeth just won't face the truth," Maria said, frustration obvious in her voice. With more compassion, she added, "But I guess I can't blame her. I'd probably feel the same way."

Barry served himself a third helping of everything on the table while the others watched, amazed at how much a teenage boy could eat. With a forkful readied, inches from his lips, he said, "Who would figure their own son would do such a creepy thing, especially against his family? Of course Elizabeth doesn't believe it."

Emily flashed him a sour look. "Where do you put all that food?"

Barry, chewing away, shrugged. "I've been working all day."

"It's not all about emotion with Elizabeth," Kent said. "As she pointed out to us last night with the subtlety of a sledgehammer, money is not a motive for Charles. So, she's asking: Why would he do it?"

Margaret rose from the table, and began clearing dishes with more gusto than usual. All the talk of money and murder made her uncomfortable.

Aubrey noticed. "That was one of the best meals I've had in a long time, Margaret," she said.

"Thank you." Margaret gentle bumped the back of Kent's head with the edge of a platter. "It's fun to cook for someone who appreciates things other than meat and potatoes."

Kent raised his eyebrows to his housekeeper. "I love your eggplant parm."

"The problem with my job," Aubrey said, "is that by the time I get home, I'm too tired to cook, even if Barry and I are starving." She motioned toward Barry, who was still intent on his food. "You see the result."

"Both of you are always welcome here," Margaret said, not even glancing at Kent. "I always cook too much."

"I'll remember that," Aubrey said, and gave Kent a how-about-that smirk.

"I'm good with that, too," Emily said. She pointed at Barry with her thumb. "You can even bring this guy along."

"Hey, I'm master of the house," Kent said, with an exaggerated scowl. "I say who gets invited here."

"Yeah, right," all four women said at once.

Out of the corner of his eye, Kent saw Lucinda over on her rug, give a quick wag of her tail, in support of the women.

"Traitor," he said to her. Then to Barry, he said, "They've got us out numbered here, buddy."

Barry nodded. "We'll go down fighting."

"Anyway," Emily said, refocusing. "How are we going to prove it was Charles?"

Kent's confidence that they had even a ghost of a chance at solving this thing was waning. The more they plotted and schemed, the more it was apparent that they were in way over their heads. They hadn't been able to come up with a plan that was any better than the infamous Lake House debacle, and he wasn't about to do that again. He looked into each of the faces around him. No way was he going to risk the lives of the people he loved. Whether they liked it or not.

"We aren't," he said, flatly. Everyone froze. All eyes shifted to him. Even Barry stopped chewing. "This is not a game. It's serious and it's dangerous. We're talking murder here, and anyone who commits one can commit another. I know what Elizabeth said about us conducting our own investigation, but I see now that's just plain unrealistic. This is way more than we can handle. Someone could get hurt badly — or worse. We told her what we found out. If she wants to follow up on it, she's going to have to take it to the police. I'm sorry. End of discussion."

Margaret looked like she wanted to applaud.

Emily let out the whine she knew her father detested. "Doc, you're kidding me."

"Does it sound like I'm kidding? It's too dangerous."

"But Elizabeth won't go to the police. She told you that. She'll let the whole thing drop before she does that. If we don't find out what really happened, no one will. Then Burton and whoever he's working with will have committed the perfect crime."

Kent accepted a cup of coffee from Margaret. "I feel as bad as you do, Em, and if there was some way we could solve it without the risk, I'd try it. But there isn't. There are professionals — police, private investigators — to do that. We don't even know where to start."

Emily pushed to her feet, nearly overturning her chair behind her. She threw her arm around an enormous casserole dish and headed toward the kitchen. Kent watched as she disappeared through the door, the glass cover clanging noisily with each of her strides.

He would not be able to live with himself if something bad happened to Emily or the others. It was better to have them disappointed now than deal with a catastrophe later.

A while after dinner, the group drifted back together in the family room. Anticipation hung like a heavy vapor as each person waited to see if Kent would resume the discussion. He sensed it. Eventually, reluctantly, he began again.

"Be reasonable," he said. "This is not a game. For the money involved and the criminal charges that could result, people will kill you!"

Aubrey put her arm around Emily. "We realize that, Kent. But we have to do something. Even if only because we have an obligation to the horses. We need to find a way to get enough information for Elizabeth to go to the police so they can solve the whole mess without ruining the St. Pierre name."

Kent pinched the bridge of his nose, eyes closed. That angry voice from the logic center in his brain screamed, No way! Only an idiot would jeopardize his family and friends for some horses and a dead man. That's what the police are for.

He drew a decisive breath, and was choosing his words to shut down this whole fiasco when he heard another voice, a child-like whisper, taunting, almost patronizing, emanating from the emotion center of his brain, *They weren't just horses.*

Silence came and lingered.

Kent braced his elbows on his knees, hung his head, and massaged the back of his neck. All eyes were on him, everyone holding their breath while Kent wrestled with his thoughts. Finally, he raised his eyes to meet theirs. "What the hell. Give me some more ideas."

For the longest time, no one offered up any suggestions.

Then, as the proverbial light bulb flipped on in Emily's head, she jerked to attention. "His apartment!" she blurted. "How about Burton's apartment? There might be something there."

"Like he's going to let us take a look," Maria said.

"Of course he won't. But we can sneak in." She watched for reactions from the others.

Maria gave Emily the side-eye. "You're saying, break into his apartment?"

"Not break in. Just sneak in, when he's not there."

"Uh-huh. Break in."

"Oh, Jesus." Kent groaned. "Burton's apartment?"

"Why not? We can find a time when he's not around, slip in, and check it out."

"Because that's breaking and entering, Em. It's against the law. A felony. That's why not."

Aubrey looked at Emily, then back to Kent. "She has got a point. Burton could have something in there."

"Already we're criminals. B&E, that's three to five years," Kent said, but no one seemed to care.

"The apartment belongs to Elizabeth. Technically, she could give us permission. Couldn't she?" Maria said.

"Quit hedging. It's still illegal entry." Then, after a pause, he said, "But I've got to admit, it would be an interesting place to start."

Everyone in the group nodded, except Margaret.

"Then we're on," Emily said, beaming with confidence.

"Not yet. It depends on what Elizabeth says," Kent said with a whole lot less enthusiasm. But, he was pretty sure hair brain scheme number two was about to get underway.

CHAPTER 25

ELIZABETH STOOD BEHIND HER DESK IN THE VinChaRo office and leaned on it like a podium.

"Well, it looks like everyone is here," she said, letting her gaze drift over the assembly of VinChaRo employees. "I think we can start. I know that it is unusual to stop work in the middle of the day. However, with Charles gone, I think it best that we all understand where we are. As you know, since Charles was a principal decision maker here at the farm, we are faced with the task of reorganizing, at least temporarily, to continue operations..."

Elizabeth's voice dissolved into a muffled drone as Aubrey's attention shifted to her role as lookout. Seated inconspicuously in back, she scanned the gathering, then eased her hand into her pocket and keyed a two-way radio.

When Kent had first insisted they use radios, she had thought it corny cloak and dagger stuff. Now she was glad she had one. She could alert her fellow sleuths immediately if anyone left the meeting. One long tone meant get out fast. A series of short beeps meant the meeting was breaking up. She glanced over at Burton who sat slouched along the wall, his red hair standing out like a beacon among the dark featured Latinos. Aubrey shuddered at her own naiveté. Could she have really underestimated him, that badly?

Kent's Cherokee was parked in front of VinChaRo's carriage house that, many years ago, had been converted to employee housing. Maria was in the driver's seat. Emily sat next to her, a two-way radio poised in her hand. Lucinda sat in back, her head and neck protruding out an open window, ears pricked, eyes fixed on her master who tested the carriage house's weathered door.

Kent had never been in the building, but Aubrey had given him the layout. There were six apartments, all small, three upstairs and three down. She had warned him that the rooms were shoddy and Kent could tell by the way she said it that it was a source of embarrassment. Every few years, Elizabeth spent large amounts of money to refurbish the building, and each time it decayed back to its dismal state. The steady turnover of young, single male tenants was too much for the old structure. Thankfully, a thick row of evergreens shrouded it from the rest of the farm.

Kent pushed open the unlocked front door. Its windowpanes, loosely glazed, vibrated as the door rubbed over warped flooring. He stopped, waited, listened for movement inside. All quiet. He heard a faint whine from Lucinda outside, but did not acknowledge it. A hallway with gray-green walls and worn carpet ran the full length of the building. Pairs of crusty barn boots lay near two of the three ground floor apartment doors. Kent stepped around a plastic bag of garbage, mostly beer cans. The air held smells of horsey work clothes, fried food, and beer. He stepped to a set of narrow wooden stairs, and took them two at a time to lessen their creaks. Aubrey had told him Burton occupied the front upstairs apartment. It would be the first door on the left. The upstairs hallway was similar to the one below, except darker. The air smelled similar, but worse.

Aubrey had told him the door would open into a kitchen area. There would be a counter with a sink and stove on the left and a small table. To the right, looking over a half-wall divider, there would be a combination living room and sleeping area. The bathroom would be straight across from where he entered.

154

He put his ear to the blistered paint of the first door on the left, then carefully twisted the brass knob and pulled.

"Jesus, Aubrey!" he said, in a loud whisper, as he stared into a disheveled broom closet.

He eased the door shut, moved to the *second* door on the left, and listened again. Still nothing. His heart beat fast. The stale air seemed depleted of oxygen. With a sweaty hand, he turned the knob – locked. He fished the master key that Elizabeth had given him out of his pocket, poked it in the knob, and twisted. The latch snapped open with a pop like small caliber handgun. As he pushed the door, a choking stench of human slovenliness poured toward him. He had just about decided the room was too foul to be anyone's residence when he noticed a kitchenette on the left and a living room-bedroom on the right, across a half-wall.

He stepped inside, accidentally scuffed an empty cereal box, and sent it skidding through other debris on the floor. A window with no curtain provided gray light. Dirty dishes overflowed from the kitchen sink to the counter. The sleeping area contained a couch opened into a bed. Sidewalk-colored sheets and an Army blanket draped half onto the floor. Against one wall, layers of expensive-looking stereo components were stacked next to speakers that could, no doubt, rattle the whole building. A cheap, portable television sat on a snack table.

Kent turned to begin his search when a flash of movement caught his eye — a dark blur low and to his right came from around the partition. His nerves, already primed with adrenalin, reacted quickly. He turned for a better look as he stepped back out of the projectile's direct line. It corrected its course and rose from the floor, a silent missile, locked on. Kent had just enough time to bring his arm up to protect his face. Ninja! They had forgotten about Ninja.

Kent reeled back as the dog's weight crashed against his chest. He felt a searing pain as the shepherd's powerful jaws sank enamel knives into his forearm.

He shook his arm to free the vice, but his flailing only forced the teeth deeper. He smashed the dog's eye with his free fist — the jaws held tight. Ninja's front feet clawed through Kent's shirt and gouged his chest. He could see red foam in the corners of Ninja's mouth and feel fire as the dog's teeth raked across bone. Searching for a weapon, he reached for a folding chair, but it fell away. The enraged dog forced him against the kitchen table, and Kent saw a butcher knife lying on it. He grabbed it, lifted his burning arm high to expose Ninja's belly, but the dog's flailing feet knocked the knife from his hand. Kent felt himself weakening. Ninja seemed to sense it and shook his arm more violently, pulling Kent to the floor.

Suddenly there was a second projectile, this one red. It came through the door and across the kitchen floor like the wrath of God, snarling and ripping. Lucinda! *He who threatens my master must die* burned in her eyes.

Ninja reeled back from the big hound's impact, allowing Kent to scramble free. She brought herself down squarely on the enemy dog, and let out a roar the likes of which Kent had never heard before. She grasped Ninja's neck in her teeth, and cast her head back and forth in a series of vicious ripping yanks. The black dog's blood sprayed across the floor and spattered Kent's legs. Ninja rolled onto his back and lay very still, eyes averted, but it was too late for appeasement. For a long moment Lucinda held her grip, then gradually she released her hold, but remained coiled like a spring, ready to attack again if Ninja so much as moved. When she was sure the shepherd was defeated, she stepped over to Kent and inspected him, passing her nose over his body and injured arm in a series of rapid sniffs. Then she whined softly. Kent stroked her scruff as the two of them watched the life drain out of Burton Bush's dog. Strangely, in spite of it all, a wave of sadness passed over him.

Kent rolled himself up onto his knees and began to tremor. He clamped his arms across his waist and wretched in revolting spasms. For a moment, the room whirled. He listed hard to the left and caught himself with his injured arm. Lucinda whimpered. He consoled her with a feeble pat on the head. White-hot pain vibrated up through to his shoulder. He crawled across the floor, clawed a grip on the counter, and pulled himself up to the sink. He cast aside a few dishes, and splashed a handful of water on his face. Its coolness steadied him.

He looked at his arm. It was already turning blue as blood oozed beneath his skin. The definition of his wrist began to disappear as swelling enlarged it to match his forearm. Ragged tears through the skin and muscle marked where Ninja's fangs had penetrated. He drew a handkerchief from his pocket and covered the wound, more to hide it from his own view than to protect it.

Beaten, he said, "Let's get out of here, girl," and took two steps toward the door. Then a strange determination arose within him. *I'm going to quit now? After all of this shit? The hell I am!*

He pulled in a deep breath and willed the pain from his mind. Then, braced against the counter, he resurveyed the apartment. After a moment, he began pillaging through Burton's kitchen with a vengeance.

Under the telephone, which doubled as a paperweight, was a pile of mail, mostly bills, mostly overdue. Kent rifled through them. One was a telephone bill that caught his eye because it showed only two calls, both long distance, both to the same number. He tucked it into his pocket.

As he worked, the throbbing in his arm rose and fell in rhythm with his pulse. The queasiness was returning and beads of sweat coursed down his temples. The room felt like an oven.

He moved to the sleeping area, searched the shelves — nothing. Then, from behind the sofa bed, Ninja's lair, he pulled a small suitcase, actually a cheap plastic attaché case. It was surprisingly heavy. He flopped it onto the bed and popped open the latches. It was full of neatly bundled twenty-dollar bills, crisp and new, aligned in even rows. Even in his blurry condition, he knew there had to be at least twenty thousand dollars.

"Bingo, Lucy!" he said, staring at the money. "That's what I'm talking about."

He eased himself down onto the bed, and was contemplating the significance of the money when his eye was attracted to a Styrofoam mailer among the litter on the floor — maybe 4"x6"x2" thick and pristine white. It was the same type of mailer they used at the CVC to sent samples, and it seemed totally out of place in Burton's rat hole. He picked it up. It was empty. He rolled it in his hand and looked for an address. It was to Burton, but there was no return address. He squinted at the postage meter strip — postmarked Cynthiana, Kentucky.

Just then he heard a series of soft beeps. He had forgotten about the radio. He pulled it out of his pocket and signaled, *okay.*

He gave the rest of the apartment a cursory inspection, then grabbed the attaché case, and started toward the door. He was halfway to it when he stopped, as an idea struck him. He turned back to the bed, reopened the case, took out two large handfuls of bundled twenties, closed the case, and replaced it behind the bed. Then he tore for the Cherokee.

He let Lucinda in, then fell into the back seat. He signaled Maria to drive. As the wheels spun up gravel, he breathed deeply, allowing the sweet fresh air to flow over him.

They were out on the highway before Emily or Maria felt at ease enough to speak.

"Did you find anything?" Emily asked.

"Yeah, I did. Enough to tie Burton to foul play of some kind, but I'm not sure it's anything that will help the police prove he killed Simpatico."

"What was it?"

"I'll tell you all about it after we stop by Dr. Marshall's."

"Why Dr. Marshall's?"

Kent held up the arm that he had hidden from view. Emily's gasp startled Maria, who whirled around to look, throwing the Cherokee into a violent swerve.

Kent grunted as his shoulder slammed against the vehicle's door. "Maria, you pay attention to the driving."

"What happened?"

"I forgot about Ninja."

"Ninja!" Maria cried. "Oh, God. He was in the apartment? He bit you?"

"To say the least." Kent winced as he gently lifted the handkerchief jellied with clotted blood. "If it hadn't been for Lucy, I might not have made it out of there." He tried to make a fist, but the slightest movement of the forearm muscles sent high-voltage pain ripping up his arm.

"We didn't hear anything, but she must have. Or she just sensed you needed help. She shot out of the window before we could stop her. We figured better to just let her go. Good thing, I guess. Right?"

"She got Ninja off of me."

"Wow."

"She killed him. I never saw her like that before. I found out one thing, for sure — you don't mess with Lucinda when she's ticked." He hugged the red coonhound like a child, burying his face in her scruff. Lucinda whined softly and licked his cheek.

When he looked up, he saw Emily studying his arm, a frightened look on her face. "A few stitches, a little ice, and antibiotics and I'll be as good as new," he said with false bravado.

It turned out to be twenty-six stitches installed during a tongue lashing by their family physician, Dr. Marshall. "You're too careless about these animals, Kent. A bite like this can land you in the hospital. You've got assistants to hold them for you, and restraint devices. Use them. As many dogs as you handle at your clinic, you need to take better precautions."

"You're probably right," Kent said, letting Dr. Marshall remain under her misconception. He held up his arm for the last tape to be applied, and listened to instructions about keeping it elevated, applying ice packs, and the importance of rest and antibiotics.

"Kent, be careful," Dr. Marshall said. She looked over her glasses at Emily and Maria. "You heard the instructions I gave him. I expect you two and Margaret to see that they are carried out."

"They will be," Emily said, and the expression she made at her father told him she meant it.

Just like Lucinda, Kent thought. Don't mess with Emily when she's ticked.

CHAPTER 26

BY THE TIME AUBREY ROARED INTO PINE HOLT late that afternoon, Kent's arm felt like it was tangled in red-hot wire. He couldn't find a comfortable position in the bed the girls made for him on the family room couch. Dr. Marshall's pain prescription was so totally ineffective he considered getting himself some horse painkiller. Ice packs helped a little. Margaret's tea was a distraction. Petting Lucinda's head as she lay on the floor by his bed helped as much as anything.

"What the hell, Kent?" Aubrey said, as she burst into the room. "What happened?"

"Half-assed plan number two."

"I'm beginning to agree with you. Maybe we aren't too hot at this detective shit."

"Uh-huh."

"What did happen?"

He held up his arm. "I got into a dog fight."

"Yeah. I guess so. Who won?"

"I did, of course. With Lucy's help."

Aubrey looked at his arm. "Was it worth it?"

"I think so."

"I hope so. Burton was absolutely crazy around there after he found out someone broke into his apartment and killed his dog.

161

He went right up to see Elizabeth, and carried Ninja with him for proof. He stormed around about her having a bunch of worthless S.O.B.'s working for her. He made all kinds of threats. He really lost it." Aubrey's face darkened for a second. "I have to admit, I do feel bad for Ninja."

"Did Burton say anything incriminating?"

"No, just a lot of ranting and raving. He swore he'd find out who killed his dog. Do the same thing to them. You know, that kind of stuff."

"I hope he doesn't have any luck at that. But like you say, it's a little weird, but I feel sorry for Ninja, too. And Burton, as far a losing his dog. Ninja was a jerk of a dog, for sure, but he was Burton's best buddy. I get that."

Aubrey huffed a sad laugh. "Yeah, I get that part, too. Elizabeth offered to call the police for him. She knew he would say 'no'. And, of course, he did. He didn't want them anywhere near. She asked him why not, but he wouldn't say."

"That's a relief. My reputation is bad enough without getting arrested for burglary."

"Tell me all the details," Aubrey said, easing down onto the couch, as Kent pulled his legs up to make room.

He told her the whole story — his encounter with Ninja, Lucinda's rescue, the phone bill, the money, and the mailer. She listened without interrupting.

After some thought, she said, "Why didn't you take the money? Then he would think the motive for the break-in was robbery. Might have taken some of the pressure off us."

"I thought of that. In fact, I had the case in my hand, but I put it back. I got to thinking maybe we'd get a better reaction if he realized the motive was *not* robbery."

"What do you mean?"

"Well, if he figured it was robbery, all he'd do is harass the other farm hands, or worse, trying to figure out which of them had the money. But when he sees that someone broke in but *didn't* take the money, even though they could have, even a dunce like Burton will realize that something else is going on. It may force him to make some kind of mistake. Either way, he's not likely to put any of us very high on his list of suspects, and this way the other boys at the farm will have to endure a lot less undeserved hassle."

"You devious thing, you."

Kent squinted into a nefarious smile.

"You sure he's going to know someone found the money?"

"Yep."

"How?"

Kent stood slowly and crossed the room to a bookshelf. With his arm that was not in a sling, he reaching behind some books, and extracted the bundles of twenties he'd not mentioned till now. "Because he'll see these are missing." He tossed them on the couch.

Aubrey stared at the money. "You took *part* of it?"

"Yep. Just enough for him to figure someone found the case."

"No wonder he went ballistic."

"That's just what we want. Plus, I might talk to Merrill about finding someone who can check out the serial numbers on these bills. Maybe that will tell us something."

"No police."

"Right."

Aubrey picked up a bundle of twenties and stared at it. "I take it all back, you should have been a P.I."

"No thanks."

She tossed the bundle back into the pile. "So what's with the phone bill?"

Kent pointed toward the end table, "It's right over there."

Aubrey scanned it. "This bill is old. He must have paid it by now or his phone would have been disconnected."

"True. But does anything strike you as odd?"

Aubrey studied the bill again. "Well, Burton wasn't one of AT&T's biggest customers."

"That's what I thought. Burton only made two long distance calls and both are person-to-person to the same number in Cynthiana, Kentucky."

"Okay, I'm with you there."

"It pays to have a Chief of Police for a brother. I had Merrill check the number for me. I didn't tell him why. Get this, it belongs to none other than Hector Figurante." He let that fact sink in.

"You're kidding," Aubrey said, sitting up straight as it registered. "You think this is *the* Hector Figurante?"

"Doesn't he live in Kentucky? How many Hector Figurantes can there be in Cynthiana, Kentucky?"

"What would a ne'er-do-well like Burton Bush be talking to a guy like Figurante about?"

"That's a good question. And the first step in answering it is for me to learn more about Mr. Figurante. All I know about him is what I've read in the Thoroughbred magazines, and a few rumors at the sales."

"Did you ask Maria? She worked for him last year, didn't she?"

"Yes. And no, I didn't ask her yet. I haven't mentioned anything about the phone bill or the money to anyone except you."

"Not even the girls?"

"Just you. I wanted to make sure you didn't have some logical explanation for Burton talking to Figurante."

"I've got no clue. And about all I can tell you about Figurante, you already know. He's a real wheeler-dealer. I think I heard he made lots of money somehow, then decided to live out a dream in the world of Thoroughbreds. You know the type. I know he's very controversial. A lot of people hate his guts and won't deal with him, but just as many think he's been a real shot-in-the-arm for the industry."

Kent stretched out on the couch again, letting his foot stroke Aubrey's hip. "Sometimes that means he's a good businessman. People get jealous."

"Right. You know, another person to ask would be Elizabeth. I don't think they've ever struck a deal, but I know they've talked. She can tell you more." Aubrey glanced at her watch. "You want me to call her? She's probably home."

"Sure. I'd like to hear what she has to say."

Aubrey pushed Kent's feet aside and padded silently, cat-like, toward the phone in the privacy of Kent's office. As she passed the kitchen, she greeted the three women at work there.

"Nice bite your dad has there, huh, Em?" She motioned to her forearm.

"Looks like a bear got him," Emily said.

Aubrey stepped into the office and closed the door.

When Aubrey returned to the den a few minutes later, Maria and Emily were tending to Kent.

"Well, Elizabeth was home and I was right. She knows Hector Figurante. Apparently Charles considered some deals with him, but nothing came . . ."

Aubrey was interrupted by the clatter of a teacup rattling off its saucer and onto the floor, as the side table Maria was lifting, jolted violently in her hands. "Sorry," Maria said, her face ashen. As she dropped into a chair, she whispered, "*La pesadilla ha vuelto.*"

"Are you okay?" Kent said.

She gave a weak nod.

"Maria, you worked for Hector Figurante. What's your take on the guy?"

Maria was silent for a moment. Then she made an expression like she was going to spit, and said, "Hector Figurante is a bastard." She stood abruptly and started to leave.

"Wait, Maria," Kent said. Shocked by her reaction, he made his voice as soothing as he could. "Do you have any idea why Burton would be talking to Figurante?"

Maria wheeled around. "I know nothing about Hector Figurante or his dealings." She disappeared down the hallway toward her bedroom.

Kent's gaze trailed after her. He felt a mix of surprise, confusion, anger, but mostly sympathy for Maria. He remembered the day Maria arrived back in Jefferson and her strange comment about Pine Holt being a safe place to be.

"What just happened there?" he asked Aubrey and Emily who were just as dazed as he was.

"I think we hit a sore spot."

"I guess so," Kent said.

Emily followed down the hall after her friend. Then her head reappeared around the corner. "Think about this — maybe Burton talked to Figurante about a job." She didn't wait for a reply.

Silence hung between Kent and Aubrey as both mulled over Maria's reaction. Eventually, Kent turned to her. "He wouldn't talk to Figurante about a job. He'd talk to Figurante's farm manager. Right?"

"That's how it works at most farms. I'm going to go check on Maria."

Kent took her hand. "Let Em do that?"

"But she's really upset. Besides, I want to ask her a few questions."

"So do I. Later. When she's settled down. Could Figurante have an interest in Simpatico, Charter Oak, or Solar Wind?"

Aubrey glanced down the hallway, then reluctantly focused on Kent's question and shook her head. "Not Simpatico. Even if he did, he'd talk with Elizabeth, not Burton."

"What about Charter Oak or Solar Wind?"

"Elizabeth doubts it. I do, too."

"I'll call Louise Stanford and Art Kelsey tomorrow. Just to be sure."

"What else did Elizabeth have to say?" Kent asked.

It took Aubrey a second to clear her mind enough to recall what Elizabeth had told her. "She said most people in the Thoroughbred business know Figurante, at least by reputation. He's from South America originally, she thinks maybe Ecuador."

"Maria's from Ecuador," Kent said, more than a little surprised by the coincidence.

"And it's not that big a place, is it? Hmm. According to Elizabeth, he came from a fairly wealthy family down there, but really made his fortune in the coffee importing business here in the states. A few years back when coffee prices took such a jump, he made a killing. He moved his headquarters to the U.S. about ten years ago, supposedly because of a better economic climate, and to allow himself to fulfill a life-long dream of owning a horse farm."

"You can't own a horse farm in Ecuador?"

Aubrey just shrugged. "His detractors, of which there are many, say it was for other reasons. One rumor is to better manage his illegal import business, that being drugs. According to Elizabeth, his ethics are marginal at best. Apparently, he has clawed his way to the top of the Thoroughbred world over several old and well-respected Kentucky farms by using some really questionable tactics, to put it mildly. Elizabeth hasn't gotten burned, but she knows several people who have, and she says she discouraged Charles from dealing with him. And, as far as she knows, he didn't. She also said she has some back issues of a couple of trade magazines that featured him as a premiere breeder or something. She's going to try to find them for us."

During the silence that followed, Aubrey wandered to the bookcase where Kent stashed the bundles of twenties and found the Styrofoam mailer.

"What's up with this thing, anyway?" she asked.

"That's a medical mailer."

"So."

"It has a Cynthiana postmark. Another odd coincidence isn't it? Figurante being from there and all."

"What would Figurante be mailing Burton?"

Kent let her question hang.

Finally he said, "Ed Holmes told me Kentucky is the only state in the U.S. that has the VanMark strain of EVA."

CHAPTER 27

KENT SAT ALONE IN ELIZABETH'S OFFICE, WAIT-ing. The pain in his arm had subsided to a constant ache, and by twisting sideways and draping it over the back of his chair, he could just about make it bearable. Earlier, Emily and Maria had changed the bandage. Twenty-four hours post-attack and the lacerations were healing as expected — his entire forearm was now a revolting purple and yellow bruise under glistening skin, stretched tight. The swelling went from his palm to his elbow. To occupy the time, he wiggled his fingers, then squeezed them into a loose fist. It was an excruciating exercise, but it reassured him that, eventually, his hand would be functional again.

He had tried twice earlier that morning to broach the subject of Hector Figurante with Maria. Both times she had gone silent, quaking like a rabbit. The second time she actually walked out on him. Again.

He hoped the plan he was about to propose to Elizabeth was not half-assed plan number three, but without Maria's input, all he had to go on was Elizabeth's back issues of several Thoroughbred industry trade journals and some newspaper clippings. Aubrey had dropped them off at Pine Holt, and Kent had spent a good part of the morning poring over them.

In general, the articles confirmed what Elizabeth had said. The periodicals were nothing but complimentary; Hector Figurante was the nouveau star in the Thoroughbred world. A new thinker, a future force in the business. They mentioned his Ecuadorian background, his highly successful coffee business, and that he was forty-six and never married. There was a quote by Figurante about the need for new blood in the horse breeders as well as the horses, and how he approached the selection of his sires using modern science rather than by traditional whims. There were several pictures of him posing around his farm, Criadero del Jugador. Kent noted that he had thinning black hair, brown eyes, sienna skin, and dazzling white teeth.

In one, he was next to a sale-record-setting yearling. In another, he was gazing out across his training track. And in a third, he was smiling proudly in front of a glass cupboard filled with trophies, plaques, and ribbons. There was a photo taken at Churchill Downs showing Figurante in the winner's circle holding the bridle of a horse blanketed in roses.

Kent noticed that in several pictures Figurante carried a black cane with what looked like a gold horse head for a handle. He wondered for a moment if the man carried it more for style or intimidation. Then he thought, maybe he just has a bad leg. Kent was raising a daughter with a crippling birth defect. He could have a soft spot for a guy with a bad leg.

The newspaper clippings were not so gracious. They homed in on Figurante's sinister side; investigated, but never indicted, on drug charges. Possibly linked to the South American cartels. Convicted and fined substantially for import and tax improprieties. And currently embroiled in a lawsuit with the United States Department of Agriculture over coffee importation, and, not surprising, one with the Kentucky Bureau of Livestock Sanitation that claimed Figurante circumvented laws for importing horses.

"Morning, Elizabeth," Kent greeted the matriarch as she pushed through the barn-side entrance to her office.

"Sorry I'm late, Kent. I've been helping with the paperwork in the breeding shed. We're running a little behind this morning."

"No problem."

"I take it you had a chance to look over the stuff I sent you."

"Yes, I did. And I've got to say, Figurante is definitely a question mark. Plenty of dark shadows. Maybe he's a killer, I don't know. No motive, though."

Elizabeth gestured at his arm and made sour face. "You paid quite a price for your little foray."

Kent brought his arm down into his lap. "I think it was worth it."

Elizabeth looked a little skeptical.

"I think we should follow up on Figurante. I'd like to go down to Cynthiana and meet him myself." He paused, waiting for a reaction and was disappointed when Elizabeth revealed nothing. "What I thought we could do is have you contact him with a story about how you are looking to buy a stallion — maybe to replace Simpatico, whatever. Then, at some point after you've supposedly reviewed video tapes, pedigrees, progeny records, and that other preliminary stuff, you'd like to send your veterinarian down to look over the prospects. That's totally plausible, happens all the time in the horse world."

"I think we could make it believable," Elizabeth said, each word measured.

"I'd have a better feel for the guy if I met him face-to-face. Plus, I might be able to find out if he and Burton are connected, and if he has a motive for killing our horses."

After batting around details, they settled on Kent's scheme, whereby Elizabeth would make the initial contact under the pretense of wanting to buy a stallion, and request information on prospects. After a brief time for review, Kent would be sent down to examine them on her behalf.

As Kent drove back to Pine Holt, the feeling that they were in too deep swept over him again. He looked at his bandaged arm. If simply entering Burton's apartment could result in an injury like that, what would happen when he entered the realm of Hector Figurante?

CHAPTER 28

THE FORD TAURUS KENT RENTED AT THE AIR-
port had thirty-five thousand on the odometer — hard, stop-and-go
miles, no doubt. Its brakes were mushy, and it negotiated turns like
a ship in heavy seas. The radio carried a background hum of engine
interference that crescendoed and decrescendoed as Kent worked
the accelerator. He leaned over, flipped on the air, and ignored the
cigarette smell it emitted. None of it mattered. All he cared about was
getting to Hector Figurante's place.

He thought about how Aubrey and the girls had balked at the
idea of him meeting someone as questionable as Figurante on his
turf without any back-up. Finally, they had agreed to let him go, but
he was under strict orders to be extra careful, and to call them on a
regular basis.

The road between Lexington and Cynthiana wound through
a mix of depression-era Kentucky towns with worn brick buildings,
their countless coats of paint blistering in the midday heat, and elegant antebellum homes, some remaining on their vast estates, others
diminished by progressive taxes or highway construction.

Along routes 75 and 62, there were dusty little farm houses
floating in seas of corn and tobacco. A few had a handful of scrawny
white-faced beef cattle basking behind tangles of barbed wire, or pigs
in pens cobbled up between rusting trucks. And, of course, there

were majestic horse farms with crisp, clean buildings and endless miles of white board fence rolling over Kentucky bluegrass.

The first thought that struck Kent as he approached the gate to Criadero del Jugador was that the farm did not fit with the rest of the Kentucky motif. There was no sense of history. From Kent's windshield vantage point, Hector Figurante's farm had an air of abruptness, as if it had just appeared, a garish display of opulence. The stone archway of the gate was impressive in its massiveness, yet all subtlety was lost in its construction of pink granite and mirrored silver lettering that shouted the farm's name.

The house was a jumble of architectural styles. A slate, mansard roof spanned like a hat between two stylized Queen Anne turrets that jutted skyward from the north and south ends like huge ears. The windows, which were more or less contemporary, and a tongue of stairs spilling from the entrance, combined to give the place the look of a giant clown, laughing at his own gaudiness.

Since there was not a car in sight, Kent wheeled the Taurus to a stop close to the front door on the circular driveway. He climbed the stairs and struck a heavy iron doorknocker. The door swung open instantly, and Kent saw before him Hector Figurante. He was wearing a loose print shirt and cream trousers. His black hair, brushed straight back, contrasted with the whiteness of his smile. He was leaning on his cane. Now, seeing it up close, Kent saw its thin, straight shaft had a carved snake coiling up like a corkscrew. At the top, where the snake's head should have been, was a gold horse head for a handle. Kent wondered if the snake-horse beast had some Incan relevance. Figurante would be keen on that, coming from Ecuador.

"Ah, Dr. Stephenson, I presume," Figurante said, then laughed at his own joke. His speech was precise, without the slightest accent. He extended a hand, soft, no calluses of a horseman. "Sorry, it just popped out. I'm Hector Figurante, and it pleases me immensely to meet the head of the CVC." He waved his cane. "Come in."

Kent tugged at the front of his shirt. "It does feel like I've been in the jungle."

"Right. Right. I'm delighted you could come down for Mrs. St. Pierre. I've always been impressed with Elizabeth, but this time she has outdone herself. The renowned Kent Stephenson leaves the CVC to do her bidding."

"We're close friends."

"Yes. You must tell me about that. But first, let's get you settled in, and then something to drink. I'm dry myself." He lifted a small bell from a nearby table and gave it a shake. In response, a fair-skinned, young woman in a summery floral dress appeared. She had auburn hair and deep blue eyes. Judging from her Irish features, Kent would have bet her name was Mary O'Something.

When Figurante touched his hand to her shoulder, she responded with a slight crouch, like a pup expecting to be disciplined.

"Renee Reilly, this is Dr. Kent Stephenson. He is here to evaluate a horse or two for Elizabeth St. Pierre. Kent, Renee. Renee is my farm manager."

Kent nodded hello. She smiled weakly, eyes downcast.

"Renee will help you with your things. I'll meet you in the solarium in — say — twenty minutes." He turned and walked away using the cane to support his left leg, which dragged slightly.

He really did have a bad leg, Kent thought, and was immediately disappointed. Not because of any sentiment for Figurante, but because it would be harder to dislike a person with a limp.

"If you can show me some shade where I can park this clunker, we can leave most of my stuff right in the car," Kent said to Renee, as they walked toward the Taurus.

She pointed to a pull-off under an enormous oak. "How about over there? You can pull it around to the barns later, when we check the horses."

"Perfect," Kent said, as he hoisted his suitcase from the back seat. "We can leave the vet equipment in the trunk for now."

Renee seemed cordial enough, polite and accommodating, but Kent sensed a subtle evasiveness. He wasn't sure if it was her quietness, or her reluctance to hold eye contact.

"How long have you been at Criadero del Jugador?" he asked.

"Four months."

"Oh. So not that long then," Kent said. "Where'd you get your training?"

"Mostly here."

He considered asking her why a farm manager would be so fresh groomed and clad in a sundress in the middle of the day. He pictured what Aubrey would be wearing at that moment — boots, dusty jeans, and a tank top clinging with sweat.

"I'm eager to see the horses," he said.

"We've got the most handsome boys in Kentucky. Which ones are you interested in?"

"Several, but mainly the four-year old, Snow Din. Mrs. St. Pierre likes his breeding, out of Snow Crane, and his race record. If he's healthy and the price is right, he's our boy."

"Good choice. He's as good as they get. Probably the best horse ever sired at Criadero del Jugador."

Renee showed Kent to a huge, overly-appointed guest room and departed. Standing alone, he pondered Renee's last comment, and then let it pass.

A few minutes later, when Kent entered the solarium, he was surprised to see that he was first, and had the room to himself. He moved to a massive wall of windows, and took his time admiring the spectacular view of the south fork of the Licking River. Then he crossed the tile floor to a wicker chair nestled in a cluster of exotic-looking plants, and sat. He drew a paper from his pocket and reviewed a summary of information about several horses Elizabeth was supposedly interested in buying.

"That's what I thought," he whispered to himself after studying the sheet. Renee had been wrong when she said that Snow Din was sired at Criadero del Jugador — Figurante *bought* him as a yearling. The horse was not born on the farm.

Kent leaned back and rolled that information around in his head. She may have just misspoken, he supposed, but any farm manager he had ever worked with knew the breeding of every horse on the place, backward and forward. It was part and parcel of the job.

He was pulled from his thoughts when Figurante entered the room.

"Sorry I'm late." Figurante made a sweeping gesture with his cane. "Duty called. I trust you are feeling better."

"Much."

"Good. Renee will be here in a minute with some iced tea. I have something stronger if you'd like."

"No. Tea is fine."

Figurante lowered himself into the adjacent chair. "So, VinChaRo is in hopes of further bolstering its position in the Thoroughbred world, eh?"

"Looks like it," Kent said. "I'm sure you heard about Simpatico."

"Everyone in the business did. A terrible loss. He was a magnificent animal. And still no cause of death, I understand."

"That's right. We're going to miss him. He was a major contributor to the New York Program."

"Sometimes these things have a way of working out for the best. Maybe introducing some new stallions will strengthen your program even further. What do they call it? Hybrid vigor?"

"Maybe."

"The New York Program actually began about the time I started here at Criadero del Jugador, you know. Over the years I've watched it grow into one of the better programs in the U.S. But I've got to tell you, Kentucky is still the world capital for Thoroughbreds. Don't get me wrong, there are a lot of good horses in New York. Fine horses. But, it speaks for itself when people like Elizabeth St. Pierre, on top in the business, come to Kentucky looking for stock to improve their own."

"We're gaining on you all the time."

Figurante puffed a short laugh through his nose. "Let's say we are all moving ahead. I doubt the gap is closing much."

Arrogant bastard, Kent thought, even as he held a smile.

Renee entered with a tray of iced tea, complete with mint leaves — southern style — and some tiny sandwiches. She accepted their thanks, turned and quietly slipped out of the room.

"You are originally from Ecuador, right?" Kent asked Figurante.

"Yes, I grew up in the Andes. Quito. My family has a plantation over along the coast. I come from a long line of coffee growers." He chuckled. "No Juan Valdez jokes, please."

"You could have fooled me. No accent, I mean."

Figurante smiled, and gave Kent a slight nod. "I'll take that as a compliment. I had the good fortune to be one of the 10 percent of Ecuadorians of white European ancestry. Most of my schooling was at English-speaking prep schools, then Colorado State."

"When I first moved here with my business, I could barely get anyone in the horse industry to talk to me. When they heard I was in the coffee business, from South America, they expected me to wear a sombrero and serape. They figured me to be a stall mucker." Figurante's voice became as empty as his face. "But they acknowledge me now. Every one of those pompous asses knows who Hector Figurante is. They come to me for horses, and pay what I ask."

Kent watched the real Figurante moving behind those dark eyes, knuckles clamped tight around his cane.

"They complain about my business practices, but they respect me — maybe even fear me. The old school Kentucky breeders have seen me rise to become one of the biggest farms in less than ten years. Can you imagine how that irks them when their ancestors took generations to build what they flaunt as their own great achievements? They have tried to discredit me. I'm sure you've heard rumors. They are all lies. And those who try to take away my dream?" He jabbed the floor with his cane. "I make them suffer."

Figurante downed the rest of his tea, dousing the flames. He set his glass on the table with theatrical flare, and smiled broadly at Kent, signaling that it was all a jest. Kent knew it was no jest.

"Tell me about yourself," Figurante said, more calmly. "I get the feeling that you are more than just a veterinarian doing a job for a client."

"As I mentioned before, Elizabeth St. Pierre and I are close friends."

"I meant your involvement with the New York Program."

Kent stared at the rivulets of condensation trickling down his glass. "I don't own any horses myself. That is, not race horses. My daughter has a couple of riding horses. That's all. But I'm a staunch supporter of the Program and very much involved in it from the veterinary standpoint. Like you, I've seen it grow from some politician's brainstorm to a major role in the Thoroughbred world."

"You are obviously proud of that."

"I am. I was in on the ground floor, and I feel like I contributed a little."

"Like which blood stock to pilfer from Kentucky?"

The guy definitely didn't mince words. "Yes, early on, to get started, I guess. And other places, like Florida, California, Europe. We still buy some now. That's why I'm here, obviously. But we breed our own for the most part. Like Hubris."

"Ah, the great son of Simpatico? I've heard of him."

Kent knew that was an understatement. Anyone who followed the horses as closely as Figurante did, knew of VinChaRo's Hubris.

"Is he as good as they say?"

Kent played along. "Check out his racing record. And while you're at it, check out the records of his first foal crop to race."

"Good, huh?"

"Superb. We sell our own horses, too. To Kentucky and all the others. And we win with our horses."

Figurante mulled over Kent's words. "Personally, I am not so sure the New York Program is as strong as you say. But I'll tell you this, your success with horses like Hubris has struck fear into many of the gutless gentry around here."

"I'll take that as a compliment. But you can tell them to relax. We're not a threat to Kentucky or anywhere else. We simply want New York to have a top Thoroughbred business in its own right."

"And so it shall, if you buy my horses." Figurante said, as he rose from his chair. "Let's go look at some of them."

CHAPTER 29

IN SPITE OF THE OAK TREE'S SHADE, THE TAURUS
felt like an oven. Kent turned on the air, but it was no match for
the direct rays of southern sun that lasered through the windows.
Figurante sat in the passenger seat. An oily shine coated his brow.
Otherwise, he seemed unaware of the heat. He directed Kent down
a meandering drive to the barns, then into a parking spot near the
training track.

They were walking along a cinder pathway that ran around
the outside of the track's white rail when Kent caught the sound of
pounding hooves. He paused to watch a lone horse and rider, dust
trailing behind, round the turn at the head of the stretch, and race
toward them. Leaning on the rail, he was once again mesmerized by
the strength and beauty of a racing Thoroughbred.

A look of pride was just breaking onto Figurante's face when
the rider pulled back hard on the reins, pulling his horse up abruptly.

"What the hell is that all about?" Figurante said, as he ducked
under the rail, and crossed the soft dirt track with surprising quick-
ness for a man with a bad leg. He met horse and rider as they bounced
to a stop. Kent, still at the fence, saw the jockey leap down, stroke the
horse's neck, and speak to Figurante in rapid fire Spanish.

Figurante ripped the reins from the tiny man's hands and sent
him reeling backwards with a vicious swipe of his cane.

"That's bullshit!" Figurante screamed in the man's face.

"He's hurt! I'm telling you. Look at him," the rider said, this time in English. He pointed at the horse's left front leg with one hand, and rubbed his cheek with the other. The horse stood with the leg off the ground.

"Cut the goddamn leg wraps off," Figurante said, tossing the man a pocket knife.

The jockey sliced at the wrap with quick strokes until it fell away, exposing an ugly swelling of the flexor tendon just above the fetlock. It grew in size as they watched. Figurante bent down and touched it. The horse grunted and pulled back.

"Whoa, you pea-hearted bastard! Stand up here!" Figurante said.

The horse stood trembling as his owner examined the leg.

After a few seconds, Figurante said, "It's just a bow. And not much of one, at that. A horse with any guts wouldn't even have noticed it. Ice him. Twenty minutes. Then hit him with some bute, and wrap him up with a poultice. I want that son-of-a-bitch back on the track tomorrow. I don't care how he looks. Tomorrow. Got it?"

"Jesus! That's enough of that," Kent said, and ducked to slide between the rails. He had one leg through when he remembered why he was at Criadero del Jugador. If he alienated Figurante now by pointing out his cruelty, he'd never get any information out of him. Reluctantly, he resumed his place at the rail, gripped it like he'd tear it out of the ground, and bit his tongue.

Figurante spun and took three steps toward Kent, then turned back to the jockey. "And if you can't get any more speed than that out of my horses without breaking them down, I'll be looking for someone who can. You hear what I'm saying?"

The jockey nodded.

By the time he had crossed the track, Figurante's demeanor had changed, as if controlled by a switch. He smiled and gave Kent a *no big deal* gesture. "Just a bow. Not bad. He'll be fine."

"Do you want me to take a look at him? I don't mind."

"No. I don't think so. We won't take the time now. I might have my vet look at him later. We'll give him a few days off. He'll come around."

Kent turned and glanced over his shoulder. The horse hobbled three-legged, head down, at the coaxing of the tiny man pulling his reins. Kent had seen enough lame horses to recognize, even at a distance, that the injury was not a mild bowed tendon. It was something serious — a bad sprain or, worse yet, a fracture. Possibly surgery, and six months off, for sure, and the horse might make a comeback. He fought the urge to go to the horse's aid.

Figurante seemed to have dismissed the incident entirely.

He said, "Renee should be at the other end of barn three with Snow Din by now."

They headed down the row of stalls in that direction. Figurante commented on several of his best horses as they passed their stalls. One Kent remembered from the Preakness four years ago, another had sired several stakes winners that Kent knew of.

The string of horses was impressive. There was no denying that. Figurante had managed to amass a splendid group. But, two things were obvious to Kent as he peered into the stalls at the awesome horseflesh that stared back at him. First, and not surprising given Figurante's reputation, most of the really top-notch horses, the world-class ones, were purchased, not born and raised at Criadero del Jugador. Second, and far more alarming to Kent, there were a lot more injured horses than he would expect on a well-managed farm. Throughout the barn, he saw knees and fetlocks swollen hard from sprains and joint damage. Many of the horses showed tiny scars coursing up and down their cannon bones like the tracks of a small rodent, grim vestiges of the firing iron, a painfully cruel and long ago discredited treatment. Kent saw cracked and weeping skin on the legs of several horses, the hideous result of harsh blister liniments once prevalent in the Neanderthal days of equine medicine, and now considered barbaric.

"Who does your veterinary work?" he asked, forcing himself to keep a casual tone.

"Mostly I do it myself. I take a bad problem over to Lexington once in a while, and the rest I figure out. Unfortunately, I find the vets around here difficult to work with."

Kent's face twisted into a *that's pure bullshit* expression.

"Hector, I may be out of line here, but," he tried to wring a compliment out of his anger, "you've got a barn full of fabulous horses. They deserve the very best. You're within a stone's throw of some of the best horse veterinarians on the planet. You ought to be able to find at least one you can work with."

Figurante kept walking. No reply.

Kent wanted to grab the man and shake him until his head rolled off his shoulders. Instead, he jammed his hands in his pockets, fists clenched so tightly his nails cut into his palms.

They found Renee at the end of the barn brushing the finishing touches onto a magnificent black stallion standing on cross ties. Kent recognized him instantly as Snow Din.

"There's the boy," Figurante said proudly, pointing with his cane.

Renee slipped into the shadows. Kent played his role. He circled the horse from a distance, carefully scrutinizing Snow Din's head, neck, and torso, giving extra attention to the all-important legs. The stallion was one of the few clean-legged ones in the barn, a testimonial to his durability.

"Nice horse," Kent understated, dickering for his client.

Figurante smiled. "VinChaRo should have such a nice horse." He waved his cane. "Renee, trot him off for the good doctor."

Obediently, Renee, whom Kent noticed had changed into more appropriate jeans and T-shirt, snapped a leather shank onto Snow Din's halter, released the cross ties, and walked him outside onto safer footing. Kent and Figurante followed.

"To the left. At a trot," Figurante said impatiently.

Renee glanced back at Snow Din to be sure that he was paying attention and tugged lightly on the shank. They commenced to trot along a gravel lane adjacent to the barn.

Suddenly, a covey of doves blasted out of a patch of tall grass along a drainage ditch two horse lengths to Snow Din's right. The birds cackled loudly, beat their wings, and executed perfectly their natural defense — escape by startling the enemy.

No one could have known the birds were there, dusting themselves in the sandy soil. Kent felt his body jolt reflexively and saw Figurante do the same. Snow Din, his equine reactions a hundred times quicker than a human's, was already spinning hard away from the birds. Renee held tight to the startled beast as he twisted to run. She looked like a marionette in the hands of an angry puppeteer as Snow Din swung his head.

"Whoa!" she shouted, refusing to be shaken free. She braced herself in front of him, both hands fisted on the lead, shoulders stretching from their sockets.

Kent rushed to help.

"Hold him, damn it!" Figurante shouted.

When Kent stepped behind Snow Din, the stallion realized there was no escape. He allowed himself to stand, still wide-eyed and quivering.

Figurante grabbed the lead rope in one hand and swung his cane with the other. It landed on Snow Din's neck with a sharp crack. The horse jerked back.

"You goddamn fool!" Figurante roared.

He was drawing his cane back for a second blow when Kent grabbed his arm. "Hey. Take it easy. The birds startled him. That's all."

Figurante spun toward Kent and ripped his arm free. His eyes were on fire. Kent saw the cane drawing back and braced himself to deflect the kind of blow the jockey had received. But Figurante froze mid-swing. Still holding the cane above Kent's head, he burned his eyes into Kent's. An electrified silence surrounded them. Finally, Figurante tore his eyes from Kent and fixed on Renee.

"You call yourself a farm manager and you let a stallion go crazy in your hands?" Figurante said. "A horse worth more than you will make in your lifetime, and you treat him like some skate!"

"I didn't know the birds were there."

Figurante pointed his cane at the mansion. "I don't want to hear it. Get up to the house. You've got the horse skills of a gorilla."

Renee stared at him in disbelief. Just as it appeared Figurante would strike her, she wheeled and headed toward the house, rubbing her blistered palms on her shirt.

Kent was preparing to strangle the man, when Figurante's disposition switch flipped one more time.

"Shall we try again?" he said, with a mellifluous smile.

For the next two hours Kent conducted the prepurchase examination he'd done hundreds of times before on hundreds of horses. He reminded himself to appear genuinely interested and make the exam authentic. Snow Din was the picture of good health. The only fault Kent could find was a raised red welt on the side of his neck. It was a perfect imprint of the serpent spiraling up Figurante's cane.

Figurante's treatment of Renee kept playing back in his mind. How could anyone work for such a man? His split personality would have been fascinating if it weren't so terrifying.

Through it all, Figurante watched in brooding silence.

"I can't find a thing wrong with him," Kent said as he repacked his veterinary equipment in the Taurus. "Barring any unforeseen problems with the x-rays or blood work, I'm going to tell Elizabeth to go ahead. The rest is between you two."

"I didn't think you would find any problems. At Criadero del Jugador, if they are not healthy, we don't keep them. I'll send a contract to Elizabeth."

CHAPTER 30

FLAME AND NEAPOLITAN CARRIED EMILY AND Maria along the trail on loose reins. Their saddles creaked in rhythm with the peepers. Long shadows crisscrossed the trails as orangey light filtered to the forest floor. They pulled up facing west on the bluff, where Emily knew they would get the best view, and were rewarded by an explosion of blue and gold as the sun sank below the horizon.

"Doc will be home tomorrow evening," Emily said, letting her eyes adjust to the near darkness. "He's only been gone overnight, but still, I'll be glad to have him back safe and sound. I wonder if he found out anything."

"He'll tell us, I'm sure," Maria said in a tone that made it obvious she resented having to revisit the subject of Hector Figurante. She twisted in the saddle. Neapolitan perked up his ears, aroused by the stir on his back. For a moment he was attentive, feeling for additional cues. Receiving none, he relaxed again.

There was another long silence, then Maria spoke out of the dark. "I want to block that place out of my mind."

"Why?" Emily asked, her frustration causing it to come out too loud. She had not had any better luck than her father getting Maria to opening up about her time at Figurante's.

"Because I hate Criadero del Jugador and I hate Hector Figurante."

"You have to tell me what happened down there, Maria," Emily begged.

"He's a terrible person. He is why I left Criadero del Jugador."

"Did he do something to you?"

When Maria didn't answer, Emily tried a different tack.

"Is Figurante mean enough to hurt our stallions?"

Maria maintained her silence for a long time, then with caustic huskiness in her voice, she said, "He is capable of anything."

"What do you think, though? Do you think he could be behind everything that's been going on?"

"I don't know, but I'll tell you this, if he felt he had a reason to do it, he would do it. He's ruthless."

A horrifying thought crossed Emily's mind. "Maria," she said cautiously, "he wouldn't hurt Doc, would he?"

Maria didn't answer.

Emily repeated her question more forcefully. "My father is safe down there. Right?"

Still Maria said nothing.

Emily did not ask again. Instead, she said, "Come on, Flame," and drove her heels into the pony's flanks so hard he leaped a stride, then took off at a gallop. Ignoring the darkness, Emily pushed Flame to his max with clucks of her tongue and heels in his ribs. They charged toward Pine Holt at a dead run.

As she reined him in at the barn, she remembered the phone number Doc had left for Criadero del Jugador was next to the telephone in the kitchen. She spun Flame toward the house and forced him back into a gallop. Flame bolted across the lawn, but when they reached the patio, he instinctively slowed. Emily urged him on one last time, and the bewildered pony leaped onto the slippery flagstone surface. She pulled him up within inches of the French doors, and dismounted as he stopped skidding.

"I love you, little man," she said, over her shoulder. "I'll cool you out as soon as I'm off the phone. I promise."

She raced into the house. She glanced back over her shoulder in time to see Flame watching her through the glass. His chest was still heaving, his face looked confused. Then, to her relief, he sighed deeply, stepped to a pot of ornamental grass and began nibbling.

In the kitchen, Emily snatched up Doc's note and punched the number for Hector Figurante's farm into the telephone.

"Hi. This is Emily Stephenson in Jefferson, New York," she said to the bored voice that answered the phone. "My father is Kent Stephenson, a veterinarian there on business. I need to speak to him right now. It's really important."

"Yes, ma'am. They are at dinner. Hold, please."

While she waited, Emily stretched the phone cord for a look at Flame. A smile flickered across her face — she'd worry about an explanation for the stump of grass in the pot later. Kent's voice came over the line and her smile vanished.

"Hello?"

"Doc, it's me. Are you okay?"

"Yes, Em. I'm fine. Are you? Why are you calling?"

Emily allowed herself to breathe again. "Yes. I'm okay. But Maria just scared the crap out of me. She told me Hector Figurante really is nasty enough to hurt our horses or even people. I think he must have hurt her, too, but she won't talk about it."

Emily's voice cracked. There was a pause. Then Kent heard her swallow hard.

"I got afraid for you, Doc," she said.

"Em," Kent said, the panic in his voice giving way to relief, "thanks for looking out for me, hon. But, hey. I'm fine. Nothing bad is going to happen to me."

"You promise?"

"Cross my heart. Actually we're having a nice dinner right now."

"I wanted to warn you."

"I appreciate that."

Emily brushed her fingers over the itinerary Kent had stuck to the refrigerator. "When are you coming home?"

"Soon. Tomorrow. You and Maria are still picking me up at the airport, right?"

"Yes." Silence again. Then, "I miss you. Be really careful."

"I miss you, too, honey. I will."

● ● ●

Emily's warning played in Kent's head as he returned to dinner with Figurante and Renee. His appetite for sea bass had faded, but the Riesling hit the spot. What happened to Maria? What had she told Emily that got her so upset?

A few minutes later Figurante was called away from dinner for a telephone call, and Kent and Renee were left alone at the table. Kent made sure her wine glass was never empty.

"How is it around here?" he asked, as he poured. "Up in New York it's hard as hell to find good farm workers. You know — no one wants the long hours, low pay."

"It's the same here. Everyone wants an eight-hour day, week-ends off, big pay – doesn't work that way on a horse farm."

"I'll drink to that." He took a sip of wine, she drank half a glass. "In fact, just last week a guy who's been at VinChaRo for a long time gave his notice. Said he'd been looking for work down this way, around the Cynthiana area, and got a couple of good offers. His name is Burton Bush."

Renee showed no reaction.

"Burton Bush," Kent repeated. "Did he make it over here to Criadero del Jugador? He's a heavy-set guy with wild red hair you wouldn't forget."

"Doesn't ring a bell."

"It doesn't much matter. From what you say, he's in for a surprise when he finds out the work situation's the same here as back home."

She emptied her wine glass and refilled it herself. "Worse if you get a boss like Hector."

"He does have a short fuse."

"Understatement of the year."

"Hair triggered."

She rolled her eyes. "Yeah. Like today, when the birds scared Snow Din. You know, when I first came here he treated me super. He was teaching me, introducing me to the right people, paying me great. I really thought this job was the break I'd been looking for."

"What went wrong?"

"Hell if I know. Him, I guess. He insisted that I moved in up here at the main house, and it's gone downhill ever since. He wants one hundred percent of my time. I've got no life. He doesn't want me to see my friends, I can't dress like I used to, anything. Lately, he has a fit every time I'm around the horses. I mean, Christ, that's what he hired me for, I thought."

She finished the rest of her wine, but made no move to refill it. Kent let it remain empty this time. Her voice was starting to slur.

"I don't know," she said. "He's got an ego that won't quit. He wants to own everything he sees. He can't stand to think someone has something better than him. It makes him furious. Once he . . ."

Renee's voice tapered off as Figurante re-entered the room.

"Sorry," He said in a tone that usurped the role of host back from Renee. "I think we've got the boat on an even keel again. Any food left?"

Renee and Kent sipped coffee and watched Figurante eat his dinner, held warm by the kitchen staff. When he'd finished, he lit a cigar, large and brown, still girdled with its gold label. He made the briefest of eye contact with Renee, who then said something about barn check, and excused herself.

When the two men were alone, Figurante exhaled a blue cloud toward the ceiling, and said, "There really has been a run of bad luck at VinChaRo, hasn't there?"

"Been a tough last few months."

"First Simpatico, then Elizabeth's son. That's more than a lot of farms could take."

"They'll keep going. Remember what I told you about Hubris."

"You mentioned him. What about Charles St. Pierre's death?"

Kent turned slowly to look Figurante in the eye. "It was an accident. He drowned."

Figurante sat perfectly still. Kent watched the man's Adam's apple rise slowly then drop back.

Kent would be leaving tomorrow and so far the trip had turned up nothing. He decided to lay his cards on the table.

"Even so, there's a few of us that aren't buying it." He spoke at a measured pace, studying Figurante's reaction. "We have reason to believe he may have been killed — by a farm hand."

"Really?" Figurante said, his voice rock-steady. "Someone who worked at VinChaRo?

"Yep. Still does. For now, anyway." Kent hedged. "Allows the police to keep a better eye on him. The Burning Bush."

"Say again?"

"That's what they call him around the farm. He's got blaze-orange hair and his last name is Bush. Burton Bush."

"Burning Bush. I get it." Figurante didn't manage to conceal the wave of anger that crossed his face.

It was midnight when Kent dismissed himself to bed. Sleep was out of the question. He was in the house of a man mired in deceit and cruelty. Now he had to connect him to the events in New York.

Was Figurante capable of killing a horse? Yes. Would he? Maybe. Why? Who knows? At least Emily and Maria thought so. Whatever that crazy phone call was about. And, how were Figurante and Burton Bush connected?

CHAPTER 31

EMILY AND MARIA MET KENT AT THE AIRPORT right on schedule. They showered him with kisses and hugs.

"Wow," he said, finally. "I was only gone one night."

"You feel like you're getting too much love?" Emily asked.

"Nope. Just the right amount. You going to carry my bag, too?"

"Nope. Welcome home."

Several times as they drove to Pine Holt, he started to tell them about his trip, but each time the girls redirected the conversation to superficial topics. Eventually, a little perplexed but too tired to question it, he turned to gaze at the familiar terrain streaming past the window. His thoughts drifted as the girls continued to chatter.

It was when they pulled up in front of Pine Holt that he started to suspect something was up. Aubrey's car was there. That in itself was a good thing — he had not talked to her while he was away, and the prospect of seeing her buoyed his spirits. He also noticed Margaret's car was not in its usual place. That too, was odd, being that it was near dinnertime. He looked from the cars to the girls. Their expressions registered mock innocent.

"Where's Margaret?

"We gave her the night off."

"Oh, really?" He wondered what Margaret would do with a night off.

"There's a covered dish supper in Jefferson tonight she kind of wanted to go to, so we decided we'd fix dinner."

Kent gave them a dubious look. "You two are fixing dinner? Okay. That's Aubrey's car?"

"We invited her and Barry."

"Uh-huh. So, what are we having?"

"We're firing up the grill. Steaks for those who want them, portobellos for those who don't."

"Nice."

Just then Barry and Lucinda emerged from the house, Barry with his slow teenage amble, Lucinda at a dead run. Kent got a high-five from Barry, and a faceful of licks from Lucy.

"You go on in, Doc. I'll get your stuff," Barry said.

Kent found Aubrey chopping greens into a large wooden salad bowl. When she saw him, a sultry smile broke onto her face. She wiped her hands on the apron that protected her shorts and blouse.

"You look domestic," he said.

She curled her arms around his neck, and gave him a full chest-to-chest hug. The peck on his cheek meant *welcome home*, the hug meant much more. He let his tired body relax into her warmth.

Instinctively, they stepped apart when the kitchen door rattled.

"Don't mind me," Barry said. "Did you start the fire, Mom?"

Aubrey smoothed her apron. "Not yet. I thought we'd have a drink while it gets going."

"Okay. I got it covered." Barry disappeared back through the door.

"You already lit the fire, whether you know it or not," Kent said.

"Different fire. I'm hoping to stoke that one later."

"Well then, if that's a promise, I'll see if Barry needs any help." He left Aubrey to her salad.

Kent took a seat on the patio glider, and stroked Lucinda's head, which was instantly in his lap. The two of them watched Barry tow the Webber out of the corner, pour in a pile of briquettes, douse them with lighter fluid, and touch it off with a match — just the way Kent had taught him.

Aubrey was groaning that she should not have eaten that second mushroom, and the others were gnawing the last bites of steak off the bone, when the conversation finally shifted to Kentucky.

Kent sipped coffee and said, "Figurante is, without a doubt, dangerous. He's bitter about the success of the New York program and, the odd thing is, he despises the other Kentucky breeders just as much. And, for sure, the guy is schizo."

"Does he know who Burton Bush is?" Emily asked.

"Not that he admitted. And there's no direct tie that I could find. At least Burton didn't apply for a job. Renee Reilly, his farm manager, didn't seem to know anything about him. I think she would remember if she'd met him."

"Farm manager. She'd be doing the hiring," Aubrey said.

"So what's your gut feeling?" Emily asked. "Is Figurante in on it? Yes or no?"

"I've been trying not to let my gut reaction influence me. But honestly? I've got to believe the S.O.B. is behind it — somehow. For sure, he *could* do it."

Maria, who had been quiet through the whole discussion, suddenly balled her fists and shook them in the air. "Yes, yes. He could do it! And he would do it, without a second thought. He did it to me."

She hid her face in her hands, and began to cry.

"I can't stand this anymore," she said, through her hands. "I came back to Jefferson to get away from Hector Figurante. I never wanted to hear his name again. Just when I think I am free, there he is again, right in the middle of my life!" A deep growl rolled in the back of her throat.

Emily and Aubrey enveloped her, as Kent and Barry watched helplessly. Eventually her sobbing was replaced by sniffling, and then by a long, cleansing sigh.

Maria took a tissue from the box Emily offered and blotted her eyes.

"I'll tell you about Hector Figurante," she said, her words still seething, even as she forced herself to stay in control. "When I graduated last year, that's where I went. You know that. It was going to be my opportunity to work with one of the top breeders in the country. I was going to get some super experience, make contacts, work with some awesome horses. Well, at first Figurante seemed interested in teaching me. He talked about us both being from Ecuador and how he wanted to see me succeed. He introduced me to the right people and gave me some real responsibility. I thought I had the perfect job. In no time, he made me farm manager. What a fool I was."

She brushed aside the water Emily offered. Her face darkened as she thought back.

"But then it got to where if I even suggested something, he'd jump down my throat. He'd get crazy. He started giving me less and less work at the barn and more at the house. One day he suggested — more like ordered — that I move out of my apartment and into his house."

Maria looked directly at Kent, then dropped her gaze to the floor.

"I should have left then, but I wanted that job so bad. So I moved into his house. After that, it was like I was his personal property or something. He didn't want me to see my friends or do anything on my own. He told me just how he wanted me to do everything. He even bought clothes he wanted me to wear, if you can believe that. Then one night…"

Maria paused, glanced nervously at Emily and Barry.

"Then one night he came up to my room. It was late and I was asleep. Before I knew what was happening, I thought I was dreaming, he was on top of me. I tried to scream, but he covered my mouth. He said that there was no one to hear, and did I think he gave me the job and stuff for nothing? He was too strong, I couldn't get away. The more I struggled, the more angry he got until finally he hit me, hard, in my face. After that, he got what he wanted."

Long rivulets ran down Maria's cheeks. "I hate Figurante for what he did to me. I hate myself for letting you go to his house, for letting you walk into such danger."

For a long moment, the only sound was Maria's crying. Emily, Aubrey, and Barry simultaneously turned desperate looks to Kent.

He was sure his head would explode as hatred for Figurante rose within him. He stepped to where Emily, Aubrey, and Maria were coiled, and bent so that his forehead just touched the top of Maria's head. He could feel her quaking.

"He'll pay, Maria. You have my word. He will pay."

He stood up and stared back at the others. Finally, he said, "We're taking this to the police. We have no choice. I don't care what Elizabeth said about not wanting them involved. We've got leads we can give them now. Getting the police on him is the surest way to see that he pays."

"No," Maria said, her face still buried in her hands.

"What do you mean, *no*?" Kent said, and instantly wished it hadn't sounded so harsh. He figured Maria would be the last one to object.

She raised her head. Her face was blanketed with defeat. "It would be my word against his. I'm not going to go through all that police stuff, to face him again, then watch him walk away laughing."

"Maria, we are amateurs. We don't have the means to get him."

"Then just let him go."

"That ain't happening."

A silence came and it lingered.

Then, out of nowhere, Maria's demeanor changed from utter defeat to an icy, frightening calm. She pushed Emily and Aubrey aside, and rose to her feet, shoulders back, no longer trembling. Her eyes impaled Kent. "I want him dead," she said. She spit the words, and they sent an army of wet-footed spiders racing up Kent's back. "Nothing less."

Before anyone could respond, she turned, and headed to her bedroom.

Long after the others called it a night, Kent and Aubrey cuddled on the patio, Lucinda at their feet. They pushed slowly back and forth in the glider, sipping wine, and studying the stars. But even in that perfect moment, Kent could not get what Maria had said out of his head.

"It may have happened in the very room where I slept last night. And," he shook his head in disbelief, "the sonofabitch is doing it again! To Renee Reilly, the farm manager he has now. The same things that happened to Maria are happening to her."

He pictured Maria as he had seen Renee, trapped in Figurante's palace — frustrated, lonely — wondering how things had gone so terribly wrong.

"Aubrey, I swear, I could kill him myself!"

From his contact with Figurante at Criadero del Jugador he knew the man was evil, but now, after Maria's revelation, he knew just how evil. Killing horses or people would be nothing for him.

He just had to connect the dots — Figurante, Burton, and the horses.

The night chill had settled in by the time Aubrey took his hand and led him toward the bedroom.

"Come on," she said, the wine her in voice, "I'm going to help you get all this stuff off your mind, at least for the rest of the night."

"I'm good with that. You are my favorite sleeping pill."

CHAPTER 32

HECTOR FIGURANTE STARED DOWN THE LENGTH of his conference table at the handful of people around it the same way a hawk stares down at meadow mice.

The mice were pale and shaken because Figurante had just confirmed what they had all suspected anyway.

"Yes, I admit," he told them, "that I initiated activities in New York. But keep in mind, you are all accomplices." He paused for effect. "The Bluegrass Conspiracy." He laughed at his own cleverness. The mice were stone silent. "So don't get cold feet."

Lettie Hook, Chairwoman of the derby committee at Churchill Downs and wife of the Lieutenant Governor, squared her shoulders and tried to sound defiant.

"Wait a minute, Hector. We formed this group to discuss a business matter — a problem. We did not authorize you to sabotage New York's breeding program."

The others nodded in nervous agreement.

"Oh, really," Figurante baited her. "Just discuss?" He stood, and paced behind his guests. "Corbett, do you remember making me — us — a diagram — a map, if you will — of Keuka View Farm?"

Hamilton Corbett, who had recently inherited one of Kentucky's oldest and most prestigious horse farms, nodded and then mumbled a weak denial.

"You drew it right here at this table," Figurante reminded him. "It was very useful."

He turned to Dean Nolan. "Mr. Nolan, excuse me, eminent *Doctor* Nolan, PhD., University of Kentucky virologist extraordinaire, you were kind enough to enlighten us about the VanMark strain of EVA when we batted around the possibility of germ warfare. Remember?"

"Of course I remember," Nolan said, "but we were just talking — thinking out loud." He waved at the rest of the group. "None of us intended for you to carry out anything like that."

"Yet you made a vial or two available to me. You told me right where to look. Just which refrigerator to search in your lab."

Nolan gave Figurante a deflated look and said nothing.

"So," Figurante continued, still pacing, "throughout the course of our meetings here, I dare say all of you have made some rather damaging contributions."

He smiled, but did not look at them as he listened to their sputters of disagreement. For a long time he did not move. Then he slowly circled back to the head of the table. "I am a man of action, you all know that. But, what you may not know is that I am also a cautious man. I realize that you people are not used to having your integrity impugned. Nevertheless," Figurante shrugged with palms up, "I thought from the beginning I had better ensure your loyalty in case the going got rough." With dramatic flare he turned, reached up, and opened a hidden cabinet high on the wall.

There was a collective gasp as everyone at the table recognized a camera.

"That's right, folks. I've got you all on tape, with all your incriminating comments and contributions." He smiled broadly.

All the unwilling members of the Bluegrass Conspiracy stared at each other. Trapped meadow mice.

"However," Figurante began again, his tone relaxed, "I have no intention of using the tapes for any purpose other than insurance.

I'll do the dirty work. I know that's the way you southern gentry prefer it.

"So now, let's get back to the reason I called the meeting tonight. In our *discussions* of key New York stallions, we overlooked one — VinChaRo's Hubris. Do you recall the horse?"

Every head nodded.

"He's got to be dealt with."

Anguished groaning noises rumbled up every throat.

"He may be even *better* than Simpatico, his sire."

Clayton Davis, one of Churchill Downs principal stockholders, held up both hands. "Hold on, Hector. Enough is enough. I am not going along with any more plans to kill horses. Period." He pushed back his chair, and stood to leave. Several others did the same.

"Careful now, Clayton," Figurante said, with false sincerity in his voice. He pointed to the hidden cabinet. "Remember the tapes."

"Forget the goddamn tapes!" Davis roared. "You'll get caught sooner or later, and I'm not going to be there when you do. You can't eliminate every horse you don't own, Hector."

"Sit back down, Clayton," Figurante said, "Let me finish. I do not intend to eliminate Hubris."

Figurante turned to the others, each one waiting for Clayton Davis to fight on. "We don't need a wholesale rebellion here. Listen to what I'm about to say."

Clayton sank back into his chair, and the others followed his lead.

"Thank you," Figurante said, letting them refocus. "I said that Hubris must be *dealt with,* not *eliminated.*"

"Let's not play word games, Hector," Hook said.

Figurante remained composed. "Actually, Clayton hit the nail on the head when he said, 'you can't eliminate every horse you don't own.'"

"Meaning what?"

"Surprising as it may seem to you folks, I agree." Figurante smiled an evil smile, and let his words hang.

"Then how do you propose to eliminate him, or deal with him — whatever — get rid of him?"

Figurante stayed silent for an infinite moment. Finally, he leaned forward, braced his arms on the table, and said flatly, "We buy him."

No one made a sound as the mice mulled the possibility. Now Figurante was talking their language. They knew money talked. They knew wealth was power, and they had used money to achieve their goals many times before.

"You think Elizabeth would sell him?" Corbett asked.

Figurante let out a short laugh. "If the price is right, she will."

"She's got tons of money."

"So do we."

"I think Elizabeth is more interested in prestige than money."

"Come on, Hamilton. You've spent a lifetime in this business. There is nothing more prestigious than a big sale."

Corbett conceded that with a nod, "True."

"We could syndicate and offer her a price that would set a new record," Figurante said. "*That's* prestigious. She'll go for it."

Corbett nodded again, but said nothing.

"Besides, think what a fantastic addition Hubris would be to Kentucky's breeding stock. We'd be killing two birds with one stone."

Corbett raised his eyebrows, drew his lips tight, beginning to see Figurante's point. "We may even be able to recoup our investment."

"Of course we will," Figurante said. "After an historic sale like that, breeders will be breaking down the door to book their mares. We'll make his stud fee astronomical."

The others began a buzz of conversation among themselves. Figurante watched their heads bobbing a positive reaction. He moved his eyes around the table, making eye contact with each person.

When he was sure everyone was on board, he said, "Good. I'm glad we're all in agreement. I will work out the details and let you know. Consider the members of the Bluegrass Conspiracy the new owners of yet another premier stallion."

Then with the shrewdness of a born salesman, he concluded the meeting while sentiment was favorable.

CHAPTER 33

FIGURANTE HEADED EAST ON ROUTE 20. THE lush green hills of Central New York were a pleasant change from Kentucky's unrelenting heat. He drummed his fingers to the beat of his rented Lincoln's radio. It felt good to be behind the wheel. He stomped the accelerator in giddy experimentation, and the luxury cruiser's engine hesitated as if startled by the unfamiliar prodding, then lurched ahead in response. He pushed his shoulders back into the seat, and roared toward Jefferson.

He swung a sharp right at the blinking light as Route 20 became Albany Street and paid little attention to the quaint side-walks and storefronts or the quiet square guarded by the statue of Willard Covington, founder of Jefferson. Figurante scoffed at the appropriateness of the perfectly white Presbyterian Church, morning sun glinting from its steeple.

One block farther, on the intersection that was Jefferson's main hub, Figurante found what he had been watching for. It was a colonial brick building, large for a small town, yet elegant, with three stories of windows each flanked with black shutters. A wrought iron arm suspended from a white signpost stated simply, THE RED HORSE INN, established seventeen eighty-one.

He cranked the wheel hard and pulled into the inn's parking lot. *Perfect. Just the place for an old blueblood like me.*

A few minutes later, Figurante was shown to his room. It was appointed with delicate cut glass lamps and rich patterned carpet encircled by a border of polished hardwood. Fine lace curtains. A marble fireplace with carved mantle occupied most of one wall. All of it wasted on Figurante. As soon as the bellman was gone, he flopped onto the canopy bed that was the room's centerpiece, and collected his thoughts. After a minute, he pulled a black book of phone numbers from his coat pocket, riffled through it, reached for the telephone, and dialed a number.

"Yes. I'd like to speak with Burton Bush." He listened to the receptionist's reply. "That's all right. I'll hold, it's important."

After a long wait, Figurante heard a dull voice come over the phone.

"Burton, I need to talk to you," Figurante said. Not bothering with an introduction. "Where can we meet?"

He knew Burton recognized his voice by the dolt's alarmed response.

"Why? Where are you?"

"I'm in Jefferson. When do you get off work?"

"Four o'clock. You're in New York?"

"Where can we meet?"

"Uh. Kolbie's, I guess."

"What's Kolbie's?"

"A bar."

"Is it in town?"

"Hell, no. It's out in the sticks. Maybe five miles."

Figurante wrote down the directions. "I'll meet you there at four-thirty this afternoon."

"Why?" Burton said, his voice a mix of fear and distrust. "Can't you just say what you gotta say right now?"

"I'll see you at four-thirty," Figurante said, and hung up. He glanced at his watch — just after ten.

He forced himself to wait a full fifteen minutes, then tapped in the number of VinChaRo Farm again.

"Hello," he said with exaggerated diffidence so that the receptionist would not recognize him as the previous caller. "Is Elizabeth St. Pierre in today?"

"Yes she is, but she's busy in the barn. Can I take a message?"

Figurante had guessed Elizabeth would be too busy to talk. "No, thank you," he said vaguely. "I need to talk to her about an insurance matter at some point. No hurry. I'll try again later if that's okay."

"Of course, Mrs. St. Pierre should be here all day today. She'll be in and out of the office, I'm sure."

"Thank you very much." Figurante hung up.

He had travelled to Jefferson unannounced. The risk of having Elizabeth away on business was well worth the bargaining advantage he would gain by a surprise visit. Now he knew she was at the farm. Perfect.

● ● ●

It was just after noon when Figurante pulled into the only filling station in Jefferson — old style — full service without asking. From behind the shop's plate glass window a burly attendant, face covered by a bleached full beard, walked slowly toward the car. "What can I do you for?"

"I'm looking for VinChaRo Farm."

"St. Pierre's?"

"That's the place."

To Figurante's surprise, the man followed with clear, concise directions.

Within a few minutes, Figurante passed through VinChaRo's wide-open gate. He parked in front of the office, stretched as he stood next to the Lincoln, and pulled on a sport coat. It was then that he noticed a shiny mobile veterinary unit backed up to the end of the stallion barn. His face darkened.

When he entered VinChaRo's office, the receptionist looked up from the long file drawer in which she had been placing forms. "Good morning."

"Morning. Is Elizabeth around?" Figurante asked.

"Yes, she is." The receptionist gestured toward the door to the barn. "She's helping in the stallion barn. I can page her for you, Mister . . . ?"

"No. Never mind. She's through this way?" Figurante stepped toward the door without giving his name.

"Yes. But it would be better if she met you here . . ."

"It's okay," Figurante bullied. "Elizabeth's an old friend. I'd just as soon surprise her."

He pushed through the door and entered the stallion barn, ignoring the receptionist's protests.

He scanned the alleyway — no activity. Voices were coming from the breeding shed, and he moved quickly toward it. When he pushed open the shed's door, everyone working inside turned to see who had intruded.

Emily and Aubrey registered casual interest. Elizabeth's jaw dropped. Kent's knees jerked as if he had touched an electric fence. Maria dropped the lead rope she was holding.

Figurante braced on his cane and locked eyes with Maria. His face beamed with the giddy surprise of one just presented with a birthday cake. He stepped closer, scanned her supple body, and received the sign he needed when she began to tremble and sway.

"Esta hombre es el mismo demonio," she mumbled, with a disoriented slur.

"Maria Castille. What a wonderful surprise." He opened his arms and reached to greet her.

Emily watched Maria turn on rubbery legs, flail her arms to ward off Figurante's attempt at reunion, and stagger out of the barn. *So this was Hector Figurante.*

Figurante's face registered disgust at the crooked girl who ran awkwardly after Maria.

Kent grabbed the plastic obstetrical sleeve that he was wearing and ripped it off his arm. He stepped in front of Figurante who had moved in the direction the girls had taken.

"What are you doing here?" he said.

For a moment Figurante ignored the question. He stared over Kent's shoulder at Maria until she was gone from the shed. He blinked and redirected his attention to Elizabeth. In the politest of tones he said, "I hope you can pardon my rudeness in arriving unannounced. I am actually in the area on — uh — other business. However, I have some extra time and thought I might use it to get a quick tour of VinChaRo. And maybe I'd nudge you on the Snow Din deal." He turned one last glance toward the door through which Maria had fled.

"We don't give tours," Kent said as if he owned the place. "You should have called, saved yourself the trip."

Figurante just smiled. To Elizabeth, he asked, "Where do we stand with Snow Din?"

"I'm still up in the air," she said, without the least cordiality in her voice.

Kent grabbed Figurante's arm and forcefully turned him toward the office. "You better get out of here. Now."

Figurante yanked his arm free. He stood toe-to-toe with Kent, raised his cane to chest height and ran his fingers along its black shaft. Kent didn't budge. The two men glared at each other.

"Just a minute, Kent," Elizabeth said, breaking the stalemate. "I think we should make an exception, let Mr. Figurante see the farm."

Kent's brow furrowed as he shifted his attention to Elizabeth. "What?"

"I want to give Hector a tour," Elizabeth said evenly.

"You must be kidding."

"I'm not."

Figurante flashed Kent a victorious sneer. "Thank you, Elizabeth."

Kent stared at Elizabeth in silence, then shrugged and headed toward the door. "You do what you want."

"Wait, Kent," Elizabeth said. "I would like you to join us."

Kent spun, took a deep breath to give her the million reasons why there was not a chance, but Elizabeth was smiling, her expression was knowing.

"Elizabeth, I don't . . . "

She cut him off. "Just come along, Kent."

Kent stood frowning like a child. Finally, he raised both hands, palms up. "Okay. Sure."

Calmly, graciously, Elizabeth gestured toward Aubrey, whom to this point, had watched in silence.

"This is Aubrey Fairbanks, our farm manager. Aubrey, Hector Figurante from Criadero del Jugador in Cynthiana, Kentucky."

Aubrey slid her hands into the pockets of her jeans when Figurante extended his hand.

Undaunted, Figurante gave her the same lecherous perusal he had just given Maria.

"VinChaRo's women are as beautiful as her horses. Now, here is a gene pool worth importing to Kentucky."

Kent took a step toward Figurante, fists balled, the veins in his neck like ropes, but Elizabeth stopped him with a laser look. She ignored Figurante's remark.

"I'd like you to help me show our guest around, too," she said to Aubrey, as if it were an invitation to tea.

Aubrey stared at Elizabeth like she was from another planet. "I don't think so. I'm going to check on the girls."

She turned and stalked out.

Kent admired her for it, and wished he'd done the same.

● ● ●

The tour was a stiff stroll along rows of stalls. They peeked through half doors as Elizabeth gave uninspired commentary about various occupants. Kent threw in meaningless asides and cast questioning looks to Elizabeth whenever he thought Figurante wasn't looking. Figurante showed only polite attentiveness while they viewed mares and foals, but when they moved to the row of stallions, his interest piqued.

"Elizabeth, you should be proud. I underestimated your stock. You New Yorkers have made real strides since I last toured a farm up here." The words seemed to catch in his throat.

"That is a point we've tried to make to you Kentuckians for some time now," Elizabeth said. "New York Breds are as good as the Kentucky-bred horses in every way. They represent a whole new gene pool that breeders from Kentucky, California, Florida, or anywhere else can utilize to improve their stock." She stepped to the next stall, opened the top half of the door. "And it is on this horse, right here, we place our hopes. He will capture that market for all of New York."

With an inquisitive snort, Hubris swung his head over his door and into the alleyway.

"Ah, yes, Hubris, the great Simpatico's son," Figurante said, reading the brass nameplate. "Believe me, his reputation already extends well beyond New York." Figurante stared at the magnificent animal. "He is even more spectacular in person."

Elizabeth pushed Hubris away as the horse nuzzled her. "Get back in there, Mister," she said gently. "This is the horse to watch, the number one New York Bred. Believe me, lot of people think he's even better than Simpatico."

"No doubt, Hubris is head and shoulders above the rest," Figurante said, then looked at Elizabeth. "May I talk to you in private? In the office, perhaps?"

Kent stroked Hubris's muzzle and watched the two owners grow smaller as they headed down the alleyway. "What the hell was that all about?" he asked.

Hubris shook his head and snorted.

What was Figurante doing at VinChaRo? Elizabeth knew what he did to Maria. Why would she even talk to him, let alone give him a tour?

CHAPTER 34

FIGURANTE SQUEALED THE LINCOLN'S TIRES AS he hit the road outside VinChaRo's main gate. He swore a loud curse in Spanish. Elizabeth had flat-out refused to sell Hubris. He could not believe it. He had offered her the heaven and stars. '*No, no, no,*' that's all she'd said.

The New York Breds were far better than he had imagined. He had underestimated Simpatico's ability to transmit his genes to his son. So, if Elizabeth won't sell Hubris, he must be eliminated. To hell with buying him. To hell with his lily-livered co-conspirators in Kentucky. He had tried to play by their rules. Now, Hubris must be *eliminated*, pure and simple, just like the others. But how?

● ● ●

Figurante parked his Lincoln in a secluded spot behind Kolbie's Tavern. Through the windshield he studied the back of the ramshackle building. A discarded deep fat fryer lay on its side in some tall weeds, an overflowing dumpster buzzed with flies, and several beer kegs pretty much blocked the rear entrance to the kitchen. He hoped he would not have to be there for long.

Thankfully, a few minutes later, Burton's dilapidated pickup rumble into the parking lot.

"Right on time," Figurante said, his tone a mixture of relief and anger.

Burton pulled in close to the Lincoln and stuck his red head out the window. "The place looks dead now, but it'll pick up in the next hour or so. Come on, I'll buy you a beer," he said.

Burton's swagger didn't conceal his nervousness.

"No. You get in here," Figurante said. He leaned across and pushed open the Lincoln's the passenger door. Its springs sank as Burton's hulk descended into the seat.

Figurante wasted no time. His calmness oozed an aggressiveness that made Burton press against the door.

"My original plan was to just talk to you while I was up here in New York — tell you to keep your damn mouth shut, and be more careful. Which, for sure, you need to do. But now . . ." Figurante let his voice trail off. For a moment he sat in silence, working his palm on the handle of his cane, thinking, deciding whether or not to recruit Burton one more time. Finally, he nodded and said, "I'm going to need you to do another favor for me. Naturally, you'll be paid."

"I'm not sure I want to do any more favors, Mr. Figurante," Burton said, his voice shaky.

"I'm not asking."

"It's harder, now. They're watching me."

"I paid you a lot of money."

"And I delivered."

"Yeah. You delivered, all right. And you couldn't keep your yap shut about it. That's why we're in the shit we're in right now. Not to mention, you killed Charles St. Pierre."

"Someone broke into my apartment. They found the money."

"You kept all that money in your room? Jesus!"

"Where else would I put it?"

Figurante ignored the question. "I need you to get rid of Hubris."

Burton's face folded into a look of fear and dismay. "I can't do that!"

"Why not? You are the expert, right? You said you could kill any horse, any time, without any trace. Isn't that what you told me? How many times have you been hired to kill horses for insurance, or whatever?"

"But, like I said, they're watching me."

"Now. Tonight. Kill him."

Burton's expression morphed from fear to anger. He jerked his fist to within inches of Figurante's face, middle finger extended straight up.

"Fuck you! You want Hubris killed, you do it yourself," he said, and reached for the door handle.

"Well, I pretty much figured it would come to this," Figurante said, not the least bit ruffled by Burton's response.

His tone was so deadly placid it caused Burton to turn. When he did, he saw Figurante's cane pointing at him. The humor of that was just rising in his brain when Burton noticed a hole in the end, and realized he was staring into the gaping bore of a gun barrel.

"What are you, fucking Yancy Derringer or something?" Burton said, and tried to laugh, but only gurgled.

Figurante's expression was like stone. "It's just a .38, but that's plenty at this range."

Burton swallowed hard and kept staring at the cane gun.

"You're a screw-up, anyway," Figurante said. "Talked too much. Killed Charles St. Pierre. I was an idiot to figure you could do this. Get out of the car."

That suited Burton just fine, and he moved quickly, but Figurante kept his gun trained on him as they came around to the trunk. He tossed Burton the keys and motioned with the muzzle. "Open it."

Burton raised the lid. Instantly, his face paled to the color of polished lead. The trunk was empty except for a plastic tarp that had been carefully spread over the floor. He turned a terrified look at Figurante just in time to see his former boss swing his cane like a baseball bat. It caught Burton on the left temple, full force. His knees buckled. Figurante pushed him into the trunk as he wilted. Burton never even quivered.

CHAPTER 35

EMILY TAGGED ALONG AS MARIA BUSIED HER-self between bedroom closet and bathroom mirror, preparing to go out for the evening.

"Tonight, Maria? That's what the phone call was about?" Emily asked, still surprised by the sudden invitation. "It sounded like a man's voice when I answered the phone."

Maria pulled a summery shift over her head, then shook out her hair. "That was one of the girl's boyfriends you heard."

"Your friends don't give much notice."

Maria checked her makeup in the mirror. "It's a spur of the moment thing." She headed down the stairs, Emily in tow.

"Sounds like it. What videos are these, anyway?" Emily asked.

"Last year, the Clinton Equestrian Team went to Nationals. Remember?"

"Yeah."

"Well, some of the other girls from the team are back in town visiting. They called me to see if I wanted to come over to watch a tape of the Nationals with them."

They reached the kitchen just as Aubrey wedged the last supper dish into the dishwasher and wiped her hands on her apron. She had insisted that the girls stay with her and Barry at her place, so she could keep an eye on them while Kent went about his work and whatever he had to do with Figurante. Not to mention, she had her own ulterior motive — keeping an eye on Maria. Aubrey had mentioned her suspicion to Kent when they last talked, and he flatly refused to even consider it. But there were just too many coincidences: Maria coming back in the midst of all the problems with the stallions, having worked for Figurante, both of them from Ecuador. If Kent wouldn't face it, she'd check it out herself. The girl definitely bore watching.

She handed Maria the keys to her Outback. "So, where is this videofest going on tonight?"

"On campus somewhere. I'm not exactly sure. We're all supposed to meet at the equine center, then I guess we'll find a video machine wherever."

"Okay. You go ahead if you want," Aubrey said, making it sound like a tease. "Em and I are going to chill on the couch with a couple fuzzy blankets, a huge bowl of popcorn, and a movie. Sounds like fun, eh?"

Maria sighed. "Actually it does." She jingled the keys. "Thanks for the car."

"We'll let you know what you missed when you get back," Aubrey said as Maria headed out the door.

● ● ●

Aubrey sat with her arms around her knees at the foot of the couch where Emily was stretched out. The young girl's breathing was deep and slow. Freddie Krueger's hideous face and slashing fingernails hadn't been enough to hold Emily and now she slept like the dead. Aubrey half watched the TV screen that still played the last gory minutes of the movie even though she had muted the sound. She stewed about Maria and Figurante. The employer-employee relationship, the Ecuadorian thing, there had to be something there.

Now she wished she had talked Maria out of this evening of horse videos, with Figurante still in town and all. Granted she's out of harm's way with friends over on campus, but still weird stuff happens.

Then her newfound mistrust of Maria raised its head again. What if the whole video night was bullshit? What if right now Maria wasn't with friends at school? Aubrey hit the remote and sat in darkness as the screen popped off, extinguishing the room's only source of light. What if Maria was meeting Figurante? She listened to Emily breathe as she collected her thoughts. Screw it! Emily wouldn't be budging till morning. Plus, Barry would be home from the CVC soon, too. He could keep Emily company. She had to know.

She tiptoed into the kitchen, jotted a quick note for Em just in case, found the keys to the F-250 pickup she used to run farm errands, and headed out, closing the door quietly behind her.

Jefferson didn't have more than a dozen blocks plus the college. This time of night, sidewalks rolled up and all, she knew she'd find her Subaru in no time. She figured she'd give Maria the benefit of the doubt and start searching at the college equestrian center, so she took a left off the main drag and headed toward campus. She hadn't gone a hundred feet along the first block when she saw her car, big as life, parked at the curb next to the Red Horse Inn.

"Dammit to hell, Maria," she said. For a second, she felt validated for having been right, then she felt like crying, then she felt like stomping in there and decking the girl. Instead she hit the gas and headed back home. Kent was going to be crushed.

● ● ●

Figurante fumed. Getting angrier by the minute, he sat concealed in a dark booth in The Groggery, the Red Horse Inn's mahogany and brass taproom. He batted a coaster back and forth on the table, then picked it up and read it: Löwenbräu, imported from Munich. He sipped impatiently from a gold-rimmed mug. "Where the hell is she?"

It hadn't been all that difficult to ferret out Maria's whereabouts. Another disguised call to VinChaRo's office — Jesus, that secretary had to wise up sooner or later — she had informed him that Maria lived at Doctor Stephenson's house. He didn't have to guess what the good doctor had in mind with that arrangement. Then, a call to the house and a chat with Kent's amiable, eager-to-please housekeeper, and — voila! — he had Maria's location at Aubrey Fairbank's home, and the phone number to boot.

When he'd called her, he had specified eight o'clock sharp. His watch said nine o'clock. He hated waiting.

But the very next time he glanced toward the entrance, his eyes were rewarded with Maria's unmistakable silhouette; all features strong yet perfectly feminine. His palms moistened against the cool table. Lewd memories of that hot summer night at Criadero del Jugador stirred his groin. Such a prize, and taken with just the right amount of resistance. He half rose, leaned out of the booth and signaled her over with the congeniality of an old friend.

Maria hesitated, then slowly she started toward him. Her cold stare was the antithesis of his congeniality.

"Maria, I'm delighted that you could make it," he said, with an oily politeness.

"One rarely refuses the invitation from someone who threatens harm to their family should they decline," Maria said, ice crystallizing on each word.

"For that, I apologize. I wanted to be sure that you would come." Maria slid in across from him. "I'm here. What do you want?"

As Figurante drew a breath to speak, a waitress in a short, tight skirt stepped to their table. "Can I get you something, ma'am?" Maria waved away the distraction.

"Another for you, sir?"

Figurante covered the beer mug with his hand. "Do you think we could have a bottle of champagne sent up to my room, instead?"

A knowing smile crossed the waitress's lips. "Sure," she mentioned a brand, wrote down his room number, and departed.

When she was out of earshot, Figurante turned to Maria and smiled darkly. "Shall we go up?"

Maria leaned across the table, her face within inches of the man she despised. "No, we shall *not* go up! What do you think you're doing? Surely even you don't think you can appear in this town, find me, and then demand that I go to your room with you! You're crazy. Not after what you did to me at Criadero del Jugador. Not on your life."

As she slid across the booth to leave, Figurante grabbed her arm. She twisted to pull free, but he was too strong.

"Maybe not on *your* life, senorita, but what about Antonio's?"

It took a moment for Maria to grasp his meaning. When she did, she stiffened. "You absolute bastard! You would hurt my family, wouldn't you?"

"You tell me if I would," he said, his voice a roaring whisper. "I'm sure your family told you about the bomb, and Alicia's little ride, and Antonio's cheating ordeal?"

Antonio *had* written to Maria about disturbing things that happened to her family back in Ecuador. A phony mail bomb had done nothing more than fill the room with smoke when her mother opened it at the kitchen table. Little Alicia, Maria's five-year-old sister, had been lured into a car by two men, driven once around the block, then released with a note to deliver to her parents: ONE MUST KEEP WATCH OF ONE'S CHILDREN! No signature. And there was the anonymous call to the head master at Antonio's school describing in great detail how Antonio had cheated on his university entrance exams. He had endured an embarrassing three-week inquiry before being absolved.

In South America, threats and vengeful acts were not uncommon, especially against wealthy families. She had told Antonio to be careful, but not to worry. Then she had dismissed the whole thing. Now, suddenly it became clear.

"You did those awful things to my family?" she asked in disbelief. "You?"

Figurante conceded with a shrug.

"Hijo de puta!" Maria swung hard at him aiming for his left cheek. He caught her wrist so that her fingertips only grazed him.

"Such a nasty mouth you have. They were just little jokes. No harm done, was there?"

"You scared the hell out of my parents!"

"Nobody got scared to *death*."

"But that was *after* I left Criadero del Jugador. Why?"

"I thought it would force you to come back when you realized who was behind it. But, you didn't even figure it out, let alone return. I gave you too much credit."

"Like I would ever come back to you. I'm glad I didn't understand," Maria snapped.

"I can still do any of those things to your family, you know. And I will, if you don't cooperate."

"If you think I am going . . . "

Figurante held up a hand. "This is not the place. Let's continue this discussion in my room." He gestured for her to lead the way.

"Forget it, Hector, I'm out of here," Maria said, but it did not come out with the intensity she intended.

Figurante let her rise. "As you wish," he said, then with an ominous dryness he added, "But, don't forget about Antonio, and Alicia, and the rest of your family."

The very utterance of her family member's names by this vile man made her knees weak.

"I just want to talk," he explained.

She knew that was a lie.

"I have something important to tell you about Hubris," he said.

Now Hubris! My God. She could feel the web he was spinning wrap still tighter around her, cutting off her air.

Figurante placed his hand on the small of her back, nudging her toward the stairs. For an instant she resisted, holding her ground. *Run from this monster and endanger her family, or submit?* She closed her eyes.

Figurante pushed her again, more firmly this time.

She could hear the sound of her teeth grinding as she allowed him to guide her up the stairs to his room.

● ● ●

As they stepped into Figurante's room, he motioned her toward the bed. "Have a seat."

Maria sidestepped and took a seat in a straight-backed chair.

He flashed a disdainful smile at her prudishness. "Relax. I just need some cooperation from you."

"Is that what you call it?"

"You are always in such a hurry," Figurante said. He crossed the room and took his time uncorking the bottle he had ordered. He offered Maria a glass. "Champagne?"

"No. I don't care to talk over old times."

He huffed a laugh. "Of course not." Figurante took a long, slow drink.

Maria heard his splashy swallow. He moved slowly to a position behind her. Terrible memories of that night at Criadero del Jugador rushed into her head and took away her strength. She could feel herself shaking and knew he could see it, too. She felt a feathery touch on her neck as Figurante rolled a lock of her hair in his fingers.

"Why do you suppose I invited you here, Maria?" he asked, a moan of arousal in his voice.

She knew what she supposed. She knew *he* knew what she supposed. No answer came from between her lips.

She heard Figurante swallow more champagne.

"Do you think you can stop me this time any more than you could at Criadero del Jugador?" he said.

His hands began kneading her shoulders. Maria wanted to die.

"You were the best of any of them, Maria," Figurante said. "I was so disappointed when you left."

"I'll scream if . . ."

"No you won't. Remember my little bag of tricks? You wouldn't want anything to happen to your brother or sister. Would you?"

Maria began to cry quietly. She did not want to, but irrepressible tears erupted onto her cheeks and trickled down. She had no doubt that he would carry out his threats.

He laughed and swilled down the last of his drink. Then his hands were under her arms ordering her to her feet. He was right; she had no way of repelling him before, and none now. Her hands squeezed into white knuckled balls as Figurante loosened the row of buttons down the front of her dress, slid the straps from her shoulders, and let it drop to the floor.

With a forefinger under her chin he raised her head so that she stood, in submission, looking directly into his eyes.

"Maria. Do you want it again? Do you want it like before?"

"Let me go home."

"Yes, Maria. I'll let you go home," he said. "But in return you must do something for me. Is that agreed?"

She looked away. "Whatever you want. Just let me go."

"All right, then. Tomorrow, you will rid us of that obnoxious beast, Hubris." He let the silence hold, as Maria comprehended what he had just said. Then he said, "Do we have a deal?"

Maria's stunned eyes met his. The thought was too bizarre, even for this monster, but she was not about to ask questions or argue. Not now. Not the way he had her.

CHAPTER 36

IT WAS DRIZZLING, THE FIRST RAIN OF WHAT THE weatherman predicted would be a wet week. Kent sat in his truck in the Mattson Cemetery. He held a sandwich that he barely tasted in one hand, and massaged Lucinda's ruff with the other. Mostly, he stared through the windshield at Maria who ignored the misty rain as she twirled a wildflower in her fingers, deep in thought. He couldn't believe what Aubrey had told him. To outright lie so she could meet Figurante. He tossed his sandwich out the window for the birds to finish. How could she? He watched Maria gently weave a flower into Em's hair. Granted, he wasn't the best judge of character, but not Maria. She was so open, so innocent, so — perfect.

They hadn't said anything to Em, and they wouldn't. Not yet. But he and Aubrey had agreed that one of the two of them would watch Maria every second. He let his head rock back until he was staring at the roof of the cab. Now they had to keep tabs on Figurante *and* Maria.

When the mobile phone rang, he jumped. It was Sally. "Elizabeth St. Pierre wants you to call her. Something about dinner tonight."

Kent pushed memory and a number, and was talking to Elizabeth in less than two minutes.

"Thanks for returning my call," she said politely. "Sorry for interrupting your rounds."

"No problem. What's up?"

"Hector Figurante invited me to dinner tonight at The Red Horse. He wants me to reconsider."

"Reconsider what?"

"Selling Hubris."

"What?" The words flew up Kent's throat. "You can't do that!"

"Of course not. I'd never sell Hubris." She took a deep breath and released it slowly, giving Kent a chance to regain his composure. "Let me back up. Remember yesterday when Figurante wanted to speak with me privately, after we gave him the tour?"

"Of course. And it was you who gave him the tour. Not me."

"Okay. Have it your way. I figured he was up to something. And I was right. He made me an offer to buy Hubris."

"You can't do that!"

"You said that, already."

"I know."

"It was a very serious offer. His visit to VinChaRo was not as casual as he would have us believe. He and his friends have actually formed a syndicate to try and buy him."

"You told him 'no.'" Kent wanted to hear her say the word *no*. He wanted reassurance that Hubris was not leaving New York State. It was going to be tough, but the New York Bred Program would survive the loss of Simpatico, Charter Oak, and Solar Wind. But, if they lost Hubris, it would be finished. He had no doubt about that.

"I said, 'No.' But I have to admit, he caught me flat-footed," Elizabeth said. "I had no idea he was even interested in Hubris until he blurted out his offer. And, let me tell you, they are willing to pay a remarkable amount for him."

"How much?"

"A new record."

"Jesus!"

"He got hot when he realized that I had no intention of selling Hubris, no matter what he offered. Finally, he made some rather rude remarks about my business sense and left in a huff."

Kent breathed again. "Good riddance."

"That's what I thought, until I got a call from him this morning asking me to dinner. Ostensibly he wants to apologize for his behavior, but I suspect he wants to renew his offer."

"Refuse his invitation."

"I almost did. Then I thought, we still have a lot of loose ends to tie up regarding Charles, Simpatico, and the other horses. Maybe we should keep talking to the guy."

Kent gave a soft humorless laugh. "Elizabeth, you are one sly lady. But, no, he's too dangerous."

"Oh, I'm not about to meet him alone. I want you to join us."

"If you're going, I'm going."

"Excellent. Then I'll see you at The Red Horse. Seven o'clock."

Kent loaded up the girls and pulled out of the cemetery. His brain was sagging under the weight of what he had just heard. He drove so slowly, a car behind him honked. Emily and Maria gave him odd looks.

Figurante and a crew from Kentucky wanted to buy Hubris. Now there was a testimonial to the success of the New York Bred Program. Let them drool. Elizabeth would never sell Hubris.

Kent crept along down the highway. With each mile, his stomach twisted tighter and tighter. Figurante was not one to take rejection gracefully. He'd go nuts once he realized Hubris was not within his grasp.

The mobile phone rang again, and he pounced, startling the girls.

"What?" he said, sending his question flying at whoever was at the other end.

"Kent, it's me," Aubrey's voice came back at him. "Are you all right? You sound upset."

"I'm fine." He hesitated, returned Emily and Maria's bewildered looks with a defiant one. "No. I'm not fine. Actually, I'm anything but fine."

"What's the matter?"

He considered dropping Elizabeth's bad news on Aubrey, but changed his mind. He needed to think about it more. Besides, he wasn't sure he wanted Em and Maria to hear it yet, either.

"I've got a dinner meeting at the Red Horse at seven tonight. I'll call you after that. We'll talk."

"With who?"

"I'll tell you tonight."

"You may not want any dinner when you hear why I called you."

"What's up?"

"Elizabeth just got a call from the police. They want her at the morgue to identify Burton Bush's body."

"Burton's dead?"

"According to Elizabeth, the police figure he jumped off the Falls Creek Bridge. Fishermen found him downstream."

For a brief moment, thoughts like *you reap what you sow, he had it coming*, and *no great loss* sailed through Kent's head. He held the phone behind his head so Aubrey would not hear the growl that rose from his throat. Even with all the ill will he felt toward Burton, he did not wish him dead.

"When did they find him?"

"I'm not sure."

"I just got off the phone with Elizabeth," Kent said. "Has she left yet? For the morgue, I mean."

"No. She says she can't do it. Too much death for her lately. She asked me to go in her place. Will you come with me?"

"Of course I will."

● ● ●

This was nothing the girls needed to see, Kent thought as he pulled up in front of Community General Hospital. Their horrified reaction when he told them what Aubrey had said about Burton's death was enough for him to know that, for sure.

"You ladies sit tight and keep an eye on Lucinda. I'll be back in a minute."

Jefferson's morgue was in the back of the hospital on the ground floor. It was nothing more than a walk-in cooler the size and design you'd see off the kitchen of any good-size restaurant. There was no wall of roll-out drawers containing bodies, no pathologist performing autopsies over wet tables — just chilled, empty space to park gurneys. Three would fill it. Today there was only one.

Kent was familiar with animal death, but human death was something different, it's impact more profound. He braced himself and took Aubrey's hand as the doctor who had escorted them into the cooler pulled the sheet off Burton's face.

He felt Aubrey cringe at the sight of Burton's gray skin. The bloated face was waterlogged from hours in the creek. It was no longer the face of the Burning Bush. Burton's trademark limbus of bright red hair was reduced to a brown mat pasted to his scalp like a helmet.

The doctor held the sheet, letting them look, watching their faces for a reaction.

As he perused at the body, Kent noticed an odd mark on Burton's left temple.

He pointed it out to the doctor. "What's that?"

"He probably landed on a rock. The creek's not deep. Skin wounds look weird after they've been in water."

Kent leaned over for a closer look. He stared at the odd welt on Burton's punky skin. It was exactly like the one he'd seen on Snow Din's neck after Figurante struck the horse for misbehaving. Kent was positive, it was a perfect imprint of a spiraled serpent — the one on Figurante's cane.

He stood up straight and signaled the doctor that it was okay to re-cover the body. "That's him," he said. "That's Burton Bush."

CHAPTER 37

THE RED HUES AND HORSE THEMES WERE CON-
tinued into The Red Horse Inn's dining room; burgundy carpet, rus-
set leather chairs, and soft lit walls hung with nineteenth century
paintings of fox hunts and sleigh races.

Kent and Hector Figurante sat at a table near windows with
many panes and carved cherry moldings. Pedestrians pass by on the
sidewalk only a few feet outside.

"You can't buy Hubris. Period. He's not for sale," Kent said, for
the third time of the evening.

"I really want to hear that from Elizabeth, herself,"
Figurante returned.

"Look, Hector. That's not going to happen. Like I told you,
Elizabeth is no longer interested in dealing with you. She authorized
me to give you that message. The Snow Din deal is off and Hubris is
not for sale at any price."

"Why doesn't she tell me that face-to-face?"

"What does it matter? You get the picture."

In fact, Kent knew it really did matter. That's why he was at the
table right now instead of Elizabeth. He and Elizabeth had agreed
that Figurante was too dangerous, too manipulative for Elizabeth
to handle. After all, they knew positively what he did to Maria and
Burton Bush. Even though they didn't have proof, there wasn't a

doubt in their minds that he was behind the catastrophes that had befallen Charles and their three great stallions. Besides, Kent wanted one last chance to look the monster square in the eye.

"I deserve a chance to convince her."

"You deserve nothing. Just pack your bags and go back to Kentucky."

At that moment, Kent felt a presence at his shoulder. He looked up into the attentive face of their waiter.

"Sorry to interrupt, Dr. Stephenson. You have a phone call." The man gestured toward his hosting podium. "You can take it at the desk, if you'd like."

"I'll be right back," Kent said, as Figurante waved him away, dismissively.

When he answered the phone, a faint, almost inaudible whisper came over the line. "I poisoned Hubris."

Kent brought the receiver around and glared into it, then turned away from the noise of the dining room. "Who is this? What did you say?"

The whisper came again, this time even fainter.

"Say that again," he ordered. "Speak louder. I can't hear you." The voice was forced, labored. Whoever was speaking was straining to get the words out.

"I killed Hubris. I'm so, so sorry, Doc. I want to die."

Suddenly, Kent recognized the voice. "Maria? Is that you, Maria? The line went dead.

For a moment, the shock of the call immobilized him. He struggled to regain control of himself. Aubrey was supposed to be watching Maria. He dialed Aubrey's number.

Her voice came over the line. "Hi, Kent. I thought you were at The Red Horse."

"I am, but something weird just happened and I need your help."

"Sure. What's up?"

"Can you, or Barry, to take a quick walk over to the barn and check on Hubris? See that he's all right, and then give me a call back." He recited the Red Horse number.

"Barry's working with Peter again tonight at the CVC," she said, resolved to her son's commitment. "But sure, I'm on my way. No questions asked, which is pretty good for me."

"And one more thing, Aubrey. Where is Maria?"

"She and Em are upstairs asleep. Why?"

"Check on them, too, will you?"

"Okay." A tinge of alarm crept into her voice. "Now you've got me. Anything special I should be looking for?"

"No. Just make sure that everything is as it should be." Kent looked at his watch. "What will all that take you? Fifteen minutes?"

"About that."

"Okay. Call me back in fifteen minutes."

He alerted their waiter to expect another call. "Business," he said, with an apologetic smile, and the waiter gave him an understanding nod.

When he returned to the table, Figurante made no attempt to conceal his interest. Kent ignored him and sat in broody silence. He envisioned Aubrey dutifully setting aside her book and forcing herself off the sofa, mumbling something about how he better not keep her hanging on this, then donning her jacket and boots, and trudging to the barn. She would cross the small parking lot and enter through the side, bypassing the office — fewer doors to open.

Inside the stallion barn, she'd pause in the dimness of the night lights. Like most good horse people, Aubrey could detect as much with her ears as her eyes. After assuring herself that everything sounded normal, she'd tiptoe down to Hubris's stall, peek in, and see him with his head in the corner, muzzle inches above the straw, standing asleep. She might step in and arouse him just to be sure, just because Kent had seemed particularly concerned. Then back to the house. A quick trip upstairs to see that Maria and Emily were safe and sound, and she would call him back — *All is well.*

The flash of Figurante's lighter startled Kent back to reality as the Kentuckian ignited a fat brown cigar and released a cloud of blue smoke. "What's going on?"

"I'm not sure." Kent gave Figurante an accusatory look. "That phone call was from . . . well, whoever it was, said Hubris may be sick. At least, I think they said that. They were speaking so softly it was hard to tell."

The information brought no change to Figurante's impassive expression.

"So I called Aubrey and asked her to check on Hubris and the girls . . ."

Out of the corner of his eye, Kent caught a wave from the waiter, and saw he was holding the phone. Instantly, he headed for it.

"Kent," Aubrey's voice was distraught. "Something awful has happened to Hubris! He's really sick. How did you know? What's going on?"

"What's he doing?"

"He's shaking all over. Really hard. He's got this wild-eyed look, and he's breathing like a freight train."

"Is anyone with him now?"

"Yes. I got Osvaldo to stay with him."

"Okay. Call Peter, he's already at the CVC. He can get there with a mobile unit faster than I can."

"I already did. He and Barry are on their way."

"Perfect. When they gets there, tell Peter Hubris has probably been poisoned, but we don't know with what. Peter will take it from there. Did you find the girls?"

"Emily is here. She's upstairs. But I don't know where Maria is. Neither does Em."

"Then see if you can get someone to find her. I'll be there as quick as I can. Okay?"

234

"Kent, how did you know all this? How do you know Hubris has been poisoned? And about Maria?"

"I'll tell you about it when I get there. Get someone to find Maria, and you help Peter."

"Okay. Hurry."

Maria! Now there was no denying it. Why? The thought of it broke his heart. She lived in his home. She was like family.

"I've got to go," he told Figurante, when he returned to the table. He was pulling out his wallet to leave some money when the waiter flagged him for a third time.

"Lot of sick animals tonight, Doc?" the waiter said, as he handed Kent the phone.

Kent ignored his little dig. "Hello," he said into the phone.

"Kent, I'm so glad I got you."

He recognized Margaret's voice and his head whirled with a dozen bizarre scenarios for why she would be calling him at this moment.

"A terrible thing just happened."

"You mean Hubris?"

"I don't know anything about Hubris. I'm talking about Maria."

"She's there at Pine Holt? With you?"

"Yes. She was, but I just had an ambulance take her to the hospital."

"The hospital? Why?"

"I heard a lot of noise and commotion coming from Maria's room. So I went to check it out, and there she was, having a seizure. The room was a wreck. She was delirious and flailing around. I called for an ambulance. She's on her way to Community General."

"You did the right thing, Margaret. Are you okay?"

"I'll be fine."

"Listen. I need you to hold things down at Pine Holt for me?"

"Of course. And, Kent, there is one more thing."

Kent winced. What more could go wrong?

"I found an open canister of horse medicine in Maria's room. A powder. The label said Ventipulmin."

"Ventipulmin? Where?"

"On the floor next to Maria's bed."

It took a moment for Kent to register the significance of that discovery. Then his face darkened, "You mean she tried to kill herself?"

"I don't know. I'm just telling you what I found."

"Okay. Call the hospital and tell them that Maria very likely has been poisoned with clenbuterol. Tell them it's a bronchodilator used in horses. Read them the label. They'll know what to do."

He hung up, ignored the disgruntled look from the waiter, and dialed Elizabeth's number at the mansion. He studied Figurante while he waited for Elizabeth to answer. The evil bastard was staring back at him with the expression of a choirboy.

"Elizabeth, it's Kent," he said, when she picked up.

"I've been waiting for your call," She said in her usual friendly voice. "How did it go with Figurante? You're back early. You must not have wasted any time telling him to take a hike."

"Actually, Elizabeth, that's the least of our problems. The night has gone to hell in a hand basket. They tried to get Hubris. Poisoned him, I think." He heard her gasp. "Aubrey is with him now. Peter should be arriving at VinChaRo any minute."

"Lord, have mercy."

"I'll tell you about it later. But that's not all. Maria just had a seizure. She's in an ambulance headed for Community General."

"Dear Lord."

"What I need you to do is find Emily. She's either with Aubrey at the barn or at Aubrey's house. She'll want to be with Maria. Can you take her to the hospital, then stay with the girls there until we know what's going on?"

"Yes. Yes, of course. I couldn't bear to see Hubris suffering. I'll be more help with Emily and Maria."

"Thanks, Elizabeth. I'll meet you over there after I help with Hubris. I'll give you all the details then."

Elizabeth's use of the word "suffering" was like a fist reaching into his chest and clinching his heart.

To no one, he said, "If one hair on Hubris is damaged, I will personally rip that bastard's lungs . . ." but cut himself off. As he stared back at their table, his blood was replaced by ice water. Figurante was gone.

The waiter made a decisive effort to take the phone, but Kent wrestled it back, and dialed VinChaRo's barn number.

"Aubrey, how is Hubris?"

"Bad. He's down now. Peter says he's in shock. His heart is absolutely pounding out of his chest."

Kent heard her start to cry.

"Aubrey, hold on. Peter will bring him around." He wanted to say more. He longed to hold her and console her. Instead he said, "Tell Peter that the poison is probably an intentional overdose of Ventipulmin."

"You think Maria O.D.'ed Hubris with Ventipulmin? No way!"

"She may have."

"On purpose?"

"The symptoms would fit."

"Could that do it? I mean, is that stuff strong enough to kill a horse?"

"Yeah, it could. Too much affects the heart. It causes arrhythmias. Just because there's a jar or two of the stuff around most horse barns, doesn't mean it's not a potent drug."

"God, I've been giving Ventipulmin to coughing horses for years. I never thought much of it. I just figured it was the veterinary version of Sudafed. I had no idea it could be poisonous. How much would it take?"

"I'm not sure right off hand."

"Would one canister be enough?"

"Probably. You think he'd eat that much?"

"With a little grain he would. The guy is a bottomless pit. Eats like a steam shovel."

"All right. Tell Peter. I'll be there in a little while."

When he was sure everyone was marshaled in the right direction, Kent apologized to the waiter and headed for VinChaRo. His brain whirled with morbid images of what he would find there.

CHAPTER 38

KENT'S MOBILE UNIT WENT UP ON TWO WHEELS
when he power turned through VinChaRo's main gate. He knew this
was the most important call of his career. If Hubris died, the last
of their truly great stallions would be gone. He tore up the drive,
then skidded to a stop at the stallion barn. Peter's truck was already
backed up as close to the barn as possible. Several of its doors were
open, drawers were pulled out, and work lights were on.

Kent pulled his grip out of his unit. He knew Peter would
already have everything they'd need inside, but there was that certain
security all doctors feel in having their own grip.

The stallion barn lights were on full. The alleyway in front of
Hubris' stall was littered with medical debris. Sterile wrappers from
catheters and syringes were strewn about, while a green oxygen cyl-
inder stood braced against the wall like a sentinel. A hose from it
snaked through the door into the stall. Kent heard Peter shouting
orders with military terseness. Deep grunts resonated up Hubris's
enormous trachea.

"Hold his head still," Peter yelled.

"We are trying, Doctor Murphy!" came Osvaldo's voice.
"Estamos haciendo lo mejor que podemas."

Kent rounded the corner into the stall just in time to see Osvaldo and Barry fly across it, catapulted from their position at Hubris's head. Aubrey was still hanging on, but barely.

Peter straddled the thin of Hubris's neck and held his right hand high, clutching a syringe of sedative, attempting to maintain sterility as the stallion convulsed under him.

"Is that pentobarbital?" Kent asked, as he crouched to help.

"Yes, but he won't hold still long enough for me to hit a vein."

As if for emphasis, Hubris thrashed violently. He struck with both front feet in vicious clawing arcs that would crush any part of a human they contacted. Peter forced all of his weight onto the massive head pressing it to the floor, but again it rose like a monster from the sea of straw.

"Give that to me and hold on as best you can," Kent said. "Osvaldo, you and Barry get a hold, too."

He wanted to tell Aubrey to stay back where it was safe, but he knew it would be wasted breath. Her eyes flashed, her jaw was set, as she ducked and dodged Hubris's flailing limbs, each time diving back in, trying for a better hold.

"Jesus, Aubrey. Watch those feet!"

Among the entanglement of humans and horse, Kent saw a ropey jugular vein. He plunged the needle in, drew back the telltale blood, and forced the sedative in. He flipped the empty syringe into the alleyway and joined the others in restraining their patient.

One sweep of pentobarbital through Hubris's brain quenched the cataclysmic electrical impulses, and the big horse began a descent into flaccid exhaustion.

Kent eased his grip slowly, cautiously. "Get the trach tube in first so we can get oxygen going." He wrenched the giant head around to allow better visualization of the horse's mouth and throat.

Peter grasped Hubris's meaty tongue in one hand, slid the latex pipe into his airway with the other, then attached the oxygen. Next, they clipped and scrubbed the skin over his jugular, inserted a catheter, and suspended a plastic bag filled with close to a gallon of lactated Ringer's solution.

Kent lifted the horse's lip. "His membranes are blue and his heart is pounding through his chest wall. We need to send an EKG."

Barry scrambled for the truck. "I'll get the transmitter."

"I'll get a phone line in here," Aubrey said.

In less than five minutes, Barry was back with the EKG transmitter and Aubrey had jerry-rigged a line from the phone in the alleyway. Peter attached the transmitter's electrodes to Hubris, and sent an EKG to the cardiology center. In even less time a specialist was back on the line.

Peter took it, and repeated the cardiologist's words for Kent to hear.

"He's in V-tach. Okay. Yes, we've got an i.v. line in. Yep, and oxygen. Probably a beta-agonist overdose — Ventipulmin. We don't know the exact amount. Orally. I'd guess about two hours ago. Uh-huh. Right, he's under with pentobarb now. He convulsed. Oh, he probably goes right around eleven hundred pounds. Yeah, I've got it. A slow i.v. bolus of Propranolol. Fifty milligrams."

Peter glanced at Kent to be sure he understood.

Kent nodded. "I'll get it."

Aubrey followed him to the truck. "What is V-tach?"

"It's short for ventricular tachycardia, a mess up of the heart's electrical system so the chambers beat out of synch — the ventricles flutter. Any kind of overstimulation can cause it."

"Like Ventipulmin."

"Yes. In V-tach, the heart beats really fast, but it doesn't pump very efficiently."

Aubrey did not have to ask what happened then.

For the next hour, the crew lavaged Hubris's stomach with huge volumes of water pumped in and out using a stomach tube the size of a garden hose and stainless steel pails. They filled him with a repulsive black paste of activated charcoal. Intermittently, Peter would call for a brief pause in the nursing to transmit another EKG.

Except for words related to the immediate task at hand, no one spoke. Mostly, they watched impatiently for signs of improvement — and worried.

When they had done all they could do, they waited. Then they sat, backs braced against the stall wall, knees hunched up, clinging to mugs of coffee, hypnotized by the drip of the i.v. and the monotony of Hubris's breathing.

Kent quietly reached over and took Aubrey's hand and moved it to rest on his knee. She rolled her head to face him with a tired, grateful smile. In the stillness of the stall, even such a tiny gesture caused the others to glance toward them. It was rare for Kent to openly display his affection for Aubrey. The exposure of emotions felt wonderfully satisfying and strangely just.

Aubrey leaned her head onto his shoulder and closed her eyes.

Peter said, "You know, there's nothing here we need you guys for. Barry, Osvaldo, and I can handle it."

Barry and Osvaldo nodded agreement.

"Why don't the two of you get out of here?" Peter continued. "Go check on Maria or something. We're all anxious to know how she's doing."

It was what Kent wanted to hear. "We'll call you from the hospital," he said, as he got to his feet. "Good luck, you guys. You did great." He stepped over to Hubris and gave the horse a slow gentle pat. He felt a wave of emotion rise in his chest that he knew he couldn't handle right then. Swallowing hard, he took Aubrey's hand and led her out of the barn.

When they were alone in the mobile unit, Aubrey asked, "What are his chances?"

"We've done all we can."

"How did you know Hubris was sick? And Maria? You knew something was going on with her, too."

Kent kept his eyes on the road. A light rain had begun to fall.

"Okay, here's all I know," he said. "Elizabeth asked me to stand in for her in a meeting with Figurante. He and I were at The Red Horse when I got a call. I could barely make out the voice. But I finally figured out it was Maria. She said she'd just poisoned Hubris."

"Jesus."

"She said she poisoned Hubris, that she was sorry, and that she wanted to die. Then she hung up. That's when I called you. You pretty much know everything from there."

"Why, Kent? Why would she poison Hubris?"

"I have no idea. And now, it looks like she's tried to kill herself."

"Where's Figurante now?" Aubrey asked.

A ball of panic expanded in Kent's chest, cutting short his breath.

CHAPTER 39

THE VISITORS' LOUNGE AT COMMUNITY GENERAL had that eerie, late-night quiet, in spite of its bright ceiling lights, cheery murals, and fresh flowers.

Emily was stretched out on a faux-leather couch with her head in Elizabeth's lap. Elizabeth gently stroked the girl's hair. Maria was in ICU, the doctors and nurses were doing all they could. There was nothing more to do. *Now, the excruciating wait.*

"I hate this place," Emily said.

"They help a lot of people here."

"I've been in here a zillion times, and they haven't helped me."

"They're trying."

"It'll be too late."

A long pause.

"My mom's pretty, don't you think?" Emily said softly. "At least she was when she was my age."

The abrupt change of subject caught Elizabeth off guard. "She was the princess of the high school."

"Doc is a handsome man, too, wouldn't you say?"

"Uh-huh. Where are you going with this?"

"Then how come I'm not pretty?"

"You are pretty."

"What about my legs?"

244

Elizabeth sighed. Emily was too bright to accept condescending fluff about beauty being in the eyes of the beholder.

"I don't think anyone knows for sure why your legs are the way they are. I *do* know that your parents were very, very worried for you, and they tried everything they could to get an answer. No one has one."

"So they just let me grow up?"

"Right. With lots of love and attention. Then, when they, and all the rest of us, realized what an especially good mind you have, they just sort of forgot about the rest."

"I wish I was like Maria and Aubrey. They're beautiful."

Elizabeth wrinkled her brow into an insulted look. "What am I, chopped liver?"

It made Emily laugh. "You, too. You know what I mean."

Elizabeth was relieved when Emily did not continue the conversation. Soon after, she heard the girl's soft, regular breathing.

When Figurante sneaked down the hall at Community General and peeked into the visitors' lounge, he saw Elizabeth's head slumped forward, and her chest rising and falling rhythmically. He tiptoed down the hall to the ICU.

A window in room 326, Maria's room, allowed observation from the hall. Figurante stared through the eight-foot long pane of glass like a father looking for his new baby. On the left, three beds were arranged perpendicular to the wall, each surrounded by a myriad of medical gadgetry. All he could see were the knees and feet of each patient under light cotton blankets. Their bodies and heads were hidden from view by pale yellow curtains attached to a ceiling track. All three beds were occupied and each had a makeshift label on the footboard — a white swatch of medical tape with block letters of permanent marker. The middle one read, M. CASTILLE.

On the right side of the room was a nurses' station that had so many monitoring screens and other electronic devices that it looked more like a television control room than a medical facility. Among the instrumentation sat a lone nurse dutifully recording data onto clipboards. Eventually, she looked up, her young face registering momentary shock at the sight of a man peering at her through a window. Then, she smiled amiably when Figurante smiled at her.

Figurante was contemplating how to bypass the woman when she set aside her clipboard, rose, and exited the ICU. As she passed him, she nodded a simple hello. He took a few steps as if he was headed in the opposite direction — just another bored person whiling away the nighttime vigil of a family member. Over his shoulder, his gaze followed the sway of the nurse's hips as she proceeded down the hall, no doubt to the restroom.

He saluted her with a triumphant flip of his cane. What luck. No female could be expected to emerge from a restroom in less than five minutes, and now the ICU was unattended. How the sparks would fly if her supervisor were to get wind of this breach of protocol.

He eased open the heavy door and slid into the forbidding world of beeping, humming, hissing machines. Electrical smells mixed with the odor of medicines and sickness.

Three steps and he was concealed behind the curtain next to Maria. She looked so pale! The nest of pillows around her head contrasted repulsively with the blackness of her hair, which framed her face like a disheveled wig. Figurante reveled in her vulnerability. He wished there was a respirator to simply switch off or unplug. That would make it easy. Even a person on the brink of death resists the final nudge. It must be subtle and quick — and it must be undetectable.

His eyes fixed on a large plastic suction syringe taped on the wall. He peeled it down and pulled back the plunger, drawing in a full volume of air. He pulled apart the i.v. tube from a bag of fluids that trickled into Maria, and attached the syringe to the line. Without the least hesitation, he began to push in air.

"Hey, what are you doing here?" came a loud voice from behind him.

Figurante whirled around, startled. The syringe dislodged from the tubing.

It was that awkward little girl he remembered from the breeding shed at VinChaRo. Her glance darted from him, to the syringe, to Maria, and back to him.

He returned to his task, struggling to reconnect the syringe, but excitement made his hands clumsy.

"Get away from her!" Emily screamed, lunging at the man she hated. One sweep of Figurante's cane sent her sliding across the tile floor.

Elizabeth, who had been lagging behind, suddenly approached, alerted by the commotion. "Hector? What are you . . ."

"He's trying to kill Maria!" Emily yelled from the floor. "See that syringe? He had it hooked to Maria's tube."

Figurante's mind was locked on one purpose. He made no effort to explain himself, but continued to fill the tube with a lethal bolus of air.

Elizabeth grabbed at the syringe. It rattled to the floor. Figurante cursed, swung his cane again, and Elizabeth grunted, then fell onto her knees.

As Emily struggled to her feet, she searched the room for a weapon, snatched a mushroom-shaped electrode paddle from a defibrillator, and swung it with all of her strength. It made a dull thud as it hit the bone above Figurante's right ear, and sent him crashing to the floor. He lay there momentarily, quaking. Then he regained consciousness and rolled onto his back. In a perfect rage, he aimed the muzzle of his cane gun at Emily, and squeezed the trigger.

The shock of impact forced the air from Emily's lungs in a choking cough. Instinctively, she raised both hands to the wound in her abdomen and felt warm fluid flowing over her fingers. She pivoted slowly and sank next to Elizabeth. Her eyes, wide with disbelief, begged for an explanation of what just happened, but Elizabeth could only stare back, horrified.

Neither Elizabeth nor Figurante moved. Finally, as blood loss darkened Emily's brain, she melted gently into Elizabeth's arms, and the matriarch released a guttural scream.

CHAPTER 40

KENT AND AUBREY WERE GOING UP THE ELEVA-
tor at Community General, deep in conversation about Maria and
Hubris. They never heard the explosion from Figurante's gun. Nor
did they realize that he managed to stumble into the adjacent elevator
and pass within a few feet of them on his way down. When the doors
slid open on the ICU floor, they were startled by the commotion.

They stayed close to the wall, out of the rush of medical per-
sonnel and equipment flowing down the corridor.

Kent hooked the arm of a nurse as she brushed by and waved
at the chaos. "What's going on?"

Her face was flushed with excitement, she made no attempt to
maintain hospital decorum. "We just had a shooting! It's crazy."

"You're kidding."

"No. A girl just got shot right here on this floor!"

Aubrey's hand came up to her mouth. Through her fingertips,
she half asked and half prayed, "Not Maria Castille?"

The nurse shook her head. "No, it wasn't her, but it happened
in her room." Instantly Kent's grip went slack, and the nurse disappeared back into the flow. Kent broke into a dead run, cutting and
swerving through the procession, following it to its destination, ICU
room 326.

The first face he recognized was Elizabeth's. She was seated on a gurney, and did her best to fend off nurses when she saw him.

"Kent! It's awful! Hector Figurante shot Emily," she said. "She was trying to protect Maria and me."

Kent reeled with denial and confusion. "Where's Emily now?"

"They took her out," Elizabeth said. "For emergency surgery, I think."

"I want to see her!"

Elizabeth gestured to the huddle of hospital staff, partially concealed by the curtain.

"I want to see my daughter," he said, and it was not a request.

A tall doctor placed a hand on Kent's shoulder. "They're taking her to surgery," he explained in a firm but compassionate voice. "You can see her as soon as she comes out."

"What happened to her?"

"She's been shot."

"I know that. Where? How badly?"

"I'm not sure of the exact nature of her injury, but I can take you over to the OR. The neurologist will be able to tell you more."

Kent followed the doctor down the hall. Suddenly, another terrifying thought entered in his mind.

"Why a neurologist?" he asked the doctor, whom he could tell was appraising him out of the corner of his eye as they walked.

"I'm not sure."

They pushed through a large set of swinging doors into the surgical section of the hospital.

"There must be some nerve damage," the doctor said, stating the obvious.

Kent's lungs discharged as if he'd been punched. Any doctor, veterinary or human, knew nerve damage was the worst — the most irreparable, the most permanent. And Emily with a spinal problem already — his knees felt like reeds.

He was looking for a place to sit when the doctor with him hailed loudly to another.

"Paige, this is Kent Stephenson, the victim's father."

The woman, who looked as though she could hold her own in a game of racquetball, brushed a lock of blonde hair off her forehead and extended her hand. "I'm Paige Nelson."

Her handshake was strong, her eye contact direct. Kent liked that she felt no need to tack *doctor, head neurologist,* or some other title onto her introduction.

She held up a large yellow envelope. "You're a doctor. Right?"

"A veterinarian."

"I have the radiographs we just got on Emily." She pointed down the hall. "Right now there's a team of surgeons getting the bleeding and soft tissue damage under control. Next, we go in to remove the bullet."

He managed to nod his head.

"From the preliminary films, we know the bullet hit her spine," Doctor Nelson said. "We're going to see what these radiographs show us. You're welcome to join us."

The unusual offer surprised Kent. Again he nodded dumbly, then followed Dr. Nelson into a room lighted only by a bank of rectangular white x-ray film viewers. She introduced other members of the team as she progressively darkened the room by snapping films of Emily's lower back on to several of the viewers.

Kent gasped the instant he saw the first film. The mushroom-shaped bullet, whiter than anything else on the film, was in the middle of a vertebrae.

"Oh, my God! The bullet's lodged in her spine."

He glanced over at the team, amazed that they showed no reaction to such a terrible finding. For a long time they remained silent, a half dozen faces illuminated by the screens like a coven of witches around a sacred fire.

Out of pure frustration, he asked, "What do you think?"

It was as if no one heard him. The team members continued to scrutinize the films without a word.

Kent moaned softly, and drove the heels of his hands into his temples.

Dr. Nelson, who was leaning forward, braced on her arms as she studied the films, turned to him. "Are you all right?" Her tone was that of a professional trying to do her job. Kent knew she was telling him to leave if he was going to be a distraction.

He swallowed hard. "I'm okay." He gestured toward the bank of x-rays. "It's just — it looks so bad."

"Of course it's bad. We knew that it would be, from the location of the entry hole, the quick neuro exam, and the films we did while they were prepping her. Then, on top of that, we have her pre-existing condition." She ran her finger down the sigmoid curve of vertebrae that was Emily's lower back. Kent had seen that lesion a hundred times.

"What are her chances?"

Dr. Nelson kept her eyes on the screen. "To survive? Pretty good. To walk?" She raised and lowered her shoulders. "I don't know."

As she turned back to her team, Kent found his way to a bench in the hallway and sat, face in hands. He rocked in a slow, delirious rhythm. Tears trickled into his palms. "Emily, how could I let this happen?"

A moment later, a hand touched gently on his shoulder. He turned and saw Dr. Nelson's face — a very somber face.

"Doctor Stephenson, we've decided it would be best to do the whole thing now."

"Whatever you think. What's 'the whole thing'?"

"The bullet shattered Emily's vertebrae right at her birth defect."

"I saw that."

"Let me finish. The consensus of the team is that since the vertebrae will have to be rebuilt anyway, the best time to correct both problems is now."

"The consensus?"

She nodded. "Yep, that's all it is. No one knows for sure what we'll find when we get in there. Maybe we can fix it. Maybe we can't. But that's the plan for now. As they say, 'subject to change without notice.'"

"That's a lot of surgery."

"A huge amount."

"Will she be paralyzed?"

"She already is. The question is, can we undo it?"

Dr. Nelson gave him a moment to reply, but there were no words. She turned and disappeared back into the xray room.

After a while, he raised his head and stared at the blank wall across from him. His eyes narrowed. Figurante. "Where is that son-of-a-bitch?"

There was no one to answer, but it didn't matter. He'd find him. He pushed himself to his feet and headed out of the hospital.

CHAPTER 41

KENT ROLLED THROUGH THE POSSIBILITIES. Figurante's too smart to head for Kentucky tonight. He's got to figure the police have an ID on his car, and they'll be watching everywhere. Besides, he's hurt. The CVC? Maybe he'll try to get medical attention there. No. The place will be crawling with cops. Back to VinChaRo? Cops there, too. Kent drove and brooded. Then it hit him, as if a Clydesdale had kicked him. I bet he'll head to Pine Holt. He knows Margaret is there alone. It's the last place anyone would expect him to go.

Kent turned his mobile unit toward Pine Holt and cursed the rain that coated the road with an oily sheen. The beam from the truck's headlights danced off the highway. He squinted against the glare, then glance down at the speedometer. It read seventy. He roared through Jefferson, then on to the narrow backcountry roads. Each time he rounded a curve, he caught gravel, but managed to wrestle the tires off the shoulder and back onto the macadam.

It was one of those swerves that caused the truck's headlights to sweep across a field of freshly cut alfalfa and flash for a second on a car. Startled, Kent twisted for a better look as he sped past. It was a few yards into the field, resting on its roof, four wheels to the sky. His instinct to stop and investigate, make sure that there was no one in need of help, kicked in. He pushed it out of his head. Not this time, he couldn't stop now. If the driver was still out there, he was on his own. He turned his attention back to the road. Then, a burst of recognition lit up his brain and he slammed on the brakes. The truck skidded a stop. That car looked like the Lincoln Figurante had been driving. The tires squealed for traction as he rammed the truck into reverse.

He nosed the mobile unit just into the field so that its lights shown on the car. It was still rocking when he jumped out. No signs of life. He pulled a flashlight from behind the seat, and headed toward the car. He could smell the odor of smoke as he crossed into the field. He beamed his light onto the car. Yeah, it sure looked like Figurante's Lincoln. He circled around to the driver's side and heard a soft moan. He pointed his light in the direction of the sound, and the bean fell on a person, legs pinned beneath the wreckage.

When Figurante's blood-smeared face turned toward the light, Kent sent up a thank you to the gods of retribution.

Figurante moaned again and swung a forearm to shield his eyes. "Help! I need help."

Kent stood holding the beam on Figurante, but did not speak.

Figurante didn't know who was behind the light, and didn't care. "My legs are trapped. I can't move. Help me. Please."

When there was no reply, Figurante strained to see the person in the darkness behind the light. "What's the matter with you?" he shouted. "Get me out of here!"

"You shot my daughter," Kent said.

Ignoring the condemnation, Figurante responded with elation at the sound of a familiar voice. "Kent? Kent Stephenson? Is that you?"

"You killed Charles. And you shot Emily!"

"Burton Bush killed Charles." Figurante wailed. "Not me. Burton drowned the son of a bitch after he shot his mouth off and told Charles what happened to Simpatico."

"You gave Burton the orders. Then you killed him, too. I saw your cane mark on the side of his head."

Figurante looked deflated. He was silent for a few heartbeats, then, "I don't know anything about your daughter."

"The girl at the hospital."

Figurante's confusion transformed into enlightenment, then fear. "That crooked kid? The one that hit me? She is your daughter? Mierda."

Every organ, every cell, in Kent's body roared, *kill him, kill him, kill him*!

The light shifted in Kent's hand just enough for Figurante to see a cold calmness sweep over Kent. It terrified Figurante and he struggled to pull himself free.

Kent turned slowly and retreated to his truck.

Figurante screamed, "Kent! Come back here. I can explain everything. You can't leave me like this. Help me!"

Still in a trance, Kent opened the mobile unit and retrieved a vial. In the flashlight's white light, its contents reflected an unmistakable fluorescent blue — the same blue that had relieved the foal's suffering when he was with Aubrey. Only now he wanted it to kill *without* mercy.

He returned to Figurante and set his light on top of the car so that its beam spotlighted the trapped murderer.

"Jesus, I thought you left," Figurante said.

Kent crouched close to him, syringe in hand, extracting fluid from the vial.

"I don't need any medicine," Figurante said. "Just get me out of here."

Kent eased the vial closer so that its iridescence blue glowed in the spotlight. Horror washed across Figurante's face. "That's euthanasia solution!"

"Uh-huh," Kent said, without looking away from the vial.

Out of the corner of his eye, he saw Figurante reach for his cane that was in the grass next to him. Kent ripped it from his grasp and heaved it into the darkness. "You won't be needing that."

Kent reached across, grabbed Figurante's arm, and pulled it out straight. Figurante struggled and let out a cursing scream. Kent stepped hard on his wrist, pinning it against the ground. Another scream. Kent ignored it. He bent close, searched the arm for a likely vein, and aligned the syringe above the purple rivulet.

Then, from behind him he heard Aubrey's voice. In the tone she used to calm a frantic stallion, she said, "That will only make things harder for Emily."

Her voice in the night confused Kent for a second. Then his eyes returned to the syringe poised on Figurante's arm. "I want to kill him. I want to see him die."

"Let the police have him, Kent. Don't harness yourself with this."

Kent held his position.

Figurante lay silent. His eyes, bulging with fear, were fixed on Kent. A mumbling pray for Kent to heed Aubrey's words, gurgled up his throat.

"I want him dead," Kent said. "No trial, no lawyers, no prison. Dead!"

"I want to be with you, Kent. Forever. This will ruin it. Please, don't let him destroy our lives, too."

"He shot Emily!"

"Make him pay, not us."

Kent held steady for an eternity, then he slowly released his grip and allowed the syringe to fall away.

"We can call for help from my truck," he said, and they were the most difficult words he'd ever spoken.

Aubrey steadied him as they made their way back to the mobile unit. She was dialing when an electrical crackle broke the night silence, and a burst of sparks flashed like daylight. Kent and Aubrey spun reflexively toward the wreck. Their eyes burned, but neither looked away as they watched the nova explosion that knelled the fiery execution of Hector Figurante.

CHAPTER 42

Spring 1987

IN THE EARLY EVENING DARKNESS, CHALK-EYE
heaved his tired bones over the board fence, crossed the paddock,
and eased open the door to VinChaRo's foaling barn. Yeah, he'd
sworn he'd never stay at this farm again after what happened last
time, but that was a year ago. A year was an eternity for Chalk-Eye
— or any other bum, for that matter. By now, the terrible memory of
that night was lost in the fog of his past. Besides, bums were bums
— they changed their minds all the time. He'd hitched and walked
northward since sun up, and he was beat. He could make it work, that
was what the booze was for. Last time he stayed in the stallion barn.
He wasn't going to do that again. That was for sure. This time he was
going to hole-up in the barn where they kept the mares and foals.

He crept in, then paused, watching and listening. When he was
sure no one was around, he found a few bales of straw and built himself a cubby below a window facing east. The morning sun would
feel good. He crawled in and nestled into the clean straw. He pulled
a bottle out of his pocket, squinted to check the level, and took a
swig for supper. He shuddered, partly from the wonderful burn of
the whiskey and partly from the night chill. Man, spring was slow
to come this far north. He pulled his fatigue jacket tight around his

259

neck, curled up into a ball, and dropped to sleep, thinking about the long day he had tomorrow.

● ● ●

Cool air blew in the window of Kent's mobile unit and washed across his face as he and Lucinda drove familiar roads making his rounds through a countryside that was still mostly gray and silver. Each day, the few remaining patches of snow retreated farther into the hedgerows and shaded gullies. He breathed deeply of the fresh air, replenishing his lungs and his soul. Spring always arrived right when you wondered just how much more winter you could take.

Today was Emily's birthday. This morning she had showed him the card from Ecuador — Maria was doing well as the manager of her father's horse farm in Quito. Emily made him promise someday soon they'd visit her. Tonight they would celebrate her birthday, but *not* the fact that it was one year ago today that he'd received Aubrey's call with the terrible news about Simpatico, the call that had started the summer's strange events.

He was reminiscing about all that when the ring of his mobile phone jarred him. It was Sally.

"Doc, I just got a call from Elizabeth St. Pierre. She'd like you to stop over."

Not again, Kent thought. "Did she say why?"

"Something about a foal. She was kind of vague. She wouldn't give me any details."

"Did she sound upset?"

"Not really."

At least it wasn't one of the stallions. He let himself breathe again and slowed to make a turn that would head him toward VinChaRo. "All right. I'll head over there now."

"She asked that you bring Emily."

"Elizabeth wants me to bring Emily over to see a foal?"

"That's what she said."

"Then it's not a sick foal?"

"I don't know. I'm just telling you what she said."

Kent considered the request for a moment. "Okay, if that's what she wants. Call her back, tell her we're coming. Then call Pine Holt and tell Emily to be ready in ten minutes."

● ● ●

Elizabeth came out to greet them as he pulled into the lot in front of VinChaRo's office. Aubrey was at her side.

"Good morning," Elizabeth said. She made a sweeping gesture toward the sky. "Lovely day, isn't it?"

Kent gave Aubrey a peck on the cheek. Nowadays, he didn't care who saw.

When he noticed Barry trailing behind his mother, he knew something was up.

"Not working at the CVC today?"

"I was going to," Barry said, and gestured toward Elizabeth. "But Mrs. St Pierre asked me to stop over. So here I am."

Kent gave Aubrey a questioning look.

"Don't look at me. I know nothing," she said.

"All right. That it is," he said, suddenly suspicious of Elizabeth's high mood. "What's going on? Sally said you have a sick foal or something."

"Patience, Doctor. All in good time." Elizabeth threaded her arm through Aubrey's. "I want to be sure my soul mates are part of this."

"Part of what?"

She ignored Kent's question and pointed toward Emily. She beamed a smile as she watched Emily uncoil from the truck and stand, as straight as a soldier. Emily moved toward them with long, confident strides, then treated them to a pirouette.

"I'm a walking miracle of modern medicine," she said. "Doctor Nelson says in a few more months these legs of mine will be good as new. Actually better than new in my case."

"A sight to behold," Elizabeth said.

"You should see her dance," Barry said, laughing. "It's pretty weird. The docs fixed her legs, but they didn't do anything for her rhythm."

"Like you're Michael Jackson."

The five of them hung in silence, drawing energy from each other.

Finally, Elizabeth snaked Emily's arm, and started off with Aubrey and Emily. "Follow me," she said to Kent and Barry.

Kent turned to Lucinda, who was watching through the truck window.

"You stay extra alert, girl," he said. "I think something fishy is going on here."

Elizabeth chuckled. "You know, Kent, today I think we need to make an exception to the *no dogs in the barn* rule. I want Lucinda to be a part of this, too."

Kent furrowed his brow in an exaggerated look of confusion. "Lucy, I changed my mind. Run for your life!"

"Come on, Lucy. You're part of the team," Aubrey said, as she opened the truck door.

Lucinda jumped out, giggling with excitement. She weaved between their legs, collecting pats on the head in honor of her new recognition.

Elizabeth led them to the white board fence that encircled a small grassy paddock next to the foaling barn. It was where newborn foals were first allowed to romp and explore without straying too far from their mothers. The group could easily see the whole of it. It was empty.

"Wait here," Elizabeth said.

"What for?" Kent said.

Without answering him, she disappeared into the foaling barn.

Her friends braced their elbows on the fence. Lucinda stuck her head over the bottom board. They all gazed into the vacant paddock, and waited.

A few seconds later, Elizabeth returned. "Ready?"

Kent tried again. "For what?"

"Keep your eyes on that door."

Elizabeth pointed at one of the Dutch doors that joined each stall to the paddock, as it magically swung open on hinges still stiff from winter. Kent made out Osvaldo moving surreptitiously in the shadows, and smiled as he saw what was happening.

Elizabeth, no doubt, had ordered Osvaldo to turn out a mare and foal, but remain hidden so as not to distract from her theatrical display. Unfortunately for Osvaldo, the mare, sensing something was odd, refused to take her baby from the security of the stall. She stood with her tail out the door, glaring at the little man, who was desperate trying to follow Elizabeth's instructions. He flailed at the mare and tried to stay out of sight at the same time.

Finally, the mare made a break for daylight. Instinctively, the foal followed. Osvaldo's relief was obvious.

Kent's laughter stopped the instant he saw the foal. He had seen hundreds of foals over the years, but never, ever, one like this one. It was magnificent.

Aubrey's trained eye recognized the mare instantly. "That's Carnation Castle."

"Correct," Elizabeth said, with a nod, then looked at Kent. "Remember her? We bought her last year in California. I knew she'd do great things for us. And, do you know what? She did. Look at that guy."

Kent's eyes remained locked on the foal as he spoke. "He's huge!"

"Yes. I think the reason he's so big is he's late. Castle went *way* over."

"Really?" Kent admired the young horse. "How much over?"

"A month."

"You're kidding. How come you didn't have me check her?"

"I've got to tell you, I almost did. Aubrey said I should. I kept talking her out of it. I wanted this foal to be a secret."

"Risky."

"It was worth it just to see your reaction. What do you think of him, Em?"

"He's perfect. Look at his legs. He's fantastic."

Elizabeth nodded again. "Look at his eyes. They tell the story."

As if enjoying the critique, the foal tore out ahead of the mare with the long strides of a racehorse. Lucinda, ears up and alert, let out a whine of approval.

"He moves well, too," Kent said. He spoke softly, "He is something special, all right."

At the far end of the paddock, the colt stopped, head up, chest out. He waited for his mother, who followed slower, still feeling the effects of foaling.

"Goes to show," Kent said. "Hubris makes super foals."

"Yes, he does. And, no thanks to Hector Figurante, he'll be making them for a long time. But this guy is not by Hubris."

"Too bad."

"He's the last foal by Simpatico."

"Oh my God," Kent said, and it came out like a prayer. "He'll be an awesome racehorse."

Elizabeth kept looking at the foal. "No. I don't think so."

Kent turned to his old friend. "I'm telling you, he'll be great."

"He's not going to race," Elizabeth said. "He's going to be a jumper."

"What?"

"The next Olympic games are in '92. That gives us five years for Emily to be ready." She pointed at the foal. "And there is the horse that is going to get her there." She reached into her pocket, pulled out a white legal-size envelope, and handed it to Emily. "I signed his papers over to you, Em. Happy birthday."

For a moment, Emily seemed frozen. Then, she said, "Are you kidding me? For real?"

"For real."

Emily attacked Elizabeth with a long, swaying embrace. Words would not come, but the tears that flowed from both women sealed the deal.

Finally they separated to arm's length. Elizabeth held Emily's cheeks in her palms and gently wiped away the tears.

"I'll do my best to make you proud of me," Emily said.

"I don't doubt that for a second."

Emily looked over at her father, who was watching, his arm around Aubrey.

"We have to name him," she said.

"I already took care of that," Elizabeth said, her eyes widening into a mischievous smile. She let the silence hang. Then, with theatrical flair, she said, "His name is Simpatico's Gift."

● ● ●

Not long after the others had left, Chalk-Eye snuck out of the foaling barn.

"Now, that's more like it," he said to himself.

At first, he'd panicked when he'd overslept, and was scared awake by people's voices. Trapped in his cubby, he dreaded the thought of witnessing another horrible crime against the horses. But this time what he saw and heard had been wonderful. He drew a deep breath of spring air through his nose, then released it out his mouth. Maybe the world wasn't such a bad place after all. He hopped the fence with more bounce than usual, jumped the ditch along the road, stuck out his thumb, and let the sun bathe his shoulders. As he waited for a ride, he thought of home.

ABOUT THE AUTHOR

Frank Martorana grew up working with animals on several farms around Schenectady, New York, and at the veterinary hospital of Dr. Stanley E. Garrison in nearby Burnt Hills. In 1976, he graduated from the College of Veterinary Medicine at Cornell University. Since then he has been the "family doctor" for countless horses, cows, dogs, cats, and many other creatures around Cazenovia and Hamilton, New York. When he is not treating animals, he is hard at work readying the next book of the Kent Stephenson series.

Please visit his website at www.frankmartorana.com.

Don't miss the next thriller in the Kent Stephenson Series.

THE COLOR OF WOUNDS

It's been a dog's age since Kent helped an old classmate expose inhumane animal testing at the research center of a prominent university. But now, after all that time, his good intentions are coming back to haunt him. Ex-members of the US military-industrial complex have Kent in their cross hairs. When threats and blackmail don't stop him, they bring on the bombs. But Kent brings on his coonhound, Lucinda.

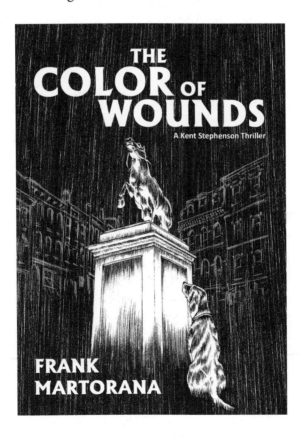

Visit www.frankmartorana.com for update